HANDMADE
MYSTERIES

Cover design copyright © 2025 by Sperrico Designs

Printed by Hillary Sperry, Author.
First printing: Apr 2025

ISBN: 978-1-960985-12-5 (paperback)|ISBN: 978-1-960985-14-9 (ebook)

The Jenny Doan name and the Missouri Star Quilt Company are trademarks of and property of the Missouri Star Quilt Company, used with permission. This is a work of fiction. Names, characters, business, events, and incidents are the products of the author's imagination. Any resemblance to actual persons, living or dead, or actual events is purely coincidental.

Copper Crow Publishing
Bella Vista, AR

Copyright © March 2025 Hillary Sperry

All rights reserved.

This book or parts thereof may not be reproduced in any form, stored in any retrieval system, or transmitted in any form by any means—electronic, mechanical, photocopy, recording, or otherwise—without prior written permission of the publisher, except as provided by United States of America copyright law or by a reviewer, who may quote brief passages in a book review. Electronic distribution of this book or the facilitation of such without the permission of the publisher is prohibited. For permission requests, write to the publisher, Copper Crow Publishing.

HANDMADE
Mysteries

A Cozy Mystery Anthology of
Missouri Star Mystery Novellas

By Hillary Doan Sperry

To my readers,

Thank you for the joy,
the positivity, and the hope.
Your enjoyment makes this all so worth it.
I'm sending prayers to you and yours
For love in your homes, success in your quilting,
and quiet while you read!

— A Missouri Star Mystery —
Hillary Doan Sperry

HANDMADE
Mysteries

Dear Reader,

Hi! I'm Hillary, and I'm so excited to share this anthology with you! It includes two of my very first mystery novellas. These short stories have been updated and polished so even if you've read them before, they'll feel brand new!

I've also included two quilt block patterns designed as a mystery quilt along! With each chapter, you'll receive a few quilting directions, and if you follow them by the end of the story, you'll have a complete quilt block! I designed both patterns—one even has a Jenny Doan tutorial, while the other is my take on a classic. The link to the tutorial is at the end of the book, including several tips and tricks for new quilters.

To listen to the stories online or as audiobooks, scan the QR code at the bottom of this page!

Happy reading and happy quilting!

SCAN CODE

Choose your listening option on the website to hear Jenny read the audiobook.

www.hillarydoansperry.com/listen

MYSTERY IN THE OLD QUILT

PART One

A Seam of Secrets

No one understood growing old quite like a quilter. Age spots and sagging sections were easily assumed badges of honor. Jenny adjusted the tension on her sewing machine and pressed the foot pedal down. She was on a deadline. This project had to be finished today.

As the sewing machine hummed along, she considered the observation. It wasn't just that she was well into her sixties. Or that most quilt shop patrons were closer in age to the Golden Girls than the Gilmore Girls. It had everything to do with the fabric running under her fingers and the hum and warmth of the sewing machine as she sat stitching together a legacy.

Every quilter's dream was to create something that stood the test of time. Twenty years, forty—each was a triumph. If a quilt survived a lifetime, it was a treasure, and if it outlived the quilter, passed on to children and grandchildren . . . that was the holy grail—an heirloom of their own creation.

Growing old was, after all, the epitome of success. Any quilter worth her pins knew when it came to quilts, the older, the better.

"But you have to start somewhere," Jenny said, completing the thought she'd been mulling over. Lifting the presser foot, she removed the finished quilt with practiced hands. Jenny should have been concerned to be talking to the fabric, but she made friends with her quilts. Naturally, there were a lot of one-sided conversations. "You're halfway there," she encouraged the soft fabric. "Only a few decades to go."

Jenny slid her hand down the smooth side of the sewing machine, finding the toggle switch. She flipped the switch, and the sewing machine's light went dark.

A sense of accomplishment settled around her as she headed up the stairs. It was as if she'd wrapped up in the quilt instead of folding it and leaving it on the table in the dining room.

Mystery in the Old Quilt

She moved quickly to her room, eager to get ready. With each glance, the seconds seemed to slip away faster. She pulled a thick cardigan from her closet and checked the time again. She was dangerously close to running late.

Slipping on her sweater, Jenny was careful not to muss her dark hair. It was beautiful outside, but she would need the extra layer. Experience had taught her not to trust Missouri's blue skies and spring sunshine. It might look warm, but the heat only extended to where the sun hit the hardwood below the windows. As soon as she stepped outside, the chill would find her.

She checked her reflection and the clock and hurried out the door.

At the bottom of the stairs, Ron stood waiting, the quilt over one arm and a small brown bag in the other.

Her heart involuntarily hitched at the sight of the man she'd been married to for over four decades. "When did you get back?"

"Just now." He shook the paper bag lightly, and the space between them filled with a delicious, savory scent. "Hungry? I'm pretty sure you skipped lunch."

A familiar logo peeked from beneath his fingers. The silly cartoon peanut from *In A Nutshell*, Sam Peters' new food truck. The image lounged lazily, arms crossed and feet kicked out, against the bag in two-dimensional charm. Jenny had heard about the truck when she hired his daughter as her assistant, and they had been visiting almost daily ever since. She inhaled the warm scent of spices mingling with the nutty aroma that made Sam's food truck so popular.

"You went to Sam's without me?" she asked, eyeing the grease spots on the to-go bag as she reached the bottom of the stairs.

"Peanut-crusted chicken strips," Ron said, smile lines splayed from the corner of his eye.

The bag swung between them, and Jenny lunged for the quilt instead. "Careful!" She clutched the fabric close, giving it a quick once-over. For a moment, her misgivings outweighed hunger, but only briefly.

Ron raised an eyebrow, clearly unimpressed by her priorities, but Jenny refused to return his smile. Not until the scent snuck up on her, triggering a deep growl in her stomach. She sighed, glancing at the bag. Torn. She wanted the food, but—

"This is the guild quilt," she said, her voice firm. "More than twenty members contributed to this. You can't wave your fast food over it."

"*Your* fast food," Ron clarified, holding the bag out to her. "I would never threaten your hard work."

She gave in to a grateful smile, already reaching for the bag. "I *am* hungry."

Mystery in the Old Quilt

Pulling out a chicken strip, she took a hurried bite and mumbled, "Here—please?" She gestured at the quilt, desperate for an extra hand. "Help?"

Ron chuckled, shaking his head as he took the quilt and headed to the car. Jenny followed, stuffing another bite into her mouth.

"Oh, and Sam threw in some of those dates you love, the peanut butter stuffed ones," Ron added casually.

Anticipation rippled through her as Jenny perked up, peeking into the bag. "Mmm, grownup peanut butter and jelly dipped in chocolate." She grinned, swallowing quickly. "I'll save one for you."

Ron cleared his throat. "Oh, you don't need to do that." He busied himself opening the car door, avoiding her gaze.

Jenny narrowed her eyes, realization dawning. "You already ate some, didn't you?"

Ron hesitated. "Define *some*."

Laughing, Jenny tapped the bag against his arm. "Well, thanks for saving me a few anyway."

With a final kiss goodbye, she climbed into the driver's seat and drove the few blocks to the church where the local guild held their meetings.

With the quilt resting safely in the passenger seat, contentment settled in her chest. It was a guild project, created after the passing of Gina Sloane, a friend and fellow member. When the quilt had been left unfinished for weeks, Jenny offered to help, but Loretta, the guild president, had brushed her off—until yesterday morning, when she showed up unannounced on Jenny's porch.

With half the blocks sewn together and a bundle of border fabric in hand, Loretta hadn't so much *asked* Jenny to help as *challenged* her to complete it.

"I thought I'd get a head start for you," Loretta had said, handing her the pile. "You sew so fast, I'm sure you don't need it. Impatience is really working out for you, isn't it?"

Jenny had swallowed down a sharp retort. Loretta had a way of twisting compliments just enough to make them sting. But the quilt was for Gina's family, and Jenny knew she could finish it on time.

So, she had.

In a single afternoon, she pieced the top, added the borders, and sent it off to the machine quilters with a special priority request. That morning, it had arrived back, and with her friend Bernie's help, she spent the afternoon hand-tacking the binding in place.

The finished quilt was beautiful, and Jenny couldn't wait to show Loretta—not to prove her wrong, but because Gina deserved to be honored and remembered.

Mystery in the Old Quilt

BEVELED WINDOWS GLINTED WITH golden light as Jenny pulled into the parking lot. The small church bore a fresh coat of white paint, covering everything from the clapboard siding to the bell tower. Tonight, the guild had chosen to combine their meeting with Gina's memorial.

Even if Jenny hadn't known Gina's daughter, Blair, would be attending, the activity outside the church would have given it away. More women than had attended a meeting in months now clustered near the front steps. Feminine voices wove softly through the fading sunlight as friends and neighbors carted quilt bags and foil covered pans inside.

In her generation, grief and love tended to spill out as freezer-safe, reheatable meals. By the end of the meeting, Blair would walk away with the quilt they'd made in Gina's honor... and a freezer's worth of casseroles and kindness.

A redbud tree bloomed near the sidewalk where Jenny parked her car, its tiny pink buds stitched along the branches like French knots in a spring embroidery. Bernie and Dotty waited by the stairs as the crowd thinned, and Jenny hurried to meet them.

The two sisters stood side by side in near matching pantsuits. Dotty wore pale blue, her short silver curls burnished to a warm gray in the glow of the setting sun. Bernie was several inches taller and wore deep purple with her long gray braid over one shoulder.

"What a beautiful quilt." Dotty winked, giving Jenny and the fabric in her arms a wide-eyed look of admiration.

Bernie adjusted her glasses. "The binding is fantastic, isn't it?" She ran a finger along the quilt's exposed edge. "Wait, is this my side? Or yours?"

Jenny laughed. "Does it matter?"

Bernie hesitated. "Not sure I should answer that." She let the binding slip from her fingers as they followed Dotty up the steps.

At the entrance, Loretta raked a glare over the fabric, her frown deepening as she absently brushed invisible dust from a ribbon-edged pin on her lapel. It read, *Loretta Manor, Hamilton Quilt Guild President*.

Jenny sent a discreet glance over the blocks. Everything was fine—no frayed seams, no loose stitches, not even a forgotten pin in the corner. Loretta's large status brooch should have read Hamilton Quilt Police.

With forced confidence Jenny held out the quilt. No way was she letting Loretta's nitpicking get to her tonight. "Finished and here, as promised."

Mystery in the Old Quilt

Lifting the corner of the quilt, Loretta huffed and let it drop. "It's about time. Blair's been waiting inside for fifteen minutes."

"It's good to see you too, Lo. You're welcome." Bernie stirred the air in response to the questioning arch of Loretta's eyebrow. "For all the extra hours we put into completing this, you're lucky we had time."

"Oh, Bernadette. I am lucky." Loretta primped the ribbons on her badge and gave a tiny, pained smile. "I just don't have those kind of hours. Thank goodness you're never as busy as this, right?"

Her emphasis on Bernie's full name sent a twitch through her jaw. "I asked you to call me Bernie, Lo."

"I don't care for nicknames." Loretta plucked the quilt from Jenny's arms, opening it halfway.

Bernie scoffed loudly, and Dotty stepped between them. "Gosh, you look nice, Loretta." Dotty herded them through the doorway with a smile. "I don't think anyone will notice that's the same dress Gretchen's wearing." She tapped a finger to her lips, glancing over her shoulder. "No. It looks much better that way."

"Gretchen?" Loretta blustered, scanning the last few women on the stairs. "That's impossible. I wear it better."

A small table inside the doorway held Gina's picture and the guild sign-in sheet.

Dotty marked their names off the list as Jenny found a seat, and Bernie watched the door to heckle Loretta one last time.

"Sit," Dotty insisted. Bernie glowered at her sister but she obeyed and sat down.

When the last guild members had signed in, Loretta made her way through the crowd. The quilt nearly doubled her petite frame and encouraged her boldness.

"Excuse me," she said, edging past quilters and guests. "I need to get to the podium." A chorus of soft laughter drifted unnoticed behind Loretta until she reached the front of the chapel.

Jenny took a seat in the back row beside Bernie and Dotty.

"Welcome to our monthly guild meeting." Loretta smiled, scanning the crowd.

The chatty friends fell silent. As the door opened in the back of the room, a final guest entered and settled against the wall.

Loretta coughed, waiting for an appropriate amount of attention meant they usually started their meetings with long, uncomfortable silences.

Jenny still wasn't used to it.

"Think she forgot her speech?" Jenny whispered to no one in particular. Dotty smiled wryly, and Bernie rolled her eyes.

Mystery in the Old Quilt

A single laugh came from the back of the room, low and smooth. A man's laugh.

Jenny and several others glanced over. The dim lighting at this end of the room made details hard to see, but there was no mistaking the broad shouldered silhouette of a man.

"I didn't realize we had any men in the guild," Dotty whispered.

As far as Jenny knew, they didn't.

Men weren't prohibited from joining, but it seemed few had been drawn to quilting. The only ones Jenny had met were from out of town. So far, anyway.

She squinted in the dim light, trying to make out his features. Who was he?

The dark-haired figure in the corner shifted uncomfortably and shoved his hands in his pockets.

Jenny turned away, but the rest of the women did not. "No wonder we don't have any men," Jenny whispered, deliberately loud enough for the others to hear. "All these married ladies can't keep their minds to themselves."

A cough from the corner was met by Loretta clearing her throat and peering toward the back of the room, a hand shielding her eyes. Their unexpected visitor had turned the room into a quilt top of layered gossip, stitched together in whispers.

"Come now, everyone." She rapped lightly on the wooden podium as if her knuckles could act as a gavel and tried again. "I don't know what we're in a tizzy about, but let's begin. It's a pleasure to gather and, as always, a *grand* pleasure to lead this meeting." Loretta had finally launched into her welcome speech.

"Quilters and friends, tonight we have a special guest." Several heads turned back to the corner, but Loretta gestured toward Blair, who sat near the front.

Blair stood, joining Loretta for a moment of emotional poignancy that felt a bit rehearsed. "Blair, we all loved your mother so much. I, personally, spent a lot of time with Gina on guild business. I'm sure you understand when we say her passing ripped our hearts at the seams."

Blond hair fell from behind Blair's ear, a shaky smile on her lips. "I can try, but since I don't quilt that just sounds painful." Her soft laugh rang into silence. She took a breath and tried again. "My mother loved her guild. You were all very important to her."

The crowd united in a soft "Aww."

"Of course she did." Loretta gripped Blair's shoulder, pulling her away from the mic. A pinched smile stretched across her lips. "Gina was like a sister to us. At least I felt that way." The wrinkles in softening around her mouth.

Mystery in the Old Quilt

Her voice was hushed, almost reverent. "She stitched meaning into her quilts. I was so inspired to know she included names, dates ... even memories in her work. She passed too soon." She sniffled, wiping her eyes with a bold sweep of her hand.

The man in the corner shifted forward. His expression stiff and unreadable, before slipping quietly out the side door.

"I'm sure everyone's anxious to share their memories, but before I open the floor, we have a gift for Blair." Lifting the quilt, she handed one corner to Blair and held the other out so the quilt fell open and everyone could see. "We made this quilt for you in Gina's honor."

"Thank you for such an incredible gift." Tears glistened in Blair's eyes, and compassion pricked Jenny's chest. The late nights and hurried stitches were worth it.

Once the quilt was folded back down to a manageable size, relief flickered across Blair's face. "My mother's love of quilting was an inescapable part of her. I can't tell you how often she invited me to join her at her cutting mat." A murmur rumbled lightly around them. "I didn't take her up on it enough. Maybe one day—" Blair looked away from the crowd, her eyes unfocused. "Maybe, one day, I'll learn to put thread through needles and fabric effectively. I'd like to understand why she loved it so much. Until then, thank you for sharing her memory with me."

Without stepping into Loretta's wide-armed hug trap, Blair crossed the podium and beelined toward the stairs. She didn't make it all the way to the back.

Crisp air greeted Jenny and Bernie as they gathered outside after the meeting. They'd visited with friends for nearly half an hour, and the lingering conversation still swirled around Blair and the loss of her mother.

"Mrs. Doan?" a voice said from behind them. Blair waited with her hand extended in greeting. "I hope you don't mind, I heard you were a large part of the work done on the quilt I received tonight and I wanted to thank you."

"Did Loretta tell you—" Jenny looked over Blair's shoulder to the busy room full of quilters and let the thought pitter out. The idea that Loretta had admitted asking for her help was as impossible as never-ending bobbins.

"Not Loretta, Bernie mentioned it when we were chatting."

Bernie's gruff tone took on a surprising motherly feel. "I knew your grandmother and your mom. If you need anything, we would be happy to help."

"Of course," Jenny tried not to look surprised at Bernie's generosity. "Is everything all right?"

Mystery in the Old Quilt

"There's just a little problem." Blair's face pinched with worry. "I found my mother's quilt in the attic and I'd like to have it repaired. Our family tree is embroidered on the quilt top. There are a few weird spots though. Double layered pieces and blocks that have come undone." She sighed, looking up at the sky. "I don't know what to do. I'm not a quilter. I hoped someone could help me fix it."

"Of course. I'd be happy to look at it. Bring it by my studio. Your mother's passing was so sudden. I hope you know how sorry we all are."

"It really was." Blair hesitated. "I didn't think she'd go so quickly."

"Were there not many signs?" Jenny clipped her lips shut. "Sorry, we don't have to talk about it. Sometimes things just come spilling out—"

"No," Blair said softly. "It's all right. She had a heart condition, but . . ."

"Then you should have anticipated something." The dark-haired man from the meeting spoke up at the bottom of the stairs. He pushed away from the railing and came up several steps. "Someone should have been watching out for Gina. Maybe it was unexpected, but heart conditions can be unpredictable." His salt and pepper hair was clean cut, the scruff along his jaw was neatly trimmed.

Jenny couldn't tell if he was being pushy or comforting.

"I was watching her. She's my mother." Blair took a deep breath, her shoulders tense. "I mean, the police are waiting on the tox screen but that's only happening because I'm watching out for her. No one else—"

"A tox screen? Do you think she was poisoned? You just said she died from heart disease." The stranger moved closer.

A crease tightened between Blair's eyebrows and her fingers curled to fists. "She wasn't even fifty! Something strange must have—"

"Grief makes us see things that aren't there." He raised a hand and Blair stopped talking. Shock filled her eyes and tugged at her jaw so it hung open as the strange man tipped his head and put a hand to his heart. "Heart disease . . . it's unpredictable. No need to complicate things."

Blair didn't seem convinced. "It's actually very complicated." Her voice faltered before she backed away. "I don't feel comfortable talking about this—I need to go. I think Loretta wanted to talk with me about something." She turned and disappeared into the building.

"Sorry, I hope I didn't scare her off." The man shifted, a flicker of discomfort in his eyes.

Mystery in the Old Quilt

"Is she okay?" Jenny asked slowly.

"I'll talk to her." Bernie disappeared inside and Jenny let out a sigh.

Dotty hurried out behind them and almost ran into Jenny and Bernie. "Did you see where that man went? Several of the ladies were wondering—oh! Here he is. Welcome to the guild."

"I'm not here for the guild." He paused briefly as if hoping someone would comment. When no one did, his gaze hardened, lip hitching in silent mockery. "Anyway, tell Blair I'm sorry for her loss."

He turned and walked away, climbing into a battered, olive-green truck. It rumbled to life, taillights glowing in the dark.

Jenny frowned, watching it disappear down the road.

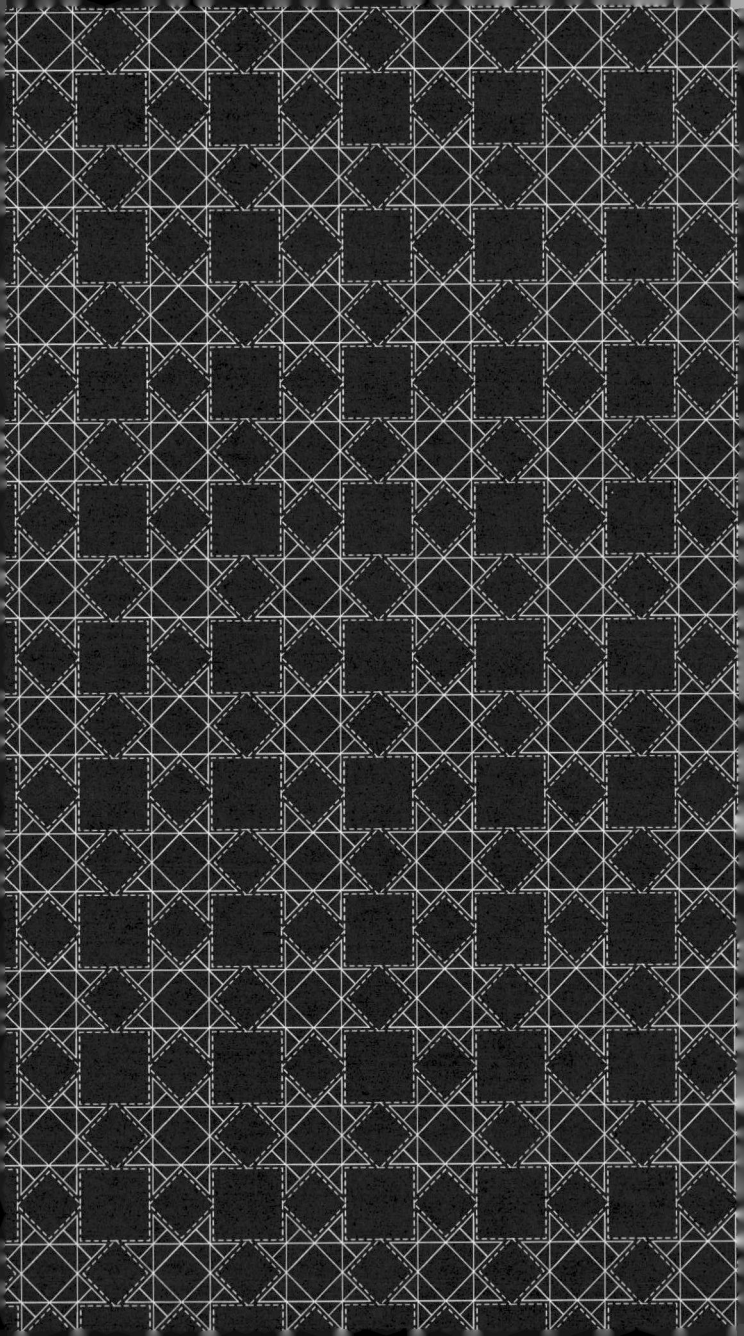

MYSTERY QUILT BLOCK 1

Clue 1

GATHER YOUR FABRICS AND CUT THEM TO SIZE
AS YOU TRIM AWAY EXCESS, ARE THEY SECRETS OR LIES

Clue 1

GATHER SUPPLIES & PRE-CUT

Supplies –
- ✓ 1 –10" sq of print fabric
- ✓ 2 –10" sq of solid color fabric
- ✓ 4 –10" sq + 1 –5" sq of white background fabric.

(NOTE: Look for sharp contrast fabric to use as your print and solid fabric squares. The white will be background fabric and can be exchanged for any preferred background color.)

Pre-Cut –

Cut all 10" sq in half to 5" x 10" strips.

Set aside 3 white 5" x 10" strips, they're good to go. Sub cut the remaining white strips into —

- ✓ 8 –5" white sq (+ the additional 5" sq there will be 9 –5" white sqs)
- ✓ 8 –2 ½" white sqs

Clue 1 – Check the Supplies and Read!

Your supplies should look something like this –

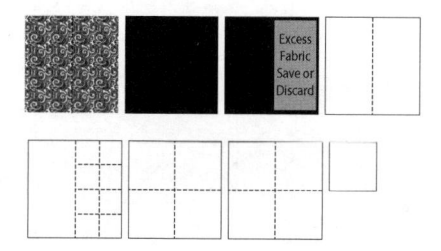

(NOTE: One of the solid color 5" x 10" strips is excess. Feel free to discard or save as you wish!)

PART Two

A Stitch Once Lost

"Jenny?"

The shush of the studio door startled Jenny away from the new pattern she was struggling with.

"Hello?" She looked up from her desk. "Blair? You're early! It's good to see you."

"Good morning," Blair said, hefting a large pile of fraying fabric onto the table. "I want to thank you again for helping me with this."

A soft 'o' formed on Jenny's lips. Heirloom quilts were her weakness. Bright pops of color peeked from the folds of the quilt. Embroidery curled around snagged threads of old stitchwork. The letters and vines piqued Jenny's curiosity.

"This is the quilt." Blair ran a hand over the fabric. "It was left in the attic for years. My mother asked me to bring it down after she got sick. We never got to work on it, but it's our family history. I'd like to make it nice." Blair opened the quilt and traced her fingers over the stitched family's names. Her parents, Frank and Gina Sloane, their wedding date, and below that Blair's name.

"What a treasure," Jenny murmured, her eyes roving the bold patterns that formed scrappy links around embroidered, white signature blocks. "I'd love to help."

"Really?" A smile tugged at one side of Blair's lips.

"Absolutely." Jenny let her fingers wander delicately over a torn piece of fabric. "Do you mind if I take a picture? I like to remember what it looked like before we fix it up."

"Go ahead." Relief eased the set of Blair's shoulders. "It needs quite a transformation. I tried to fix this section, but I think I made it worse." Haphazard sewing connected a large patch of white fabric over part of the embroidery.

"You did fine," Jenny reassured her, snapping a picture of the quilt. "It's not bad. Watch this."

Mystery in the Old Quilt

With a nearby seam ripper, Jenny snagged several stitches in one swift swipe. Half the patch came loose and in one more twitch of metal and thread the entire patch dropped away. "There we go."

Blair's jaw dropped. "Oh gosh."

Jenny handed her the piece of off-white fabric.

A string of numbers and letters peeked through the the frayed edges of the fabric. "Are you sure you want these covered? There are more dates in here. You may have found a family secret."

"Secrets?" Blair blushed. "I don't think so. I figured they were a mistake?"

"Jenny doesn't do mistakes." High heels clicked across the room, announcing Jenny's assistant, Michelle. "That's her big secret." A thoughtful expression complemented her swaying dark hair as she paused by Blair's quilt. "Where normal quilters see mistakes, Jenny sees opportunities and tricks."

"Most people would unstitch a mistake, not sew a new block over it." Jenny held a hand out to the dark-haired, blue eyed beauty. "Blair, this is Michelle Peters, my new assistant. Michelle, this is Blair Sloane."

"Actually," Michelle extended a hand to Blair. "I already know Blair. I won't blame you if you don't remember me, though. We were in school together, just different grades."

"Nice to see you . . . again." Blair pinched her brow shifting her lips into a half smile and took Michelle's hand. "I think I do remember."

"I love that you brought this in." Michelle nodded to Blair's quilt. "The embroidery is gorgeous." She admired the quilt a moment longer and moved over to her desk, sorting a stack of paperwork.

"It is lovely." Jenny pulled at the corner to see how much embroidery hid underneath. She couldn't make out the dates though, not without tearing the fabric. "Do you mind if I take a closer look?"

"Be my guest." Blair's eyes flicked between the quilt and Jenny's face before she nodded.

With a few quick flips of her seam ripper, Jenny undid the seam and lifted away the second layer of fabric, revealing four lines of delicate stitchwork.

> *10-01-1994*
> *Love anew has come to me.*
> *Love again, I must set free.*
> *10-09-1994*

Jenny's breath stalled as she read and reread the words. Something about theses hidden dates didn't feel right.

"What happened in October of 1994?" Jenny asked.

Mystery in the Old Quilt

"I don't know." Blair shook her head, "My parents weren't married till a year later."

"Ooo, it is a family secret then." Michelle arched an eyebrow suggestively.

Blair's skin turned waxy as she stared at the embroidery. The idea of family secrets seemed far less appealing to Blair than Michelle.

Something about the dates and the strange poetry unsettled Jenny. *Love anew has come to me.*

She forced a laugh, making light of Michelle's teasing. "What about other family members? Or your mother's past? Was there anyone significant before your dad? Something—anything—she might have kept from you?"

"Why would she keep something like that from me?" Blair's voice cracked slightly, as if the question itself made her confront something she wasn't ready to face. "She didn't. My grandparents passed the year I went to college, and my mom was an only child. We're it."

"If it was a relationship, it was a short one," Michelle arched an eyebrow suggestively. "Maybe he died."

Jenny could almost feel the temperature drop between the two young women. Her assistant's petulance grated against her nerves.

The snarky comment seemed to catch Blair by surprise as well. She bristled shooting Michelle an annoyed look. "Reach out if you ever need tips on dead relatives."

Michelle went pale. "Sorry, that wasn't appropriate," she said, gathering her things. "Jenny? It's almost time to meet Ron for lunch."

"I'll be right there," Jenny said as Michelle excused herself.

Once they were alone, Blair lifted and lowered the unstitched fabric, examining the hidden work. "Mom used to say if I ever learned to quilt, I might discover the family secret." Shadows crept into Blair's eyes. "I thought it was a joke, but what if she had a secret lover or child? Is that why she was killed?"

"I'm sure it's nothing," she said, putting a hand on Blair's shoulder, but the reassurance felt hollow.

"Do you think you can fix it? Secrets and all." The weight of Blair's questions hit Jenny so hard it was as if she were under water. Her chest tightened as she smiled.

"No promises on the secrets, but I'll put the quilt back together," Jenny said. It wasn't like her to pat a problem on the head and walk away. She'd do what she could. "This will be an heirloom ready for the next hundred years."

Mystery in the Old Quilt

The vines and flowers circling the Sloane family names were beautiful, if not for the torn corner.

A lump moved under the cotton as Jenny pressed her finger over the damaged fabric. The rumple ran along the center of the unstitched block. She tried several times to smooth it and failed. One wrinkle remained.

Reaching beneath the fabric, Jenny smoothed the seams and threads creating the rough patch. Something stiff scraped her, and pain pricked her finger. She jerked back.

"This wasn't paper pieced, was it?" A streak of red marred her fingertip. Jenny pinched the cut, a pinhead of blood pooling from the thin line.

"Paper—what?" A frown pressed at Blair's lips, her eyes darting back and forth as if she were working to interpret a foreign language.

Jenny chuckled softly, remembering not everyone spoke quilter. "Paper piecing is a kind of quilting where—you know, never mind."

Using her other hand, Jenny opened the layers to look for whatever had cut her. A folded slip of paper stuck out between the tacked threads, as if Gina had sewn it in place intentionally.

Carefully, Jenny removed the note and offered it to Blair.

The young woman's eyes widened, trembling fingers unfolded, the thin strip of paper. Blair smoothed it and read aloud:

> *If you're reading this, you already know my secret. You may not understand, but I did this to protect you. It's never to late to get to know your family tree.*
>
> *Secrets are best kept in the light, but should someone lost come forward, grandmas know best.*
>
> *(Her frozen heart may not provide, but what's inside will.)*

Blair's fingers trembled as she read the note aloud, the words slowly sinking in, one after another.

"What does she mean?" Jenny asked.

"I'm not sure." Worry pulled at her features, brows dipped together and lips parted, as if forming a question that wouldn't come. "I don't know her secret."

Tears threatened behind Blair's lashes as she stared at the exposed stitchwork, overfilled with emotion.

"She mentions your grandmas. Can you reach out to them?" Jenny turned the paper over, looking for any possible clues to what Gina meant.

Mystery in the Old Quilt

"No. They're gone. Grandma Sloane died when I was a toddler. I barely remember her. Grandma Rachel died more recently. But... Grandma knows best? That doesn't sound like my mom." A laugh caught in Blair's tears, her eyes distant, as if exploring a memory. "She's quoting my Grandma Rachel though. The part about secrets, anyway. I would get in so much trouble if she found out I was hiding something. Grandma always said, secrets are best kept in the light..." She looked up at Jenny. "But if not, bury them deep."

"Well, that's ominous," Jenny muttered, flipping the paper over.

Taking the note, Blair read over the words softly, forming each line in soft breathy undertones. "*—but should someone lost come forward.*" Her sudden stop was pinned with a sharp inhale. "No," she whispered. "That's impossible."

Air was the enemy as she struggled not to hyperventilate. Each pump of her lungs.came faster than the last, until Blair wasn't controlling them at all.

"Breathe through your nose." Jenny grabbed a stray Merry-go-Round precut pattern, fanning it in front of Blair. "What's wrong?" She watched as the striken girl gasped and slowly met her gaze.

"My mother's will . . . it can't be, but I've heard that before. I thought it was a weird formality. Or a typo . . ." Shifting her gaze back to the quilt, Blair took a deep breath and slowly gathered her thoughts. "In her will she included the phrase, 'Should someone lost come forward, the estate is to be split equally.'"

Jenny paused, momentarily unsure how to help. She'd dealt with plenty of crises, but this felt different. "Okay." She hesitated. "Are you worried about sharing your inheritance?"

"No," Blair whispered, almost as if the words themselves were too heavy to say out loud. "It's not about money. She said *someone lost*, like she was expecting this. If my mother left someone behind—if that's her secret—I have to find them."

"You don't have any other family, do you?"

Blair shook her head. "I don't, but more than that. Do you remember the tox screen I mentioned yesterday? If it comes back as expected it will show evidence my mother was murdered."

"Murdered?" Thoughts tumbled through Jenny's mind like a cluttered sewing basket. "I had no idea. What happened?"

"I don't know yet." Emotion glisteneed in Blair's eyes. "But if there is someone she left behind . . .maybe they would know who would want to hurt her."

Mystery in the Old Quilt

"Hello, beautiful." Ron placed a quick kiss on Jenny's cheek, as she slid onto the bench beside him.

The outdoor patio sat conveniently in front of the local bakery and burger dive on Hamilton's main street. The addition of food trucks and weekend Amish food stands made the patio feel almost like a food court.

"Hey," Jenny squeezed his hand. "You will not believe what happened today."

Blair had refused Jenny's invitation to join them for lunch, and with no need to sugarcoat things, she desperately wanted a second opinion on the quilt and its hidden information.

Ron barely nodded as he lifted a deep fried, Monte Cristo-looking sandwich. The coating had a crumbled nutty layer, adding to the classic ham and fruit flavors.

Jenny was vaguely impressed a sandwich held such control over him. He hadn't noticed her own distraction, though the words of the hidden note buzzed in her mind, but maybe this wasn't the time.

"Is that one of Sam's?" Jenny asked, deciding she could wait to share her story. "It smells amazing. Michelle, we need to order some of those. Michelle?"

Jenny's assistant had been waylaid halfway to the table, talking with one of the Missouri Star employees. Claudia, a woman from the cleaning staff Jenny had seen at the studio.

"Shush!" Dotty hissed, her finger to her lips, head tilted toward voices Jenny had ignored up to that point. "Sam and Harry are fighting over mushrooms."

"Is that good or bad?" Confusion twisted Jenny's expression.

"Drama is always good," Dotty muttered. "And this time, I'll know it before Loretta."

Jenny looked over her shoulder. Michelle and Claudia sent pointed looks flying toward the food trucks. The two women seemed as invested in the argument happening there as Dotty.

"I'm going to get lunch." Jenny stood, glancing between Dotty's focused squint and Ron's love affair with his sandwitch. "It's like a telanovela around here today."

Across the patio, Jenny found Bernie at the window of *In a Nutshell*, giving her order to the dark-haired twenty something young man working there.

Thank you notes and papers cluttered the wall near the order window. A stack of catering flyers sat beside the register, advertising *Sam's Home Cooking – Fresh,*

Mystery in the Old Quilt

Local Ingredients. Jenny picked one up and tapped Bernie on the shoulder. "Hey, Bernie," she said. "Find anything good?"

Bernie turned as Harry Millet, a local mushroom farmer, stormed into the crowd from the back side of the food truck with a basket full of orange mushrooms. "Four o'clock, Sam. I want the money by four. Or I'm taking back the shipment."

"You can't take them back. I need those chanterelles for my catering!" Sam emerged from behind the food truck yelling. His volume didn't lower until he saw the customers staring. "Maybe you forgot, but I already paid you."

"Are you callin' me crazy?" Harry yelled. He'd hit a boiling point. His face flashed red, his movements sharp and uncertain. He hesitated for a split second, then jabbed his finger at Sam again as if remembering what he was mad about. "I'm not the one pickin' fakes!"

"Where's Charlie? I thought he was in charge now." Sam raised both hands looking around at the crowd. "We already figured this out. So you don't have to worry. Just, go ask Charlie."

Jenny watched in shock as Harry grabbed a sizeable orange mushroom, waved it over his head, and launched it at Sam.

"It's your customers who should be worried if you're stockin' pois'nous shrooms. I found these jack-o-lantern mushrooms in your stash. You try'na kill people? These are poison! Even I know that."

A hidden message in a quilt, and a mushroom feud that could kill. It seemed Jenny had spent the morning unraveling one mystery, only to find herself smack dab in the middle of another.

"That's not mine!" Tension crackled as Sam dodged the flying mushroom. "I know the difference between a chanterelle and a jack! This is my specialty."

"Dotty's gotta be eating this up." Bernie chuckled, looping an arm through Jenny's elbow.

"What? The argument?" Jenny whispered.

Adjusting her glasses as if confirming they were seeing the same thing, Bernie nodded. "It was only a matter of time. Harry's been acting strange since Charlie took over the farm. Things were bound to get messy."

A truck pulled around the corner of the alley an disappeared behind the food trucks. Seconds later, the dark-haired man from the memorial appeared alongside the painted logo of *In a Nutshell*.

"Come on, Dad." He glanced nervously at the group of people watching him. Even in overalls he showed off a muscular build and strong jaw line.

Mystery in the Old Quilt

"Charlie? Good." Harry's finger twitched, amplifying his own age as he pointed at Sam. "Pay your bill, Sam. *Today*. Or Charlie'll getcha to pay. He's got my gun out back."

"What did you say to him?" Charlie asked Sam, while his eyes stayed trained on Harry. "You really got him rollin'."

"Me?" Sam complained. "Get your dad out of here before we have bigger problems."

"Fine," Charlie growled, putting an arm around Harry's shoulder. "We'll get it figured out. Sam knows what it means if he *doesn't* pay. Right, Dad?"

The men glared at each other as they passed the food truck toward the parking area.

"Whew." Bernie shook her head, "Harry must be having a bad day."

"I hope they figure it out." Jenny craned her neck watching the older man climb into the old truck. "*In a Nutshell* is the best food truck we've had in a while."

"That's true." Bernie gave Jenny a knowing glance as she adjusted her glasses. "But if Sam wants to buy from Millet, it's gonna be touch and go, at least while Harry's around."

They called Bernie's name and Jenny followed as they passed her food out the window. Jenny's gaze drifted to a glowing, handwritten, customer review tacked beside the window.

> *Sam—*
> *You made my mother's final days a little brighter. She loved the risotto. I'll never forget how much that meant to her.*
> *—Blair*

The young man disappeared from the window and Sam leaned out, grinning widely. As if the whole town hadn't witnessed him arguing over mushrooms and finances only moments before.

"What can I get you, Mrs. Doan?" he asked.

"What's this risotto Blair was raving about?" Jenny's curiosity was piqued.

Sam stiffened slightly, smacked a hand over the note and ripped it down.

"The mushroom risotto's not available from the truck. It's a catering dish." He pointed to the brightly printed pictures on the wall. "That's the menu."

"Mushroom?" Jenny took a breath of silent understanding. "Gina's favorite dish is Mr. Millet's mushroom risotto?"

"My risotto. Millet's mushrooms," Sam grumbled. "Which he's refusing to deliver. I'm sorry you had to see that. Harry's got a bit of a temper."

Mystery in the Old Quilt

"So, you're not selling poisonous mushrooms?" Jenny pointed to the basket Harry dropped spread out across the dirt.

Sam's expression soured. "What?" He leaned out the window and snarled. "No! Danny! Go get those mushrooms cleaned up. I don't want some kid to come eat 'em and get sick."

"Or die." Skepticism toyed with the information Jenny had gleaned from the argument. "Didn't the mushroom farmer seemed to think they can kill someone?"

"I don't know where Mr. Millet got his information." Sam retreated into the shade of the truck, his voice shifting into a mocking version of his usual friendly tone. "Or his mushrooms. Those weren't from me. Jacks are poisonous, but they'll make you sick and you move on. That's it. There's never been a death from them . . . that I know of." He let out a huff. "It doesn't matter, anyway. Harry Millet won't be around for long."

A chill washed over Jenny as the blood drained from her head to fill her toes. Maybe it was talking with Blair about her mother's death but Sam's phrasing made her nervous. "What do you mean?"

Sam's gaze dropped to meet hers. He soothed the tension in his jaw, settling his expression back into a smile. "Nothing. Of course nothing, just that Charlie's taking over. That'll be so much better—I hope."

"Right," Jenny choked the word out, forcing it past a suddenly dry throat. "Can I order the chicken strips?"

Sam glowered briefly, made a note, and slapped the ticket on the counter. "Here. It'll be a few minutes."

Jenny took the ticket, jumping back as the window smacked shut. She turned, but no one was close enough to witness her almost getting closed in the awning. She scanned the receipt. Sam's handwriting was all sharp, illegible lines. On one of the more aggressive markings, a hole tore through the paper.

"—if it's in awful condition, I don't see why anyone would be so obsessed with it," someone asked. "How do you know if the quilt is worth all the effort?"

Jenny's ears perked up at the sound of a quilting conversation.

Claudia and Michelle stood in debate at the corner of the food truck, while Danny moved around them, picking up poisoned mushrooms from the dirt.

"It has her whole family history, and then some!" Michelle lowered her voice instinctively. "There's even a secret message inside."

Jenny leaned in as Claudia had and chuckled, realizing Danny had done the same thing.

Mystery in the Old Quilt

"Isn't that exciting?" Michelle asked. "I would love to have something like that. It tells a story, I think that's what Jenny said, but this one has stories and secrets."

Based on the tsking sound from Claudia and her pinched frown, she didn't agree. "If that's true," Claudia said. "Someone's finding out all Gina's secrets real soon."

Danny coughed and stood. Only it wasn't Danny. Charlie had been gathering the spilled mushrooms. She'd mistaken Charlie's dark hair for Danny's.

"Thanks for your help, Charlie." Claudia reached over and knocked on the back door of the food truck. "Go on in. There's a big trash in the back for those. I'm sure Sam wants to chat with you."

"Thanks, Claudia." Charlie's voice was warmer than before. He took his time moving to the door, giving them a polite nod before he disappeared inside.

Michelle moved away and caught Jenny watching them. "Jenny," Michelle called waving her over. "Please come tell my mother how amazing Gina's quilt is, or is going to be."

"Your mother?" Jenny blinked. "I didn't realize—it's Claudia, right?"

"Oh!" Michelle jumped, gesturing between them. "So, sorry. Jenny, this is my mother—"

"Claudia Peters." Claudia returned Jenny's greeting, her firm handshake raising Jenny's estimation of the woman. "Mother to Michelle. Wife to Sam. Housekeeper of your studio and several local shops. It keeps me busy."

Both women had thick, brown hair and matching mother and daughter necklaces, but the closer Jenny looked, the less similar they seemed. One had golden brown eyes the other blue, Michelle was taller, even their builds were different.

Claudia cleared her throat, disrupting Jenny's thoughts. "Some say Michelle takes after her dad, but I think we're more alike than people realize."

"Sorry," Jenny chuckled. "I didn't mean to stare. Family connections have been on my mind today. Gina's quilt is something special. You should come see it if you'd like. Michelle can let you in anytime."

Michelle grabbed her mother's hand. "Oh you're going to love it. It's got the most gorgeous flowers stitched all over it. Blair Sloane, a girl I knew in school, she brought it in. It has their whole family history, and then some."

"You know Blair?" Surprise rang in her voice as the food truck door opened with a smack. Charlie leaned out, his gaze flickering toward the women, then he left as quickly as he'd come.

Mystery in the Old Quilt

"Mmhmm." Michelle said. "How do you know her?"

"I don't." Claudia shot a glance at Jenny and back to Michelle. "But I knew Gina. We weren't friends, but I heard about Blair coming back to town after her mom got sick."

"Oh, wow." Michelle blinked in surprise. "Sorry, mom. I didn't realize you knew each other. Did you know her—well?"

"No, just of her. It's hard to believe I'm already losing people I went to school with."

"Babe?" Sam called to Claudia. "Is everything all right?" He stepped through the doorway and shoved a large brown envelope back to the real Danny.

Jenny's name was called at the front of the food truck. She did her best to ignore it, until Michelle gave her a strange look, and she abandoned her curiosity.

"Here you go." Danny handed Jenny her plate when she came to the front window. "Would you like to pay with cash or card?"

"Card—" Jenny fumbled with her purse. "Unless I can't find it." She pulled out a pair of sewing scissors, a travel size lotion, a pill bottle, and full-size doorknob before setting her phone down to look properly.

"I don't think they take spare home repair items as payment." Ron picked up the metal handle she'd pulled from her purse. "Right, Danny?" He spun the ball of the knob on the counter, catching it as it tumbled over.

"Sorry, no doorknobs." Impatience shifted in Danny's expression, but he didn't complain.

Jenny groaned. "I don't usually carry those in my purse."

Ron chuckled, opened his wallet, retrieved his card, and handed it over.

"Thanks, Mr. Doan." Danny ran the card while Jenny repacked her bag.

"Okay," she said, her patience strained. "It's not so unusual. The knob fell off the basement door before we left. I was going to ask you to fix it."

"Not a problem, sweetheart." Ron tucked the handle in his pocket. "I'm guessing at the studio? We were having trouble with that one."

"Would you have time to fix it today?" Jenny asked, following Ron to their now empty table.

"I'll get it done before the trunk show." He winked at her as they sat, and picked one of the home cut fries from her plate.

MYSTERY
QUILT BLOCK 1

Clue 2

ONE HIDDEN THREAD CAN UNRAVEL A SECRET
BUT CAREFULLY LOST, EVEN BONES CANNOT KEEP IT

Clue 2

Pre-Sew & Cut

Pair up the fabrics –

With your 5" x 10" strips place *RST

- ✓ 1 Print & Solid strip
- ✓ 1 White & Print strip RST
- ✓ 2 sets of White & Solid strips RST

(NOTE: These will be referenced as strip sets throughout the project. Each strip set will be identified by their initials, either grouped or separated ex. PR/S, W/PR, & S/W)

Time to sew –

Sew all 5" x 10" strip sets together on BOTH long sides.

Then cut each set down the middle, lengthwise into 2 – 2 ½" x 10" strips.

Press open.

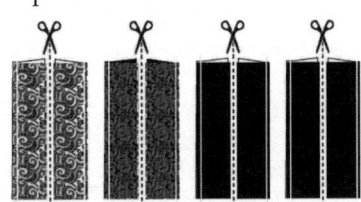

Clue 2 – Check the Supplies and Read!

The strip sets should measure approx. 4 ½" x 10"

From this step you will have –
- ✓ 8 – 4 ½" x 10" strip sets
  (2 PR/S | 2 W/PR | 4 S/W)

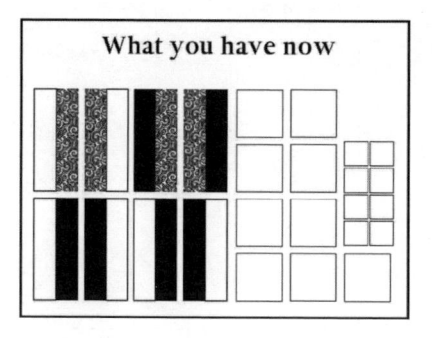

What you have now

*RST = Right Sides Together

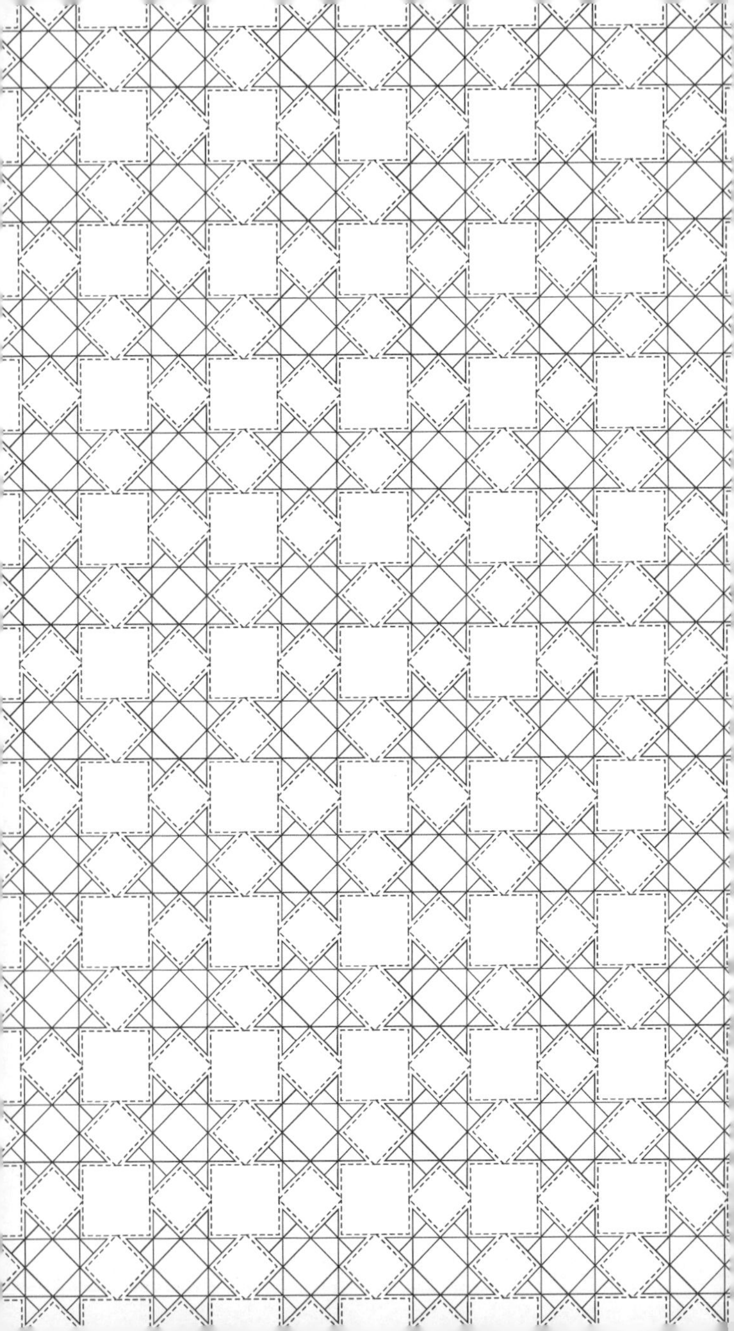

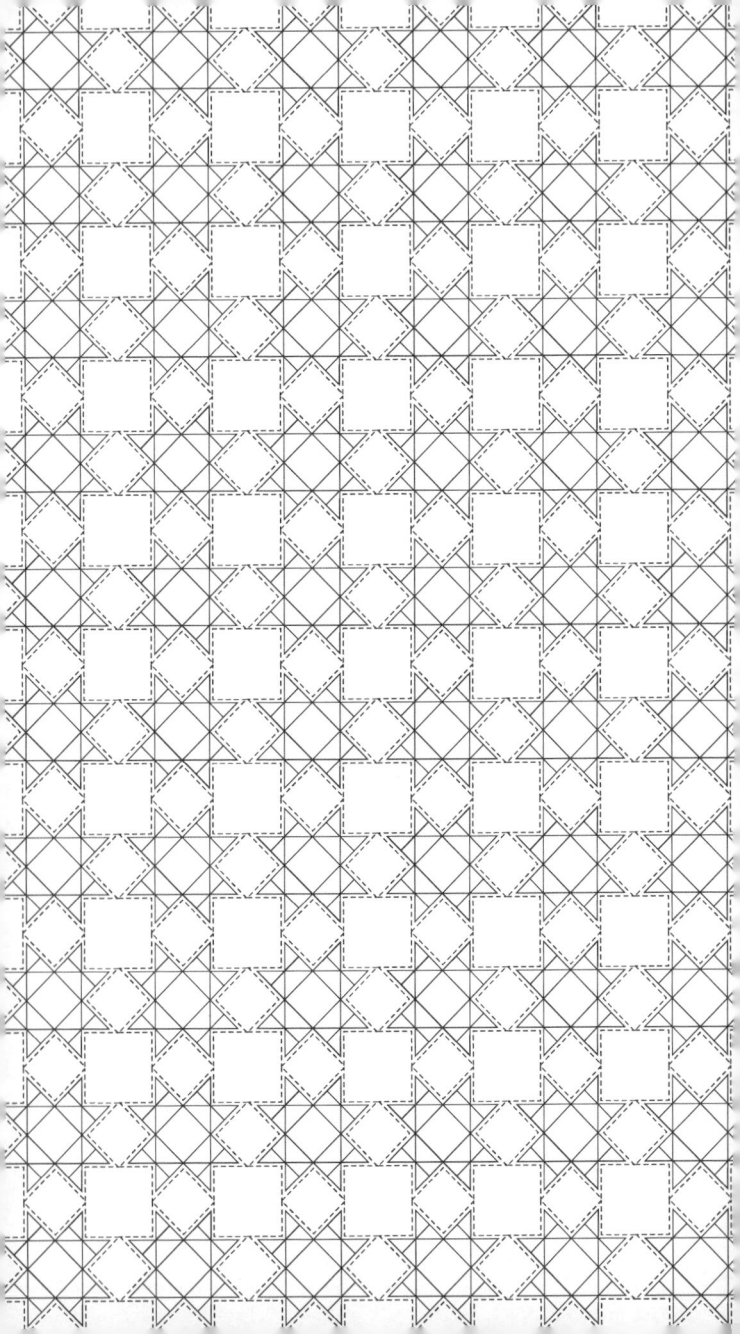

PART Three

Embroidered Lies

"IT STILL AMAZES ME TO WATCH YOUR TRUNK shows in action." Bernie shook her head as she and Dotty joined Jenny at the back of the old theater.

The sun had set by the time the trunk show ended.

"Did you see Loretta come in?" Bernie asked, pushing the door open.

"Did you see Loretta leave?" Dotty laughed. "I didn't even get to tell her about Sam and Harry's argument today."

"You know," Jenny said, and giggled as they exited

the building and entered the alley. "I don't think she enjoyed the show very much."

The theater's side entrance led them into the alley, where Sam's food truck sat closed up for the night, tucked away from the main road.

"Do we get to go see the quilt tonight?" Bernie asked.

Jenny looked up in surprise, then laughed, shaking her head. "I forgot I told you about it."

"You texted a picture," Bernie clarified. "Said you wanted me to take a look when I had time."

Focused on the mystery, Jenny had forgotten part of the plan was fixing it. "I haven't started repairs yet, but I'd love any help you can give."

Bernie grinned. "Let's go see it."

They matched stride with Dotty, crossing the deserted street to the studio. "Someone must still be at work," Jenny said, noticing the light in the window. Then something moved by the basement door and she stopped cold. "I didn't leave the door open."

"Well, it wasn't me," Dotty said.

"Me neither," Bernie whispered.

Motioning the other two women forward, Jenny moved to the side of the building. She patted her pockets and frowned. "I haven't been able to find my phone since lunch."

Mystery in the Old Quilt

The basement door creaked in a nonexistent breeze, hanging open on its hinges.

Jenny tiptoed toward the door, reached out, and it flew back.

Light flooded the darkness.

Dotty screamed, and Bernie laughed.

"Jenny?" Ron appeared behind the swinging door.

"What are you doing back there?" Jenny asked, her tone reprimanding.

"Fixing the doorknob. That's what you wanted me to do, right?" His half smile warmed Jenny as he knelt, moving a flashlight over his work. "I was going to do it before the trunk show, but I got a little distracted. It's almost ready."

"Do you mind if we go up?" Jenny asked. "I need to show the girls Gina's quilt."

"Not at all. Will you hand me the screwdriver? This one's not long enough." He pointed to his tool bag on the first step.

Jenny retrieved the tool, swapping it with the one in Ron's hand. She dropped the old screwdriver in her purse and hurried into the building. "Quick, or he'll have us fetching screws and levels."

Ron scoffed. "It's just a doorknob." He swung the door back and forth a moment. "On second thought . . ."

"Oh my." Dotty passed Jenny on her way up the stairs.

Jenny followed, directing her friends inside and to the work table. "There's a lot of history on this quilt. But these are the lines Blair and I discovered." She showed them the poem and dates. "I'd love to know if you have any insight."

Dotty fingered a few of the pins, probably wanting to rearrange things.

"Think you'll have this figured out by tomorrow?" Jenny teased.

Bernie pulled a pair of glasses from her handbag and leaned over the blocks. "Love anew has come to me. Love again, I must set free."

Dotty pursed her lips. "Love came, and love went. Maybe she was married before."

"Gina was only married once," Bernie muttered. "I was there."

"Gina's mother, Rachel, was a good friend to Bernie." Dotty patted her sister's shoulder, as if it made her proud.

"Grandma Rachel?" Jenny asked. "Would you have known her then? I mean Gina, when she was young?"

"I did. Rachel and I were friends a long time." Bernie didn't look away from the embroidery.

"Do you have any idea what might have happened

Mystery in the Old Quilt

during that time?" Jenny tried to calculate quietly. "I think Gina would have been a junior or senior."

"A senior?" Bernie looked up, her gaze shifting nervously. "Gina had normal teenage issues."

Jenny hesitated. "You know, don't you?"

"I was friends with Rachel, not Gina." Bernie shrugged, and then nodded. "But she talked to me about some things a couple times. I was sworn to secrecy."

Dotty narrowed her eyes. "But you've told me, right?"

Bernie shook her head. "I'm sorry. I couldn't."

"If you know something, it could help a lot," Jenny said.

"I don't know." Bernie swallowed and looked between them, still nervous. "I never thought I'd tell anyone, but . . . maybe it's time."

"We're not the ones leaving hints about whatever happened. She must think it's time too." Jenny reminded.

Bernie nodded, but it still took a careful moment before she spoke. "I went to visit Rachel one day. No one else was there, but she was in tears, sobbing. Rachel told me Gina—had gotten pregnant. You were right, she was a senior in high school."

"You're kidding me," Dotty hissed, soaking up a

secret Bernie had kept from her. "You've known all this time."

"Gina would have been ruined." Bernie's voice dropped to a whisper, her voice heavy as she relived the conversations. "She told her mom in the middle of summer. The baby would have been due at the new school year, and Rachel didn't know what to do."

Disbelief battled in Jenny's mind. It was a familiar enough story but she'd never known someone who'd been through it.

"I'm sorry I couldn't tell you." Bernie said to her sister. "I don't think she ever told anyone but me. The poor girl went to stay with her grandmother. And we didn't bring it up after."

Jenny tapped the table, still trying to put the puzzle pieces together. "That's the only time she mentioned it? What about when Gina returned?"

"I asked about the baby, but Rachel wouldn't talk about it. She said it was handled. I never saw the baby."

"No one knew? What about Gina's friends?" Confusion and surprise pulled at Jenny's logic.

"You could ask Claudia. They knew each other pretty well."

"Really?" Jenny asked.

Bernie shrugged and turned to Dotty. "Are you ready to go? I'm tired."

Mystery in the Old Quilt

She could have sworn Claudia said she hadn't been friends with Gina. Was she lying?

Jenny stewed over the new information as Bernie and Dotty left. She reached for her phone to call Claudia, only to remember it was still missing.

"Where did I put it?" She worked backward through the day. The last time she'd seen it was when she'd picked up her lunch at *In a Nutshell*. "I'll ask Sam if I left it, tomorrow."

The food truck was outside her window, parked by the theater and closed up for the night.

Only . . . it wasn't closed.

A light glowed through the small windows.

"Ron?" Jenny called on her way downstairs. "How's the door coming?" A clunk of metal hit the wall, and she jumped. "Sweetheart?"

Her voice sounded more apprehensive than she'd intended, but it finally got a response.

Ron leaned his head around the door. "Sorry about that." He twisted the doorknob and gave a sheepish grin. "I dropped the level."

Jenny let her relief settle. "Okay, I'm going to run back to the theater while you finish."

Ron looked up in surprise. "Do you want me to come with you?"

"No, I'll be right back." Jenny started toward the

street, shaking her head. "Someone's at the food truck, and I want to see if I left my phone there."

He nodded and glanced toward the alley. "I'll come find you when I'm done."

"Call me." Jenny winked and crossed the street. The hair on the back of her neck prickled. The empty alley felt more dangerous and creepy than when she'd left it fifteen minutes before.

The streetlight didn't do much for the space. A door slammed, and Jenny jumped. "Sam?"

No one answered.

Jenny knocked on the food truck door. "Sa—am?" The waver in her voice caught her by surprise. She cleared her throat and called again. "Sam?"

When no one answered, Jenny tried the knob. It didn't turn, but a set of keys lay on the ground. She bent to pick them up, and the door swung open.

Metal hit the wall and a large envelope swung out of the darkness toward her, smacking the side of her head with more force than should come from a paper weapon.

A sharp curse rang out, as her assailant hurried past.

"Hey!" she yelled. "I'm calling the police!" They didn't need to know she had no way to do that.

If she were lucky, Ron would have heard the commotion and he'd do it for her.

Mystery in the Old Quilt

Trying to focus, Jenny blinked, only understanding as the figure lurched back. He was coming for her. She opened her mouth to yell, but a rough hand clamped over it, muffling her cry.

"Shut up," the man hissed. "You're not supposed to be here."

The gravel tone of his voice tore through her. Panic clawed at her throat, like a serger at high speed, cutting through fabric and punching stitches at the same time. She thrashed, working her mouth free to bite his arm.

He jerked away with a yelp, and Jenny sucked in a breath, screaming with everything she had. "Ron!"

Footsteps thundered through the alley. "Jenny!" Ron's voice cut through the night.

The man cursed again and bolted, his silhouette vanishing into the shadows.

"He's getting away!" Jenny's heart pounded

Ron caught up to her and wrapped her in his arms. "Are you okay?"

Jenny pulled out of her husband's embrace, but her attacker was already half a block away. The futility of chasing him sat like a heavy iron on her chest.

"It's okay," Ron soothed, pulling her back. "We'll call the police."

She nodded, but nothing about this was okay. The fading footsteps pounded like a headache. Her attacker knew who she was, but she didn't know him, and they'd let him run free.

Jenny's gaze flickered to the ground, where a torn paper fluttered near the food truck's step. It looked like part of the envelope she'd been hit with. It didn't make much sense, but a throbbing pain still ached where the package had connected with her head.

She picked up the scrap of brown paper, flipping it over. Red hash lines covered the back, like security markings.

Ron pulled out his cell phone, holding Jenny close while it rang. His hand brushed over her back, as her shoulders trembled.

"Yes, Officer Wilkins? I need to report an attack."

BREAD AND SUGAR SCENTED the bakery as Jenny placed her order. By the time she received her quiche, she'd almost forgotten the gravelly voice in her ear. A sigh of relief escaped as she turned and found a table.

Blair sat scribbling in the corner, a large muffin doused in powdered sugar and cinnamon beside her.

"Good morning, Blair." Jenny pulled out the chair beside her. "Do you mind if I join you?" She'd been on

Mystery in the Old Quilt

her way to the studio when the smell of cinnamon and bacon had detoured here for breakfast.

She needed a moment to figure out how to find Gina's secret baby. If it even existed.

"Please, um—yes. I mean, of course. Please sit." Blair scrambled to put her papers away while standing to greet Jenny, gesturing to the open chair.

"What are you working on?" Jenny wasn't sure if the chaos of papers and thoughts was normal for Blair.

"I was just—I was telling a friend... about the quilt." Heat colored Blair's skin as she sank slowly into her seat. It took several seconds to settle herself, almost like she was avoiding looking at Jenny.

When she finally met Jenny's gaze, she immediately reached for her muffin, breaking away pieces to eat.

Jenny picked up her fork. "Is everything all right?"

"It's fine." A piece of muffin hovered near her lips.

Jenny put her fork back down, and met Blair's gaze. "What's going on?"

Blair hesitated, then slowly set her food aside. She picked up a stack of books and opened one. A folded paper marked the page, Gina's name circled in red. Several familiar names were listed beside hers, including Sam Peters, Claudia Burr, Charlie Millet, and even Frank Sloane.

Jenny nodded at the pages. "Is that Gina's yearbook?"

"Oh, yeah. I found it in her things." Blair waved it off, fidgeting with the corner of the bookmark. "I was looking at old names, but that's not what I wanted to show you." She unfolded the paper and held it out. "This note was left under my door yesterday."

Ink scrawled across the page in a single, harsh line. Nerves tingled down Jenny's spine.

Leave the quilt on her grave tonight with its secret intact.

The letters were jagged, almost frantic, pressing deep into the paper. "I thought it was some kind of prank." Blair's breath caught. "But now... I don't know."

"This isn't just some prank," she murmured, keeping her voice steady despite the unease crawling over her skin. "Someone knows about Gina's secret."

"That's what I was afraid of." Blair closed her eyes, drooping in her seat. "I keep thinking about everything she said before she died. She must have given me a hint. She kept talking about our family tree and something hidden—something I was supposed to find. She really had a secret and I ignored it. And now someone else knows. I didn't know she was going to die." Blair buried her face in her hands. "If I can't figure this out . . . someone else might."

Jenny put a hand on Blair's arm. "We're not going to let that happen. I learned about some things your mother went through that summer—" Jenny hesitated, her throat tightening. This wasn't a random teen pregnancy. To reveal a secret like this—especially when she didn't have proof—it felt like taking something away from Blair instead of giving her answers.

"I think I already know." Blair looked down at her stack of papers and books. "I found her journal from 1994. There wasn't much in it, just a few mentions of dating a guy named Charles over the summer, then a lot of torn out pages. Afterwards she only ever mentioned my dad. Something obviously happened, but my mother never spoke about a relationship with anyone else."

"She got her heart broken." Jenny let that sink in. "Was there any mention of a baby?"

"No." Blair blinked, taken aback. "She would have told me something like that. Maybe she got hurt, but she didn't have a baby."

Jenny poked at her quiche, she couldn't say anything till she had proof. Gina had been pregnant, but she would have fallen for someone first. There was a good chance anyway. Maybe this Charles was the key to finding out what really happened.

"I need to get going." Blair stood, picking up her muffin and the papers. "The police asked me to come by. The tox report came back and I think they found something."

"Do you know what?" Jenny frowned, standing with Blair.

"I'm not sure. They aren't calling it murder—not yet—but they should be. I know it." Shadows darkened Blair's eyes like gathering storm clouds. "Her heart issues accelerated much faster than they should have. I just wish I knew who wanted to hurt her." Inhaling deeply, she waited, counting to three or maybe five or whatever she needed to calm down. "It seems more and more strange."

"Can I help?" Jenny asked.

Emotion and confusion, called up tears, as the clouds in Blair's eyes began to mist. Paper crinkled in her ever tightening grip. She stepped back, darting a look at the door. "I'm sorry. I need to go."

Jenny accepted the gesture without question, moving aside to let Blair take her leave.

The bell chimed on the door as she left and Loretta pushed through awkwardly blocking Blair's path.

The quiche sat uneaten on her plate. She managed

Mystery in the Old Quilt

a few more bites before Loretta approached her table, eyes narrowed in a cultivated look of intimidation. It would've been more impressive if Loretta weren't rubbing her wrist, as if her bad mood somehow aggravated her joints.

"What are you doing here?" Loretta asked, hovering at the edge of the table.

Jenny glanced around the bakery where a dozen people were enjoying their food. "Breakfast?"

A snagged thread hung from Loretta's cuff, missing the match of the pearl button on her opposite sleeve. The rare flaw hinted at more than annoyance affecting Loretta's mood.

Jenny took another bite of her quiche and stood. "You can join me if you like?"

Loretta's lip curled. "I have a table," she snarled. "But I happen to know you're not *just* eating breakfast. I saw you chase Blair off. Maybe try minding your own business next time."

"We were talking about her mother." Jenny's reply only seemed to expand Loretta's irritation.

"You're not the only one in town," she blustered. "Quit monopolizing her time."

She turned sharply, shooting glares at the other customers like darts. Tiny explosions of negative energy began in every direction. People tripped, dropped things, and scattered, clearing her path as Loretta stormed across the room and demanded *her* table be cleared and the man sitting there leave.

Jenny chose to do so before the wave of cosmic energy shifted. The bell chimed as she pulled the door open and she met the gaze of a wiry old man, sitting by the window. Coffee and a calm demeanor had disguised Harry Millet completely.

As Jenny left the restaurant, she couldn't shake the feeling he had watched her go.

Outside, the air held a bite Jenny welcomed. It felt like a stitch had been clipped in her chest, releasing the pressure Loretta had knotted in place when she walked into the room.

"Jenny!" Michelle scurried across the patio, her heels forcing her into short steps. "Thank goodness I found you. You weren't answering your texts, and I didn't know who to call and—oh!"

Harry brushed past both of them, knocking Michelle off balance as he passed. His dark glare lingered for a second before he muttered, "People ought to let the dead rest. Nothin' good comes from stirring up old secrets."

Jenny's fingers clenched. Quiet anxiety spun around her. "Does he mean Gina?"

"How would he know her?" Michelle whispered.

Mystery in the Old Quilt

"Hey, relax." Jenny adjusted her purse and patted her pocket, expecting to find her phone. "Sorry for the radio silence. I think I left my phone on the food truck counter at lunch yesterday."

"Oh." Michelle pulled her phone out. "I think Dad should be coming in soon, but I don't know when exactly."

"It's fine. I'll get it at lunchtime."

Michelle nodded, relief washing over her. "Have you been to the studio yet?"

"Not this morning, but I'm heading that way." Jenny said, crossing to the sidewalk.

Michelle followed, clearing her throat and tapping her fingers together. "Well, um, you might notice something."

Jenny stopped them on the other side of the street. "Is anything wrong?"

"Maybe, yes. Um. The doorknob Ron fixed . . .it's, uh, it's broken again."

Jenny groaned. "Good grief. I'll let him know."

"And—" Michelle made a tiny squeak of a whimper. "—the quilt is missing."

Jenny froze mid-step. "What?"

"Blair's quilt." Her voice warbled, all her brash confidence drowning in words Jenny couldn't have heard right. A breeze blew a flurry of dark of hair in

Michelle's face as she tried to explain. "I don't know what happened. I hoped you had taken it home, but—"

"It's gone?" She wasn't sure if it was a question or a statement. Jenny finally understood Michelle's worry.

Michelle swallowed. "Yeah," she whispered.

Jenny took a slow breath. "Do I need to call the police?"

"DON'T TOUCH THAT." Jenny swatted Officer Wilkins' hand away from a pile of carefully disorganized fabric. He stepped back, hands raised, but he narrowed his eyes at her tone.

"I'm sorry." A zipper line of nerves, all cold metal and teeth, ran down her back. "I meant, please don't touch that. They're for a new quilt I'm filming."

Officer Wilkins nodded and continued around the room. "Just checking things out." He didn't push but seemed grateful for the courtesy of an explanation. His partner, however, looked eager for the chance to question someone.

"Are you sure you haven't given anyone else a key recently?" Officer Dunn leaned toward Michelle as if his glare could see through her.

Mystery in the Old Quilt

Michelle took a measured breath before answering, her nostrils flaring slightly. "I have not. And like I said before, I'm not the only one with a key—but since the doorknob is missing." She glanced back at Jenny, her eyebrow seeming permanently lifted. "I don't think a key was necessary."

Jenny gave a sad smile. The search and question session would be funnier if it weren't happening because of losing an irreplaceable family heirloom. A spool of red thread spun smoothly through Jenny's fingers.

"And you haven't seen anyone new or out of the ordinary around?" Officer Dunn asked.

Michelle flinched, and Dunn pulled out a notebook, jotting something down before she even had a chance to answer.

Jenny tossed the thread in a drawer as Officer Wilkins passed her desk. "Can't you tell him to ease up?" Both officers turned toward her, and she rolled her eyes. "What would Michelle have to gain from stealing a quilt in desperate need of repair."

"I thought you said it was some kind of '*heirloom*.' Doesn't that make it valuable?"

"To the owner." Jenny's exasperation grew, and she flung a hand toward Michelle.

Exhaustion pulled at Michelle's drooping shoulders. Outside the window the food truck drove out of the alley to its place near the food court. "Danny came in last night. He was picking me up for a date."

"You're dating?" Skepticism pervaded Officer Wilkins' question. "Is it unusual for your boyfriend to be here?"

"Not dating." Michelle corrected. "It was one date. Danny works with my dad in the food truck. He followed me in to get my purse and that's all the time he was here." Michelle leaned forward as Officer Dunn wrote something down.

"I see." The officer shifted away and finished, tapping his pen on the paper. "Do you have any questions, Wilkins?"

Officer Wilkins crawled out from under the work table. A necklace with a tiny angel dangled from his fingers.

Michelle's attention snapped to the tiny charm in Wilkins' hand, and she reached out quickly to claim it. "That's mine."

He handed the necklace to her as his phone buzzed. His radio beeped loudly at the same time and he leaned over pressing a button as he spoke into it. "Downtown, wrapping up with Mrs. Doan and Peters." He released the button and turned to the women. "We need to go. Do you know anyone who was here after you left last night?"

Mystery in the Old Quilt

Jenny shook her head. "No."

"The cleaning staff," Michelle said. "I let them in and went home."

"You went home?" Wilkins asked. "I thought you were on a date."

"I was." Michelle blushed. "But Danny canceled before we got out the door. My dad needed something. Any other embarrassing details I can share with you?"

"No, it's just—that's interesting." Wilkins sighed, rubbing the back of his neck. "This is the busiest day we've had in months. First Blair Sloane, now this."

Jenny straightened. "You spoke with Blair?"

"Yeah," Dunn muttered, looking over his notepad.

She unintentionally tracked his gaze and found the name Sam Peters scribbled along the side of the page. "What does Sam have to do with this?"

Dunn flipped the notepad shut. "It's routine," he said. "Blair's asking a lot of questions. Some tests came back, and they've got her spooked."

Jenny's stomach tightened. "Spooked how?"

"We can't really talk about that." Wilkins rapped his knuckles on the door frame, finality clear in his tone. "Anyway, thank you, ladies. We appreciate your cooperation."

"Thanks for letting us look around." Officer Dunn

turned to Michelle and Jenny before following his partner's lead.

"Anytime, officers," Jenny replied shortly.

Her tight response brought a smile to Wilkins' lips. "Relax. Things have a way of working out." He nodded to Jenny and Michelle. "You might want to let someone know about the mess under the table."

"Excuse me? Our staff cleans very well. Every night." Michelle's offense was immediate and almost humorous. "The nerve." She dropped to her knees, fishing out a small pile of debris from the corner. "A sticky note and a pearl button? That warrants a mess? Really? I wonder what we'd find at his house."

"A pearl button?" Jenny leaned closer. She had plenty of fabric and notions, but pearl buttons weren't on the list of quilting supplies she kept on hand.

Everything Michelle had pulled from under the table was covered in a thin layer of dust—except for the button. The smooth surface was immaculate. Jenny could almost see the snagged cuff of Loretta's shirt and how well the pearl button would match.

Beside it, the little yellow square had Gina's name scrawled across the top. The rest was filled with ordered points about Hamilton Quilt Guild history, key points of Gina's life, and a star highlighting the words *Memorial Quilt*.

Mystery in the Old Quilt

"Loretta?" Jenny muttered, flipping the note over. "When did you lose this?"

She pulled a scrap of brown paper from the adhesive strip, revealing a scrawl of hurried cursive below it.

"Meet Mon time at 4:00"

"Hmm." Jenny glanced at the clock. "Monday at four."

"No, it's not even lunch yet." Michelle muttered, thinking Jenny had asked about the time. She held out the chain. "Can you help me? I can't work the clasp."

"Of course." Jenny took the necklace, setting the papers down on the table. The scrap of brown fluttered over, red hash marks covering the back.

"That's weird," she muttered. "I saw something like that last night."

"Like what?" Michelle asked, lifting her hair as Jenny slipped the jewelry around her neck.

"A paper. Actually it looks like something from your dad's place. He wouldn't have been here, would he?"

"I don't think so." Michelle put a hand to her throat as Jenny released the chain. "Thank you."

"Of course."

A second later, the necklace slipped from Michelle's fingers and dropping to the floor.

"Oh!" Jenny yelped, reaching for it.

Michelle waved her off, picking it up herself. "Don't worry about it." She inspected the necklace with a frown. "I must have grabbed my mother's today. Her clasp doesn't hold well."

"That's strange. But how did it get under the table?" Worry settled in Jenny's chest.

"I don't know. Maybe I didn't." Michelle dropped it onto her desk. "She could have lost it while she was cleaning."

Jenny nodded to herself, picking up the little papers and button. She examined them once more. The scrap of brown had a hint of ink on the torn edge, the partial imprint of a peanut logo.

Tucking them into her purse, she decided she needed to run a couple errands before handing her suspicions over to the police.

MYSTERY
QUILT BLOCK 1

Clue 3

Layers you stitch, when truth makes you cry
Hide needles to draw out the blood of old lies

Clue 3

CUT ONCE MORE

Using the long strip sets you made last time, separate out the sets with the white background fabric and sub cut them into 5" long sections.

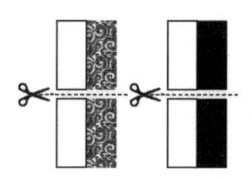

You will have –
- ✓ 12 – 5" x 4 ½" blocks (4 W/PR & 8 S/W)

✓

For the Print and Solid strip sets sub cut them into 4 ½" long sections. You will have a tiny bit of excess fabric at the bottom of these strips you can discard. Don't worry, this is intentional.

You will have –
- ✓ 4 – 4 ½" x 4 ½" (4 PR/S)

Clue 3 – Check the Supplies and Read!

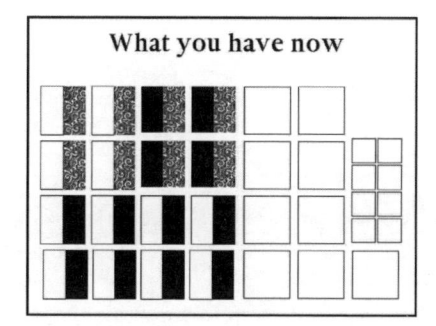

What you have now

PART Four

A Pattern of Deception

Words stumbled over words, thoughts flying through Jenny's mind as she climbed the steps of the Craftsman style home Gina had loved.

Hi Blair, I lost your hand-embroidered family heirloom quilt. The one your mother worked on her whole life, documenting your entire family history and potentially holding the truth of her deepest secrets. Yeah, sorry, it's gone.

She cringed at every painful truth and reminded herself she was determined and strong. If it were her, she'd want to know what happened. She raised her hand to knock but jerked her hand back as the door swung open.

"How did you know?" Blair beckoned her inside, eyes scanning the yard behind her.

Jenny frowned. "Know what?"

"I thought you were the police. Come in, please. They're supposed to be here soon." The taut vacancy in Blair's voice worried Jenny

Only steps inside, Jenny slowed. "What happened?"

Gina's home was usually filled with antiques, books, and knick knacks. Today boxes and furniture were pushed out of place and every surface was bare.

"Did you get robbed?"

"I don't think so . . . maybe?" Blair turned, seeing Jenny's eye on the bare room. "Oh, this? I'm moving. With my parents gone, it doesn't feel right to stay."

"I'm sorry." Instinct told her to offer a hug, but Blair's stoic gaze seemed determined to avoid everything—including Jenny. "What did you mean, you don't think you were robbed?"

Blair's eyes flickered away, then back. "Come with me."

Jenny followed her down the hall into a far from empty bedroom. "Is this—"

"My mom's room." Blair didn't go inside, but she held her hand out inviting Jenny in.

Mystery in the Old Quilt

Brass animals littered the dresser and windowsills. A shawl draped across a dressing chair, and the soft scent of perfume hung in the texture of the room.

"I found this after I got back from visiting with the police, so I get to see them twice today." Blair shook her head. "They got the tox screen back. Did I tell you that? No, I guess not. We haven't seen each other since breakfast." She took a steadying breath. "My mother's heart condition wasn't what killed her. Not alone anyway. She was poisoned."

Jenny's stomach dropped. "No, Blair. I'm so sorry."

"They didn't tell me what kind," Blair muttered. "I overheard them at the station. It doesn't take a genius to figure out what happened, though. I can't understand why Sam would want my mother dead."

"Sam?" Jenny's mind flashed to her conversation at the food truck the day before where Sam had told her— *Jack-o-lanterns won't kill someone on their own.* The scrawl of Sam's name on the officers' notes was suddenly understandable. "You mean the risotto? But why?"

Jenny had seen Blair's review, and Sam himself had said Gina's favorite meal was the mushroom risotto.

"I haven't figured that out yet." Blair sighed. "After mom's heart attack, she was weak. I hired a nurse to check on her, had her home cleaned, her laundry done. Sam catered her meals. He had access to everything."

Quiet settled around whispers in the empty room.

"We'll find out what's going on." Jenny promised. "You have too many people who care about you and your mother. If it was Sam, we'll figure it out."

Blair's watery smile didn't inspire confidence. "Sorry, you don't need to put up with my weeping. That's not why you're here."

The quilt, she reminded herself.

"Blair," Jenny started. This wasn't why she was here. She needed to explain what happened.

Blair pointed to the corner. "Someone broke in. Nothing is missing, but I got another note."

Glass shards covered a nightstand beneath an empty windowsill. The window wasn't broken but had been left open. The figurines that once sat there had fallen to the ground, taking the contents of the nightstand with them.

A picture frame lay broken on the table, the likely source of the shattered glass. Blair was centered in the image between her mother and father. The floor around the photo was littered with various items—a tiny frame, a hairbrush, a lamp, and a half-empty, expired pill bottle tipped against a framed embroidery. Everything Gina would have had at her bedside.

Mystery in the Old Quilt

Jenny nudged the pill bottle, the tablets inside rattling, and noted the use date had expired over a year ago. "Was your mother current on her medication?"

"She took it every day." Blair passed a piece of paper from one hand to the other. "Why?"

"The expiration date on the label is almost a year old. Did she save old bottles? Or is this an outdated prescription?"

Blair's expression pinched with curiosity. She hesitated, then stepped into the room and crossed to stand beside Jenny.

"That's strange," she said, picking up the bottle. The label read *Regina Sloane*. Blair opened it and sucked in a breath. "These aren't hers. Mom's medication is pink." The bottle spilled a tumble of green pills into her hand. "Someone switched her pills."

The doorbell rang, and Blair excused herself.

Jenny followed the imagined path of the intruder while she waited. She pictured them entering through the window and landing on the nightstand. The impact would have sent everything tumbling off in chaos.

But nothing else in the room had been disturbed.

The mess below the open window was no more than what would be expected if someone had climbed through unaware of what was on the other side. The only thing unbroken was the embroidery, a floral arrangement of lilies and peach roses in a dark hoop.

"Jenny Doan," Officer Wilkins said, returning to the room with Blair. "Why are you at every crime scene I visit?"

Jenny raised an eyebrow but stepped back from the debris. "Why are we having so many crimes?"

Officer Dunn came in after Wilkins, shifting around the opposite side of the bed. He slid the closet open and started touching everything.

Wilkins watched Jenny closely, then turned to Blair. "When did you discover the break in?"

"Just after I got home. I don't love coming in here. There are a lot of memories." Blair kept one eye on Officer Dunn as he sifted through her mother's things. "I wanted to get started sorting things today. Instead, I found this."

"But they didn't touch anything else?" Wilkins scanned the room, taking in its many antiques and jewelry pieces.

"They weren't looking for valuables," Jenny muttered, scanning the space.

Wilkins shot her a *look*—something between strained tolerance and mild exasperation. "Please excuse us, Mrs. Doan. Were we interrupting?"

Mystery in the Old Quilt

"She's right." Blair slumped onto the edge of the bed. "But that's not all. I found this on the table, by my family picture."

She opened a small notepaper and read aloud—

> *I missed you.*
> *Gina lost her life for a secret.*
> *Like mother, like daughter.*

A rock settled in Jenny's chest as Blair handed the note to Officer Wilkins.

"The first note was about the quilt. Now this?" Blair exhaled sharply. "Someone thinks I know something—but I don't! Who would even believe that? Michelle's the only one who even expressed interest in the quilt."

Darkness clouded Jenny's mind. "You don't think Michelle would do this?"

"No." Blair threw her hands up. "But I don't know who to trust anymore."

"This note may help us figure out who really wants your quilt," Jenny said.

"The stolen quilt from your studio?" Officer Wilkins asked, turning to Jenny.

Ice water poured through her veins. Embarrassment followed, then heat, rising up her neck and settling on her cheeks, as if a hot iron hovered beside her. Jenny had come here to tell Blair about the quilt, but somehow, Wilkins had beaten her to it.

Blair's brows furrowed. "Wait. What quilt?"

Wilkins answered before Jenny could. "The one stolen from Mrs. Doan's studio. Didn't you say it belonged to Blair?"

Jenny swallowed hard, guilt pressing against her ribs. "Yes. Blair, that's why I came over this morning." She gripped the hem of her sweater, searching for stray threads. There weren't any. "I'm so sorry. Your quilt was stolen from my studio last night. Michelle told me this morning, after we talked."

"Stolen?" Blair gasped. "What am I supposed to do now? Someone is threatening to kill me for it."

"You let us do our jobs." Wilkins turned toward Jenny, ensuring she knew the comment was meant for her, too.

Jenny moved to closer. "We'll keep learning about your mother. And Officer Wilkins has a whole team to make sure he doesn't miss anything." She caught his eye, making sure he knew she meant her comment for him as well.

"Good," Blair said, bitterness creeping into her voice as she pointed at the note in Wilkins' hand. "Because whoever's threatening me knows something about my mother. And I want to know if this

Mystery in the Old Quilt

person—" she swallowed hard, "—is the killer who murdered her."

THE PEARL BUTTON BOUNCED, hovered for a split second, and dropped back into Jenny's palm.

Confidence felt good—even if it was purely for show. Loretta didn't need to know that.

"I think I have something that belongs to you." Jenny pinched the delicate sphere between her fingers, letting the pearl coating shimmer between them.

Wheels seemed to turn in Loretta's mind. Her eyes darted from the button to Jenny's face, searching for answers, trying to determine whether admitting the button was hers would help or hurt.

"It's not mine," Loretta said, stepping back as if distance alone would validate her claim.

"Really? I noticed you lost a button identical to this off your cuff this morning." Jenny's confidence faltered as her gaze fell to the woman's deep green silk cuffs, now sporting perfectly matched gold buttons.

She must have changed.

"I found this in my studio, and seeing you had lost one, I thought I would return it." Jenny pulled the button back, and Loretta leaned forward, as if tethered together.

"It can't be mine then. I've never, and *would* never, set foot in your studio." Her soft pink nail polish highlighted her pale fingers, clenching the doorframe.

Painted china hung in precise rows on the far wall of the entry, above a collection of engraved silver spoons, and a gleaming walnut grandfather clock.

It was the perfect home, for a perfect guild president, who did everything perfectly.

Jenny dropped her hand to her pocket, making it look like she was putting the pearl button away.

Loretta's relieved sigh turned into a startled squeak, more comical than Jenny anticipated, when she realized Jenny had pulled out a sticky note instead of getting rid of the button.

"I thought the same thing until I found this." Jenny waved the sticky note like a fan.

Loretta snatched it so fast, Jenny could barely had time to blink.

"Lo? How did your speech notes end up in my studio if you 'would never set foot there'?"

"Fine." Loretta fumbled with her cuff, her fingers twisting the gold button still in place as if searching for the one she'd lost. "I went. But I only looked. I wanted to check on Blair's quilt and Claudia told me Blair

Mystery in the Old Quilt

brought it over. I slipped in when I knew Claudia would be cleaning. To make sure you were giving it the attention it deserved."

Jenny raised an eyebrow. "Your confidence is overwhelming."

"Have a good day." Loretta sneered and gestured to the porch.

Jenny stepped inside as if Loretta had invited her to tea.

"You are so welcome." Jenny let herself into the living room, where Loretta's blouse with the snagged cuff lay on the couch. A sewing basket and a jar of buttons sat beside it.

"See?" Jenny tsked. "I know how hard it is to match buttons if you don't already have a spare."

Loretta scrambled to the couch, scooping up everything in an armful of sewing supplies and fabric. "What do you want, Jenny? You know I was in your studio. You caught me. I promise it won't happen again."

The silver hands of Jenny's watch stretched wide. It was three forty-five. The note said Monday at four.

Sitting on the sofa, Jenny smiled, determined to find out what Loretta had planned. "Why?" She asked, feigning immunity to the venom in Loretta's glare. "Come on, Lo? Why were you in there?"

The intentional use of her nickname did its job. Red crept up the irritable woman's neck. "I told you," she snapped. "I wanted to see Blair's quilt. You still have it don't you? I went to your studio because that's where I was told it would be, but—it wasn't there." She crossed her arms. "What did you do?"

Disbelief knotted the breath in Jenny's chest. Did she know it was missing?

Loretta turned away, ending their conversation.

Reaching out, she caught Lo's attention. She was too close to answers to let them get away. "I lost Gina's quilt. And I'm terrible at asking for help, but when I found your button . . . I knew I needed you. You said all those things at the memorial and I thought—no, I hoped you'd come through. For Blair. For Gina. Her passing was so hard."

"Gina's passing was hard on everyone." Tears welled in Loretta's eyes.

"It was." Jenny agreed. "But you two were so close." Jenny took Loretta's hands, squeezing gently.

"I didn't think anyone noticed," Loretta murmured, almost to herself. Suspicion drowned away with the mention of Gina. Maybe all the praises and posturing at the memorial weren't all nonsense.

A choked sob, crackled through the professional façade of the Hamilton Quilt Guild president. She stared at their hands, pinned in Jenny's grip, like fabric under a presser foot. If she moved the machine might sew right through her.

Jenny would have let go, but Loretta was holding on now. She tightened the grip, alternating between convulsive weeping and loud, shuddering gasps of air.

Shock numbed Jenny's ability to respond appropriately.

Loretta didn't cry. Ever.

Reaching over, Jenny rubbed the only tiny spot on her shoulder she could reach. The sobs deepened, and then, without warning, Lo slung herself at Jenny, gripping her shoulders as if she were the last yard of a discontinued fabric line.

There was no choice but to accept the embrace.

"Gina was always so prompt and precise." Loretta hiccuped. "She helped with the guild records. And her quilting was beautiful. And her embroidery—" Her voice caught. "I can't believe she's gone."

"Yes," Jenny said, awkwardly patting Loretta's back through her heaving breaths. "She was a very thorough woman."

"She was." A sniffle and Loretta reached for a small embroidered handkerchief from a basket in the corner. She rubbed it between her fingers before holding it up. "Gina made this for me."

Flowers edged the handkerchief, tiny words stitched throughout. Jenny's breath hitched as certain phrases jumped out at her.

> *Love anew has come to me,*
> *A leaf stitched in our family tree.*
> *In quilted dreams, of starry skies,*
> *A life begins and grows and dies.*
> *Though love is spun in life for thee,*
> *My love again I must set free.*

"May I see that?" Jenny asked, reaching out.

Loretta hesitated, her fingers tightened protectively around the fabric before handing it over. "I don't know what you're getting so worked up about," she muttered.

Jenny ran her thumb over the delicate stitching, her heart pounding. "This—it's the same poem."

"What poem?" Loretta asked.

"Gina embroidered part of this on Blair's quilt."

Loretta waved a dismissive hand. "She embroidered everything. Every project had some fancy little inscription. It was her way."

Jenny frowned. "Did she say what it meant?"

"Some sentimental nonsense." Loretta scoffed. "She loved it, but it's just pretty words on fabric. It was from someone who was almost family, and she told me

Mystery in the Old Quilt

because we were such close friends she wanted me to have it. The words themselves don't *mean* anything."

Jenny wasn't so sure. If it had mattered enough to sew into a quilt and a handkerchief, there was a reason.

Loretta took the hanky back. "It was awful seeing her quilt handed off to someone who barely spent any time with her."

"Blair and her mother were close. She was with her every day at the end."

"Not Blair, you ninny." Loretta's stern glare was a complete reversal from the tearful woman moments before. "You. Gina gave it to Blair, but she turned right to you. I would have helped her in a heartbeat. I would have done anything for Gina. And the same for Blair."

Loretta clenched her fists, and Jenny took a step back. She'd never been physically violent, but Jenny didn't want to be there for the first time. "That's why I'm asking for your help."

"Blair should have known," Loretta continued bitterly. "She let everyone else help. The nurses taking care of Gina. The Peters' catering for her. Dotty embroidering with her. Even *you* fixing her quilt."

Jenny jutted her chin out slightly, unsure how to handle an emotional Loretta. "Lo?"

"My name is Loretta." Resentment simmered in her eyes.

Jenny was done beating around the bush. "Don't you have somewhere to be?"

"What are you talking about?" Loretta said, her ill humor matched with Jenny's annoyance.

"It's after four." Jenny nodded to the crumpled sticky note lodged in Loretta's sewing basket.

Loretta folded her arms and stared at her. A dark twinkle sparked in her eyes. "So."

"You made a note on the back of—that." Frustration warred with logic, and Jenny lost. "You wrote down a meeting for Monday at four. That's now. Unless you were up really early."

Loretta stared at Jenny, blinked, and then threw her head back with a loud cackle. "How long have you been sitting on that?"

Jenny narrowed her eyes. "Okay, are they coming here? If I wait long enough, will I find out someone is meeting you to buy Gina's quilt?"

"How dare you." Loretta's cheeks flushed with fury.

"Then what, Loretta?" Jenny grabbed the little note and held it up. "What else does this mean?"

Loretta's cackle returned, this time with a wicked tilt. "That doesn't say Monday, Jenny. It says M. As in Michelle, your lovely assistant."

Mystery in the Old Quilt

Jenny froze. The steam of failure inside her cooled into ice, settling over her in frozen layers. "Michelle?"

"Yes. She is quite a stickler about being on time, and four A.M. is hard for anyone."

Jenny looked down at the yellow square in her hand. M on time 4:00.

M. Not Monday.

Her entire theory crumbled. The realization sucked the air out of her, like placing the final piece of a watercolor quilt on the design wall—only to knock the rest off.

Days of creativity and work, hundreds of tiny fabric squares, tumbling to the ground. From a Mona Lisa to a mound on the floor.

It didn't sound like Michelle. Jenny couldn't shake the feeling that something was missing.

"Did Michelle give you Blair's quilt?" The question slid down Jenny's throat like a mouthful of freshly sharpened rotary blades.

"You mean Gina's quilt." Loretta smirked.

"Yes, Lo. That quilt. Do you have it?"

Her hands shook and her jaw tightened. "No."

Jenny pressed forward. "Who were you meeting?"

Loretta's gaze flickered. A pause, waiting seconds too long before she responded.

She was holding something back.

"It doesn't matter. No one showed up anyway. I only saw Sam and his delivery guy."

Jenny's cheeks tingled, heat creeping up her neck. She'd deal with the embarrassment of questioning Lo and learning nothing more than Loretta's good intentions and distrust.

Guilt and defeat seemed to feel the same just then. Hot. Like ironing over heat sensitive markings and realizing she'd ruined all her progress—but she could always start over.

And now she had to.

"Then why?"

Loretta looked away, her voice quieter now. "I wanted to help. A simple transaction. That's all it was supposed to be. I pay the money, get the quilt. Then, when it was discovered missing, I'd find it and return it to Blair. I would get to be the hero."

Her whisper, though soft, held all the sharp edges of a barbed wire fence.

"But when I got there, the door was open, so I went in. The quilt was already gone." Her breath hitched. "No quilt, no Michelle. Nothing."

She exhaled sharply. "So, no. I didn't take it. But if it had been there, I would have."

Mystery in the Old Quilt

"IT CAN'T BE MICHELLE!" Jenny dropped her head back against the headrest, gripping the steering wheel as she argued with herself.

She'd been sitting outside the studio for fifteen minutes, trying to convince herself to go inside and confront her assistant. "Why would she do it?"

She yanked her purse and dug inside for her phone, only to remember it was still missing.

"And that's why I haven't called anyone," she muttered to no one, shoving the door open and climbing out.

The studio lights glowed through the windows. If she didn't confront Michelle soon, she'd miss her. A heavy pit dropped into her stomach.

"I need to know." Jenny exhaled sharply. "I liked Michelle." The pit twisted. "Like. I like Michelle."

A shot of determination flared in her chest. She'd call Ron and let him know she'd be late. She patted her pocket for her phone—her *missing* phone. If she couldn't call she'd have to go inside. She turned toward the studio and hesitated.

A glow appeared inside the food truck parked in the alley.

Jenny changed course without a second thought. First, get the phone. That would be responsible. Phone first. Call Ron. Then talk to Michelle.

She moved toward the alley, pausing when a shadow flickered across the dimly lit space.

Something clattered near the dumpster. Jenny froze. A rustling. A muffled movement.

Then, a sharp meow.

Jenny let out a breath, laughing at herself. "Get a grip."

She crossed the final distance to the food truck and knocked firmly. Silence.

"Sam?" she called. "It's Jenny. I'm looking for my phone."

No response.

She frowned. "Did I leave it in there?"

Nothing.

"Always nothing," she muttered, leaning back against the side of the food truck.

The glow of the streetlamp reflected against the cool metal wall. If she ignored the lingering scent of fried oil and the unsettling shadows near the dumpster, the night could almost be peaceful.

Then, a movement behind her. Inside the truck.

Jenny's entire being stood still, listening. The sound was slow and quiet. Someone was inside afterall,

Mystery in the Old Quilt

and it sounded like they didn't want anyone to know they were there.

Her fingers tightened on her purse strap.

Digging inside, she searched for something—anything—useful. The doorknob from earlier would've been perfect.

Instead, her hand closed around something cold and smooth. A screwdriver.

Jenny adjusted her grip, holding the business end out toward the food truck like a dagger. Confidence settled in her stance.

The alley was too quiet.

Another crash sounded near the dumpster. And Jenny jumped, her back hitting the food truck's wall.

Inside, the light switched off.

The door jerked forward and A scream leapt from her throat as she rolled to press her shoulder against the brute force on the other side.

She wouldn't be able to hold it long.

Metal flexed beside her as something rammed her position on the entry steps from inside.

"You can't come out!" she yelped, then immediately berated herself. She wasn't a police officer, and this wasn't a game of hide-and-seek. She had no authority to stop whoever was inside.

The metal handle jiggled.

"Help!" Jenny yelled into the night. Jenny's stomach clenched. Goosebumps tingled along her arms.

The door shifted against her side, and fingers pushed through the gap.

Jenny jabbed at them with the screwdriver.

A sharp cry erupted from inside, and the metal slammed back into place.

Jenny didn't hesitate. She jammed the screwdriver through the handle, forcing it into the locking mechanism. The metal dug into the wood, securing the latch, at least for now.

Sirens wailed down the street. The sky had darkened into a dusky night, and Jenny squinted into the dimming light of the alley.

Whoever had called this in was getting free hemming for life.

A loud thump hit the wall.

She leaned up against it, breathing heavily.

Maybe she would name a quilt pattern after them.

Plus give them the actual quilt, if they arrived soon enough.

Between the screwdriver and sheer willpower, she prayed the police would get here before the door gave way.

"Jenny!" Ron's voice came from somewhere in the night.

Mystery in the Old Quilt

She couldn't see him until his hands pressed against the wall beside her.

"Ron!" She fell against him, gasping.

The person inside banged harder, more frantically. The door shuddered, then stopped.

Ron met her eyes. The sudden silence sent a chill of harrowing fear through her. Quiet before the storm.

"Stay here," Ron whispered. He turned his head, listening.

"Hey! Watch out!"

The shout came from behind.

Jenny spun around.

A figure broke from the shadows, running for the alley exit. One of the officers took off in pursuit.

Her hand flew to her mouth, stifling a scream.

The sounds from the shadows had been a second person—and she'd forgotten about them.

Metal scraped against metal. The food truck's front awning lifted and a leg swung out the window, blond hair catching in the light of the streetlamp.

It looked like a woman.

Ron lunged, grabbing the awning and slamming it down.

The culprit's sharp cry pierced through Jenny as footsteps pounded toward them down the alley.

"Freeze!" Officer Dunn raised his gun.

The girl froze, her body going completely still.

Dunn moved forward with slow, measured steps. He kept his eyes locked on the figure, hanging halfway out of the food truck window.

Jerking the metal awning up, Dunn lunged to grab the the intruder as she tumbled out.

Ron jumped instinctively to catch her, and Jenny gasped.

"Blair?"

MYSTERY
QUILT BLOCK 1

Clue 4

**Indulgent or simple when sewn without care
Make the deepest deceptions beyond all repair**

Clue 4

SNOWBALL THE CORNERS

The best snowballs are made of fabric! They are great for cuddling, and if you get all wet in a real snowball fight, a quilt with snowballed corners on the blocks keeps you as warm as a quilt without snowballed corners! Though, I'm not sure that's a selling point.

For this step, take the 4 S/PR sqs from the last step and attach 2 – 2 ½" White squares to opposite corners of each block, sew diagonally across the white squares from corner to corner "snowball" style, as shown.

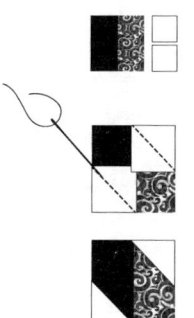

Press open.

(NOTE: Chain piecing helps ensure you put the snowball corners on the same side of every block. Line up your fabrics, facing the same direction, and add the white snowballs to the same corner on each of the four pieced blocks. Then turn them around and repeat, attaching the snowballs to the opposite corner.)

✓

Clue 4 – Check the Supplies and Read!

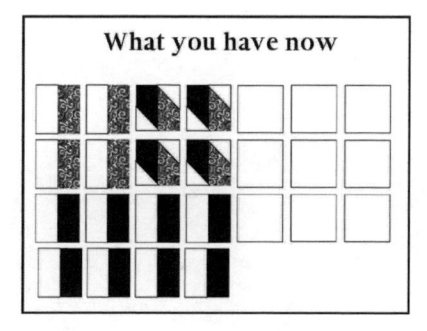

What you have now

PART Five

Piecing the Truth

"Please! You have to believe me. I was trying to help!" Red splotches spread up Blair's neck as tears streamed down her face. "It's not what it looks like! I swear it's not what you think!" She desperately searched the faces around her, looking for anyone who would listen.

Officer Dunn's steely expression didn't waver.

"Jenny!" Blair gasped, locking eyes with her as Dunn jerked her forward. "Help me! I didn't break in. The door was open." Blair's voice rose. "They're jacks! Please! He planned it! He killed my mother!"

Jenny's gut festered around a dark shadow of unease.

Blair's pleading fractured as Officer Dunn hauled her down the alley.

"Who's Jack?" Ron asked softly.

"I don't know, but this doesn't feel right." Goosebumps prickled along Jenny's skin, and she crossed her arms against the growing chill. "I wish she'd answered when I called out. Then none of this would be happening."

"She can't have meant it though, about Sam killing her mother." Ron's worry bled into his grip as he rubbed her arm harder than was comfortable.

Jenny flinched. "I think she did. But that doesn't mean it's true. And even if it is, does that make her innocent?"

Ron exhaled sharply. "That's not our call, I guess." He paused, sliding an arm around her shoulders. "Tyler will figure it out." He pulled her in, as if squeezing her close would make the worries smaller.

Jenny wanted to believe that. She wasn't always sure about Officer Dunn, but Officer Wilkins was a good cop. He wouldn't let Blair be wrongly convicted.

A soft thump pulled Jenny's attention back to the food truck. The door swayed loosely on its hinges where Dunn had removed her makeshift lock.

Mystery in the Old Quilt

"Just a second," Jenny said, pulling away from Ron.

"What are you doing?" His voice tightened with concern.

"I forgot something here yesterday, and I don't want to become part of evidence." She went quickly up the food truck's steps, her senses on high alert in case she needed to make a quick change of plans.

"Jenny," Ron hissed, "you shouldn't be in there."

His words rang too close to what her attacker had said the night before.

You're not supposed to be here.

She rolled her shoulders and shoved the memory away. She was stronger than this.

"I'll be quick," she whispered back. "I have to figure out where they put it."

Dim light filtered through the gaps in the awning and door. Shadows stretched across the vinyl covered floor. The inside of the truck wasn't exactly ransacked, just . . . disrupted.

Drawers gapped open below cupboard doors, swinging unlatched from the wall. Blair really had been searching for something.

In the back corner a row of drawers had been emptied, the contents scattered across the floor. Menus, catering flyers, and baggies full of receipts and food packaging marked with scribbled notes on recipes and quantities.

A pile of brown envelopes, stamped the front with Sam's lounging peanut logo, had fallen in the corner. Red security hash lines peeked from the inside.

Near the large order window, a small clump of papers looked as if Blair had been trying to take them with her. The top page bore the heading, *Millet Mushroom Farm*, each page listed purchase information going back months.

Identical orders, every month.

"They must make a lot of risotto," Jenny muttered, turning to the last page. The heading on this one was different, reading — *Fatal Fungi: Mushrooms to Avoid—Midwest Region*.

Her stomach tightened. Not what she wanted to find. Maybe Sam was researching, after Harry's accusations.

She shifted the pages. A small orange bottle tipped over, rolling into the line of condiments.

Pills rattled inside. The patient's name, Regina Sloane, was printed across the label.

Her breath hitched. She unscrewed the cap and tipped a single pill into her palm.

Pink.

Her body turned cold.

Mystery in the Old Quilt

"Hurry!"

She jumped at Ron's urgent whisper.

"Someone's coming." He glanced in the doorway and back to the alley, knee bouncing nervously as he waited for her.

Putting the lid back on the pill bottle, Jenny dropped it onto the papers and darted for the door, still holding the tiny pill.

"Did you find it?" Ron asked as she climbed down the steps.

Jenny blinked. "What?" The strategies stacking in her mind collapsed under his stare. She was trying to figure out Sam's motive, but Ron didn't know that. "What do you mean?"

Ron's brow furrowed. "You were looking for something."

"Oh. My phone. No. It wasn't there."

"Your phone?" His normally patient expression clouded. He reached into his pocket and pulled out the shiny red device she'd been looking for all day.

Jenny snatched it like a lifeline. "Where did you find this?"

"Sam gave it to me when I went to get us dinner. Said you left it in the food truck." His sharp glance flicked toward the crime scene behind them. "That's how I found you?"

Guilt wove long tendrils through Jenny's body. "Wait," she looked up curiously. "How did you know I was here?"

Ron frowned. "I took it to the studio first. You weren't there. But Michelle was on the phone with the police, reporting a disturbance. And after last night—"

"Right." Jenny didn't press further.

She'd already been the cause of one incident. Ron had assumed she'd be at the center of this one too.

At the end of the alley, Officer Wilkins strode forward, gripping the arm of a man in a hoodie. The stranger grumbled, resisting as he was pushed along.

"I didn't do anything," he shouted. "I was just waiting for them to leave."

"Right. You were just 'hanging around'," Wilkins muttered, unimpressed. "What, do you get a kick out of watching old women fight for their lives?"

Jenny bristled. Old? Really? The nerve. She wasn't old. She stepped closer, squinting for a better look, her irritation justifying her curiosity.

"I was here for Sam, I swear!" The man's voice scratched at a memory, jagged and familiar.

Wilkins raised an eyebrow. "Then why'd you run?" His gruff tone made Jenny grateful her interactions with the officer weren't on the wrong side of a pair of handcuffs.

Mystery in the Old Quilt

The guy yanked against his cuffs. "I got scared, okay? I've been in trouble before. I forgot to lock up, and then you guys showed up out of nowhere. I got scared." He tugged at the metal bracelets binding him. "I thought Sam called the cops. But I promise, I work for him."

Danny.

Jenny realized with a start. Her stomach sank. He'd seemed like a decent kid. She wanted to give him the benefit of the doubt—like she had for Blair and Michelle.

"Look, check my back pocket," Danny said, struggling against Wilkins' grip. "Sam's instructions are in there."

Wilkins gestured to Dunn.

"I'll look," Dunn said, lifting the edge of Danny's hoodie. He pulled out a torn brown envelope. Something clattered to the ground.

Wilkins frowned. "What's that?"

Danny shook his head and shrugged in ignorance. "I don't know."

Dunn crouched, picked up a small figurine, and turned it in his hand. "This kid still plays with toys." He scoffed and tossed it aside.

Under the streetlamp, Dunn opened the envelope, shielding it from Jenny's view.

She shifted closer, craning her neck. Daniel Long was printed over a list of bullet points.

"Looks like a list," Dunn muttered. "Maybe he's right. I really don't care if he did the dishes or figured the cost of a mushroom order."

Jenny frowned. Sam's trailer had been cluttered with drawers full of old receipts and labels—scribbled on scraps of recipe notes and half legible numbers. She hadn't seen a single organized list.

"I forgot to lock up! That's all!" Danny jerked his chin toward the food truck. "That lady was inside when I got here. She's the one who broke in! She's the one who wasn't supposed to be here." His voice rasped, low and gravelly.

You're not supposed to be here.

Jenny recoiled as her breath caught. A sharp memory shoved itself forward—the voice in her ear, the pressure of an elbow pressing into her back.

The truth hit like a falling sewing machine. She caught it, heavy and jarring. It knocked the breath out of her.

"It was you." Her words barely escaped past the knot forming in her throat.

Danny turned toward her, and the ache in her arm spidered outward. A dull pressure pulsing where she'd been slammed into the food truck steps.

Mystery in the Old Quilt

"I recognize his voice." Her pulse thundered in her ears. "He's the one who attacked me last night."

She recognized more than that. Almost like muscle memory her body replayed the experience in quick successive moments. His grip on her mouth, the sharp impact when she hit the steps, his breath on her face and that voice shredding through her.

She'd been helpless.

She was going to be sick.

Wilkins tightened his grip on Danny's arm. "Where were you around nine o'clock yesterday evening?"

"I can't remember." Danny twisted, pulling against his restraints. "On a date, I think."

"Michelle said you canceled." There was no question in Jenny's voice.

Danny's eyes widened. "I didn't do anything."

Wilkins shook his head. "It looks like we get to take a ride and talk some more."

As they pulled away, Ron grabbed her around the waist. "Mrs. Doan, sometimes you scare me."

His playful behavior spawned a pinch of guilt. Blair was being taken to a prison cell. Then she thought of Danny.

"I feel better, knowing they'll be watching Danny." Jenny leaned on Ron's shoulder as they started back to the studio. "I can't believe it was him. Ow!"

A sharp pain bit her foot and Jenny looked down finding the toy Dunn had tossed aside.

She picked it up. A wide mouthed brass frog.

"I've seen this before," she said curiously.

Ron looked over. "A frog sticking its tongue out? Where would you have seen that?"

"Not this exactly?" Jenny chuckled softly. "But something like it. I don't know but it's familiar."

She turned the figure over in her hand and almost dropped it. On the bottom of the figurine, a tiny GS was etched on the frog's foot.

The image of an empty windowsills among others filled with brass figurines flashed in her mind.

"He stole it from Gina."

"MICHELLE?" The studio was empty, and too quiet.

Light cast long shadows across the fabric piled over the cutting tables the next morning. A half finished quilt hung on the design wall. The air smelled of thread and cotton, warm and familiar, but tension coiled in Jenny's stomach.

Setting her things at her desk, she exhaled slowly, pressing her palms against the wooden surface. There were too many questions and not enough answers.

Mystery in the Old Quilt

Fabric scraps and notepads cluttered the space, but something else caught her eye—a thin slip of paper poking out from beneath her sewing machine.

She tugged it free. A flicker of apprehension hit as she registered another note.

Jenny let out a dry chuckle. "Great. Another cryptic message."

Every note she had come across lately had left her with new problems. But when she unfolded the paper, her breath caught.

If you're reading this, you already know my secret— The note from Gina's quilt.

She hadn't thought about Gina's message to Blair since she'd read it the first time.

Her eyes skimmed the words.

> *If you're reading this, you already know my secret. You may not understand, but I did this to protect you. It's never to late to get to know your family tree.*
>
> *Secrets are best kept in the light, but should someone lost come forward, grandmas know best.*
>
> *(Her frozen heart may not provide, but what's inside will.)*

Jenny pressed her lips together.

This wasn't a sentimental farewell. Gina had assumed Blair would already know the truth. But why?

I did this to protect you. Was she protecting Blair? Or . . . someone else? And from what?

Jenny's pulse quickened.

Her mind caught on the line about secrets and someone lost. Why connect them? *Secrets are best kept in the light, but should someone lost come forward.* Gina had been leading Blair, or someone, to . . . what?

Not to her secret. To proof of it?

Jenny tapped her fingers against the desk. If Gina thought Blair would already know, then what was she supposed to find?

She sighed, rubbing her temples. This was too cryptic. The only straightforward line was *It's never too late to get to know your family tree.* Gina surely meant the embroidered family tree on the quilt, but the quilt was gone.

Jenny grabbed her phone and tapped into her apps, scrolling fast.

Somewhere in here, she had a picture of the quilt.

Too soon, the images scrolled past recent days and into vacations and birthdays. She stopped and scrolled back, slower. It was only a couple of days ago.

Mystery in the Old Quilt

Jenny had shots of food and fabric and . . . no quilt.

She remembered asking Blair for permission that night at the studio. She'd clicked the camera, and the quilt had been saved in her phone.

It had to be there.

Jenny let out a frustrated breath. It had been there before. Her phone had been missing for a day and a half at Sam's. Had someone gotten into it and deleted the picture?

Her heart stuttered.

Details lined up as evidence of Sam's guilt. If only she'd had Bernie take it home the night she'd come to look at it. — *Wait.*

She'd texted Bernie the picture. Jenny switched to her messages and found the thread.

There it was.

She clicked on the quilt image and saved it back to her phone. It didn't matter who deleted it, she had it now.

Zooming in, she focused on the central square. Blair's immediate family stood out in clear, careful stitches. The next set of names were Gina's parents.

Grandma Rachel.

"All right, Grandma Rachel," Jenny muttered, scanning the image. *What do you know best?*

Gina's note hadn't said 'Grandma knows best.'

She'd written 'Grandmas know best.' Plural.

Jenny frowned. If she remembered right, neither of Blair's grandmothers were alive. So why emphasize *grandmas*?

A tiny embroidered heart stitched next to Rachel's name caught Jenny's eye. Flowers and vines decorated the quilt, but Jenny hadn't seen another heart.

She looked back at the note. *Her frozen heart may not provide, but what's inside will.*

She'd thought Gina was being sentimental. Maybe even joking, but—

The front door slammed, shaking the quiet of the studio.

Jenny startled, locking her phone and tucking the note away as Claudia stepped inside.

"Jenny? I need to talk to you." She hovered near the entrance, wrapping her purse strap around her hand. Her expression wavered, her lip caught between her teeth as if she were second guessing her reason for being here.

Jenny let out a slow breath, composing herself. "Of course. What can I do for you?"

Claudia exhaled sharply. "First, I—I need to apologize."

"I lied to you before." Claudia swallowed hard. "I knew Gina."

Mystery in the Old Quilt

Jenny folded her arms. "How well?"

Claudia flinched. "Well enough." She hesitated, then blurted, "Michelle told me about the quilt, and I told a friend. I think that's how it got stolen."

Jenny blinked. "Your friend stole the quilt?"

Tension pulled Claudia's nerves tight. "I don't know. But my friend isn't very discreet."

Jenny's brow furrowed. "Who did you tell?"

Claudia fidgeted, looking away. "Well... it was Loretta."

"Lo?" Disappointment curled in Jenny's stomach. "You don't need to worry. She didn't take the quilt."

"I told her at the memorial." Claudia bowed her head. "I heard you offer to help Blair with her quilt. I didn't care. You help lots of people with their quilts, except—" she hesitated, twisting the strap of her purse so tightly her knuckles turned white. "After you left, I got a phone call. Someone offered me ten thousand dollars to bring them the quilt."

"Ten thousand?" Jenny's pulse jumped.

Claudia nodded. "Somehow, they knew you would have it. And they knew I would be able to get it." She hesitated but squared her shoulders. "I accepted."

She frowned, but not at Claudia's confession. "How could anyone have known I would have it?

She'd barely asked me, I didn't even know I would have it before that night."

"It had to be someone at the memorial. That's why I wondered about Loretta though," Claudia admitted. "She was with me. I told her what they said and we talked and I knew I couldn't go through with it. I left the note at the church and went home."

Mind racing, Jenny fit the pieces together. "Loretta copied the meeting onto her speech notes."

Claudia flinched. "How did you know that? She made the note when we were talking. I thought she was just scribbling, but she was so insistent I not go. She was the only other person who knew."

Jenny exhaled, her disappointment deepening. Loretta hadn't taken the quilt. She had been sure it wasn't her. "Have you told the police about this?

Fear widened her eyes and she shook her head. "I can't I agreed to help, what if they blame me? I can't go to prison for this."

The anguish in Claudia's face pulled Jenny from her chair and she hurried around the desk. "It's okay, I'm sure it will work out. I can talk to them if you prefer."

"Can you wait a little?"

"I don't know. I'll do the best I can though. You didn't tell your husband about that phone call, did you?"

Claudia shook her head. "No. I didn't see how it would do anything but worry him."

"Okay," Jenny patted her shoulder. "You didn't get them the quilt, so, did anything happen?"

A weak shrug. "I got another call. Early the next morning. But this time, they didn't offer me money."

Jenny's stomach tightened. "What did they say?"

Claudia swallowed, eyes darting toward the window. "They knew where I lived. What car I drove. That I left for work before sunrise. They asked if I wanted to know what would happen if I didn't listen."

Ice dripped down Jenny's spine. "Did they do anything?"

"Not yet," Claudia whispered, rubbing her arms like she was cold. "But I was terrified. I can't answer my phone. I don't know what to do."

Jenny pressed her fingers to her forehead, rubbing her temples. Someone had threatened Claudia over the quilt. Someone who had known about it before Jenny did. And Loretta—

Jenny stilled. "Loretta's note said 'meet M.' Who was M?"

Claudia looked up, pink tinging her cheeks and sighed, shoulders sinking. "Loretta thought it was Michelle."

"Michelle?"

Loretta had been honest at least.

Claudia gave a lackluster nod. "It wasn't entirely a lie. I was going to ask her to come early and help me. She's smarter than me in so many ways. A lot like Gina. I never told her anything. I wouldn't have done it."

"Okay," Jenny frowned trying to piece things together. "Loretta thought it was Michelle. But who were you actually supposed to meet?"

Discomfort rolled in Claudia's shoulders and she looked away. "He said meet me. That's all I had. And I felt silly when Loretta asked, so I said M. Michelle came to mind, and the plan spiraled and collapsed from there."

Jenny narrowed her eyes. "He?"

"I don't know!" Claudia's voice cracked. "It was a man. He didn't say." She hesitated. "I know you've been helping Blair and I thought you should know. Someone is more worried about this than you realize and I'd hate for anyone to get hurt." Claudia pulled back as she spoke and grabbed hold of the stair railing. "If you tell the police, please don't mention me." With that, she turned and left.

Jenny exhaled sharply.

Someone had been after the quilt from the beginning. They had gone after Claudia. Then after

Mystery in the Old Quilt

Blair. And if Michelle was tangled in this, how far did it go?

And who was the man pulling the strings? Dangerous enough to intimidate Claudia, but patient enough to manipulate the whole town.

Jenny drummed her fingers against her phone, resisting the urge to text Michelle immediately.

She'd had enough half answers and cryptic messages. Enough people hiding things until it was too late. But if Michelle was involved, whether she meant to be or not, Jenny couldn't go in swinging.

She needed facts.

Her gaze flicked to her phone. Maybe one text.

Michelle should have been in by now anyway. A few taps and the quilt image came to life on the screen. It was the last thing she'd been looking at. The stitches blurred as her thoughts spun. Gina's note. The secret. The threats. And Michelle.

Jenny exhaled sharply, closing out the photo and setting her phone aside.

This wasn't getting her anywhere.

She needed to clear her head.

An old pattern lay on her desk, likely left by Michelle. Trying to focus, she picked it up, flipping it over to read the instructions.

She was supposed to be prepping for a remake of

one of her earlier designs, but this wasn't the one she was planning on.

The paper slapped against the desk as she tossed it aside. She hated wasting time.

Pushing herself to her feet, Jenny marched over to Michelle's desk. Not a note, schedule, or large neon sign saying, "work on this now!" to be found on the tidy surface.

Nothing.

Her gaze landed on Michelle's computer. It wasn't snooping. Just checking for pattern notes. Jenny tapped the keys and a password screen popped up.

"Unhelpful, remnant of a discolored fabric swatch," she muttered. Snapping the laptop shut, she plopped into Michelle's chair.

Then immediately bounced back up.

A large brown envelope sat in the seat, a peanut lounging in the corner.

She grabbed it, surprising herself with its weight. It was heavier than it should be. As heavy as the one Danny had hit her with.

Her stomach flipped.

She cringed, flopping it onto the desk and dropping back into the chair. The envelope burst open on impact, spilling cash in a smooth arc across the surface.

Mystery in the Old Quilt

Jenny froze.

Several rapid heartbeats later Jenny remembered to breathe. Twenty dollar bills. Fives. Ones. A small stack of hundreds.

She picked up the envelope, and found something solid still inside.

A thin, rectangular box.

That's why it was heavy.

Her fingers twitched around the edge, tempted to pull it out.

Not her business. Not yet.

She shoved the bills back in without looking further. Then pressed the bulging package flat, grumbling as the paper refused to cooperate.

"It's not like I had to fold anything," Jenny muttered, pressing down harder. Patterns, newspapers, maps—she never could get papers back into an envelope correctly.

Finally, closing the flap as best she could, she placed the envelope in front of Michelle's computer. Then hesitated. It had been on the chair.

She slid it back.

The studio door slammed, and Jenny jumped.

Footsteps followed, heels clicking against the floor.

"Michelle?" Jenny called, confirming her assistant had returned.

"Good morning!" Michelle's voice bounced up the stairs. "Sorry! I had to run to the warehouse. They got a shipment in for the pattern remake. We swapped fabrics to that new line. Something, something—summer."

A stack of fabric appeared at the top of the stairs, followed by Michelle. Her cheery smile pinched as her eyes locked onto Jenny, standing behind her desk. "What are you doing?"

Jenny looked down at the envelope. "Oh, nothing." She met Michelle's gaze. "Just counting the large envelope of money I found in your chair."

The sunshine returned to Michelle's expression as she came over and picked it up. "I bet that was weird."

Michelle tacked the metal prong in place and chucked it onto the desk as carelessly as Jenny had been before she knew what was inside.

"You know, drug dealing isn't considered a respectable side hustle." Jenny leaned against the desk.

Michelle's eyes sparkled. "Ha ha. You mean fabric dealer. All these fabric addicts keep lining up and handing me money. I'm not gonna tell them I can't deal anymore. They'll take me out."

"All right, Shady Chelle." Jenny grabbed the stack of fabric folds and carried them back to her desk. "So, why do you have a fat envelope full of money?"

Mystery in the Old Quilt

Michelle opened her computer. "It's from my dad's business. Nothing crazy."

Jenny nodded. "Are you depositing it for him? Because the bank isn't much further than here."

"It's for a food order from a local farmer. Danny usually picks it up, but he can't today, so I'm doing it." Michelle shrugged. "Honestly, I don't know why my dad doesn't Venmo the guy like a normal person."

Okay, it wasn't an envelope of stolen money. That was reassuring. Unfortunately, it did nothing to explain any of her other questions, including Claudia's confession.

"You know, the other day, when we discovered Blair's quilt had been stolen?" Jenny asked.

"Oh! Right." Michelle straightened in her chair. "I've been meaning to talk to you about that. I told you I'd look into those dates and the local history and stuff, didn't I?"

"Yeah." Jenny hesitated. "I assumed you hadn't been able to."

Michelle grinned. "Au contraire." She spun her laptop toward Jenny. "Honestly, it's not much, but I found some yearbooks at the history museum. They let me take pictures. Look—Gina, front row."

A group photo on the steps of old Hamilton High filled the screen.

Jenny blinked. If not for the year, she might have thought it was Blair at a decade's costume party.

"Wow." Jenny had no doubt it was Gina.

"That's her graduating class, 1994—" Michelle clicked. "Here's an individual photo. And here—"

"Wait," Jenny put a hand up. "Did you see the name above Gina's on that last image?"

Michelle switched the image back and Jenny stared at the list of names, matching the face with it.

"Charles Millet?" Jenny whispered. The name clanged in her head. She must have seen it in Blair's yearbook. More importantly Blair had mentioned Gina dated a Charles. Jenny's pulse kicked up. "That's Charlie, isn't it? Charlie Millet. I never connected that he went to school with Gina."

"The Mushroom Man? Huh. That's who I'm picking up the food order from." Michelle frowned, zooming in on the computer screen. "He hasn't gotten much nicer has he?"

Jenny laughed. "He does kinda look like he wants to knock someone off the risers."

"Pray for me." Michelle shook her head and sucked in a breath. "I guess they're one of the few organic farmers that still take cash. My dad's weird."

"I wonder if he'd remember anything about Gina." Jenny mused.

Mystery in the Old Quilt

"You could ask him yourself." Michelle offered. "Want to come with me? If we go now, we can make it back before the new tutorial meeting."

"Absolutely." Finally there was someone who'd been here during Gina's pregnancy. "If they went to school at the same time Gina got pregnant, maybe he knows who she was spending time with—" Jenny paused. In the class photo, Charlie wasn't glaring at just anyone, he was looking at Gina. And he was mad. "Or maybe he's the father."

Michelle tilted her head. "You think Charlie Millet and Gina? Are you sure?"

Jenny grabbed her purse and headed for the stairs. "I don't know yet. But I'm going to find out."

"Okay," Michelle nodded and grabbed the envelope. "I'll pick up the order, and you ask about high school gossip. Two Shrooms, one stone?"

Fifteen minutes outside of town, Michelle pulled onto a dirt packed driveway. A large wooden sign hung over the open gate *Millet Mushroom Farm* was burned across it.

Forsythia and redbuds dotted the roadside, their yellow and pink blooms softening the landscape of thick pines and gnarled oaks.

At the end of the drive, they parked beside an olive green truck. A Victorian farmhouse rose in front of them, its white siding aged but tidy. The green porch paint peeled at the edges, and a fluffy gray cat stretched lazily on a picket backed bench.

"It's pretty," Michelle said, climbing out.

The screen door banged open.

Harry Millet appeared, shotgun in hand. Wrinkles rippled beyond frown lines deepening the weatherd grooves from his downturned lips.

Jenny's heart thudded in her chest, breath caught in a loop.

"Who are you?" he racked the gun with one hand, a menacing ratchet and click came from the wood and metal mechanism.

He stepped off the porch and crossed the distance between them.

Michelle choked but held still, as Jenny's heart double flipped and landed in her gut where she couldn't feel it at all.

"No one comes onto my land unless they're invited," he snarled, as he looked down the double barrels at them. "So, I'll ask again, who are you?"

MYSTERY QUILT BLOCK 1

Clue 5

FRAGMENTS, ONCE PIECED, WILL TOGETHER REVEAL
THE SHAPE OF THE WHOLE & A TRUTH TO CONCEAL

Clue 5

SEW THE BLOCK SETS

Follow the diagram to sew the first two strip sets.

As follows–

    Block Set 1 —2 strip sets
- W | W/S | W | S/W | W

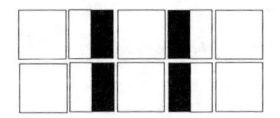

    Block Set 2 —1 strip set
- W | PR/W | W | W/PR | W

    Block Set 3 —2 strip sets
- S/W | S/PR | W/PR | PR/S | S/W

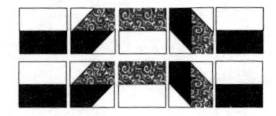

Clue 5 – Check the Supplies and Read!

(NOTE: Folow the diagram for the direction of whites and solids or patterns as you sew them together. They line up differently so watch close and piece them as shown, so the strips will complete the pattern when you put them together.)

What you have now

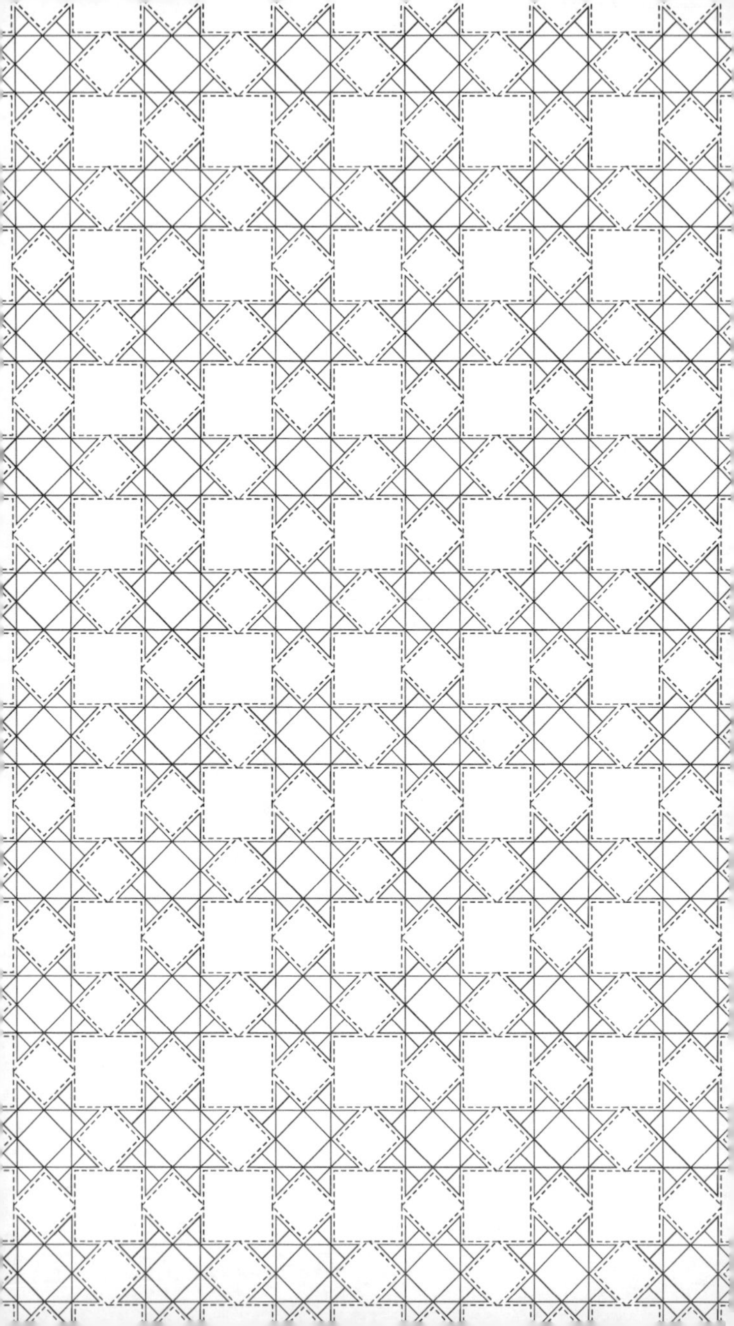

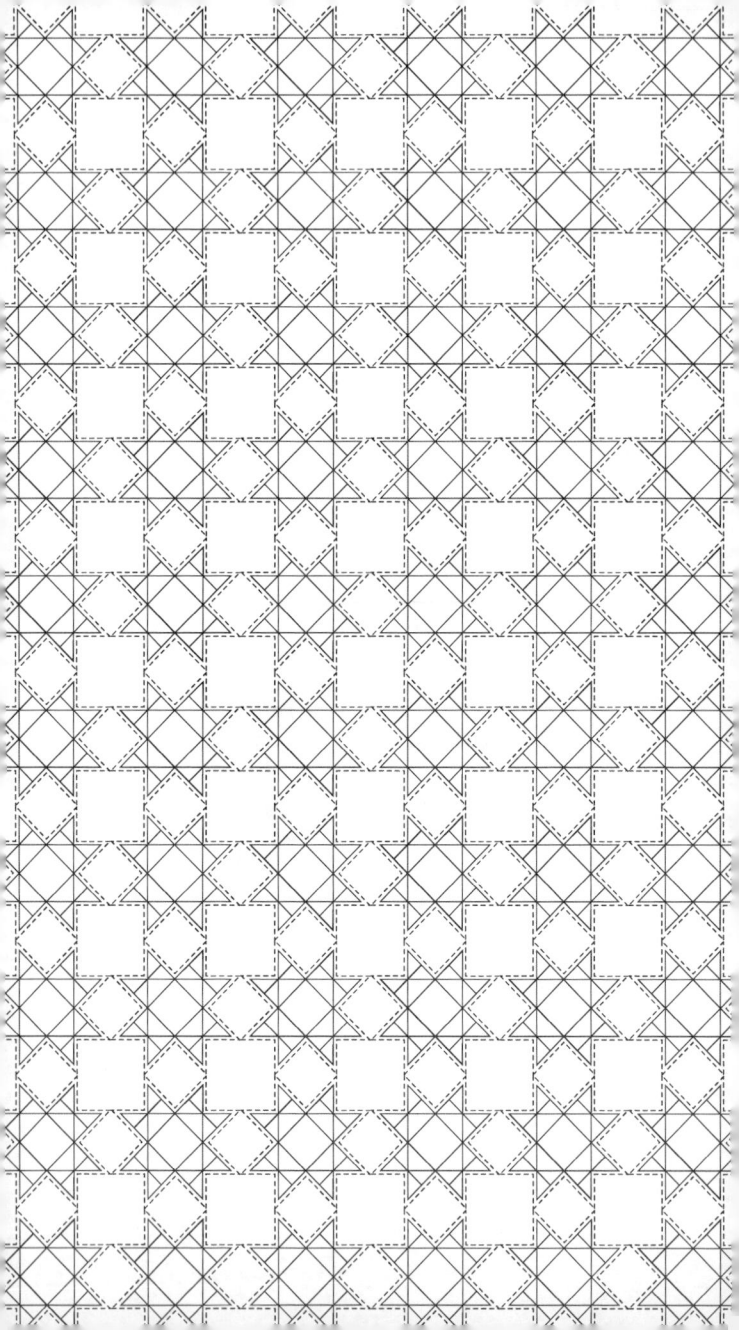

PART Six

To Kill a Quilter

D EATH ISN'T SOMETHING YOU CAN PREPARE for simply by aging. You're never so old that staring down the barrel of a gun doesn't make you question whether or not you are ready to die.

Under the attention of Harry's shotgun, Jenny couldn't move. Stuffing seemed to fill her limbs, like a giant teddy bear good for nothing but sitting. And when she sucked in air, her lungs wouldn't fill.

"Don't shoot!" Michelle raised the fat envelope of money in front of her. "My dad sent me. Sam! I was sent by Sam Peters. And I have money." She glanced at

Jenny and back to Harry's gun, shaking the envelope for good measure.

Harry's brows lifted, and he tee-heed at them. "Not for long." His tinny laughter accented the pull of the gun as he lifted it and fired into the trees. "If I shootcha, that money is mine. Now, you've got fifteen seconds to tell me why you're here. Or I'll come to claim that padded envelope for myself."

"Dad!" A dark-haired man jogged toward them, salt and pepper streaking his hair. "Put that down. We talked about this."

"Stay back, Charlie. I've got things under control. Caught me a couple of fancy bits wandering where they don't belong."

"I see that."

Charlie spoke in calm, measured tones, but when Harry loaded the gun a second time, his hand sailed out. In a fleeting motion, he wrapped the muzzle in a solid grip and lifted the barrel, keeping the two women out of danger.

"Come on, Dad." Charlie pulled the gun from Harry's hands and mouthed an apology to them. "I'll take care of our guests. You wait inside, okay?"

"Guests? I didn't invite 'em." Harry reached for the gun as Charlie led him to the house. "Don't let 'em go. The little one's Sam's kid. She's got our money."

Mystery in the Old Quilt

Charlie looked back, a touch of confusion tightening over his cheekbones. When they reached the porch, he turned to Harry and spoke softly.

Jenny's unease deepened. Michelle clutched the envelope in a white knuckled grip.

"This is still my property," Harry shouted, jabbing a finger in their direction. "Little thieves aren't allowed here." Then he turned and spit at them, like he thought it would fly and land in their faces.

Unfazed, Charlie waited, holding the gun out of his father's reach, until Harry retreated into the house.

The screen door slammed, and Michelle jumped, like she might have dived right back in the car.

A moment later, Charlie turned toward them again, flashing an easy smile. The shotgun rested against his hip, less threatening now. "Sorry about that. My dad's dealing with dementia. It's been causing... problems. He doesn't always remember we've progressed past the point of defending our land with bullets and threats. I try to keep him busy, but it's hard when I'm running a business." Charlie's laugh rolled low and warm.

Jenny forced a chuckle, as Michelle stepped forward holding out her hand. "It's nice to meet you. Sam Peters is my father."

"Yeah, Danny usually comes for Sam. Where's he?"

"I don't know." Michelle shrugged. "My dad said he has a standing order, though. I just need to pay you and pick it up. Oh, and Jenny had a few questions about Gina Sloane."

Charlie's brows lifted as he glanced between them. "Sam's kid, huh? You don't look like him."

Jenny didn't miss that he conveniently ignored Michelle's mention of Gina.

"No." Michelle let out an uneasy laugh. "I really don't."

Charlie's gaze lingered for a beat, before he held out a hand. "Okay, let's see what you've got."

Michelle passed the bulging brown envelope to Charlie.

Sliding a finger under the flap he popped it open. Instead of flipping through the money, he pulled out the thin black box and tucked the envelope into his waistband.

His jaw twitched as he opened the box, pulling out a small disposable phone.

"I'm sorry. I didn't know that was in there." Michelle blinked. "Don't you need to check the amount?"

His fingers clutched the device tightly, as he turned away. "Looks like he finally grew a spine."

Jenny tensed. "What did you say?"

Mystery in the Old Quilt

Charlie shot her a glare. "You think Sam just sends me money?" He pressed the screen, lifting it to his ear. "Yeah, Sam? I got your delivery request." He turned his glare to Michelle, looking her over from head to toe and snarled. "We need to talk." He turned away. His tone dropping to something cold and clipped.

Michelle shifted. "Jenny?" Her voice wavered. "What's going on?"

Jenny's stomach churned. Setting a hand on Michelle's shoulder, she shook her head, unknowing. She had a feeling they were about to find out.

"That's not what we agreed on." Charlie stiffened.

Jenny could only hear one side of the call, but Charlie's expression darkened. His grip on the phone tightened.

"You think I won't do it? You think I won't tell her?" Charlie's voice was quiet, dangerous. Then, with terrifying casualness, he turned toward Michelle. "Want to know a secret?"

Michelle frowned. "What?"

Charlie's warm laugh bounced around them. "Your dad's not who he says he is. You're living a lie."

Jenny stepped between them. "That's enough."

She almost didn't notice his grip adjust on the gun, but the sound of wood and metal clicked and her eye snapped to his grip, sliding down to the trigger.

Before she could react, Charlie swung the barrels around, aiming them first at Jenny and then Michelle. "I'm going to need you *both* to come with me."

THE POUNDING OF MICHELLE'S fists echoed thick and heavy against the wooden slats of the pantry door. In the cramped space, Jenny backed away from the flailing arms and hit a wall.

She couldn't see much in the dim light but Michelle's hysteria.

"Somebody's gonna find us!" Michelle yelled.

"I hope they do!" Harry shouted. Then burst out with maniacal laughter that tittered and squeaked. "It's been years since I've gotten to shoot something."

"Quiet!" Charlie's growl splintered through the chaos. The kindness and comfort he'd used to put them at ease was gone. His voice carried the same sharp edge as his father's. "Can't you keep it down? Muzzle them or smother them. I don't care!" His words trailed off as his footsteps faded down the hall.

The crack of gunfire split the air, a burst of light streamed overhead as a chunk of wood shattered.

Jenny shrieked, terror ripped through her as her

heartbeat skipped and her bones rattled like the stitches of a runaway sewing machine.

Splinters and dust rained down on them a hail of shrapnel. Jenny flinched as something sharp grazed the edge of her ear, leaving a stinging heat in its wake. She stumbled back, brushing her fingers over warm, wet blood—just a scratch, but enough to send a jolt of pain through her head. Her ears rang, nearly drowning out Michelle's stifled sob.

Footsteps pounded into the room beyond the door.

"I said keep them quiet! Not kill them! Not yet!" A thud slammed against the wall, and Charlie swore. "I can't get more money if they're dead!"

Inside the cramped space, Michelle gasped. "Yet?" Her fists froze mid-strike, her whole body going rigid. "Jenny?"

"We're not going to die," Jenny said, reaching to squeeze Michelle's hand. Her assistant's nod came with trembling fear.

After a moment, Michelle whispered. "What did he mean? When he said, I've been living a lie... why would he say that?"

Jenny hesitated. "Michelle—"

"I hear ya in there," Harry grumbled. "Don't go gettin' any ideas."

A chair scraped over the floor. Labored exhales punctuated the sound until it stopped outside the pantry door.

Charlie's voice rang through the house, smooth and slow like dripping oil. "Sam. We need to talk. You know what I want. More money. Or our baby girl finds out everything."

Michelle sucked in a breath so sharp it cut through the air. She staggered back, hitting the shelves behind her.

Jenny's stomach turned to lead. Information was slamming into each other creating more of a mess than before.

Michelle let out a strangled breath. "No."

"Blackmail," Jenny whispered and glanced over. She squeezed Michelle's hand. "We're going to figure this out."

But Charlie's words were frozen in her mind. *Our baby girl.* She glanced at Michelle. Could it be?

A door creaked open beyond the pantry, and Harry's heavy boots shuffled away.

"What are you doing here?" Harry grumbled.

"I'm here to get Sam's order." Danny's voice curled through the air, a thread of tension woven through each word.

Michelle perked up. "Danny?"

Mystery in the Old Quilt

"Is that—" A beat. A subtle shift. "Who's in the pantry?"

A dull thud followed, like a boot scuffing against the floor.

"Charlie asked me to watch 'em," Harry said, his tone puffed with misplaced pride. "Keep 'em in line."

Danny hesitated. "Right. Charlie..." A pause. "He didn't tell you?"

Another pause.

Danny sighed. "Charlie needs you to hunt some of the black chanterelles. We've got a big order. Like the ones you used to fill."

"Kansas City came back?" Harry questioned. Then he chuckled. "Of course they did. They always come back. We're the best."

"But he needs your help huntin' the rare ones."

Harry hesitated, then let out a satisfied grunt. "You're a good boy, Danny. Proud to call you family."

Jenny stilled.

"Family?" she whispered.

Michelle turned to her, confusion tight across her shadowed face.

The pantry door creaked open. A sliver of light slashed through the darkness.

"Danny?" Michelle barely had time to say his name before he pulled her into a tight hug.

"Michelle," Danny whispered, and pulled her out of the closet.

Jenny kept her eyes on the kitchen doorway, keeping her voice low. "What are you doing here? I thought the police arrested you."

"Police?" Michelle pulled back, blinking hard. "What's going on? I thought you were staying away from all that?"

Danny hesitated, then ran a hand through his hair. "I was. I—" he glanced toward the door. "I'm figuring it out. My job at the food truck only happened because I was helping Charlie with . . . things."

"Danny?" Michelle's confusion pulled her back further, pushing both her and Jenny into the opening of the pantry. "Charlie's a terrible person. You know that, right? I think he's blackmailing my dad."

He winced, guilt pressing his shoulders lower. "I didn't get it. I thought I was causing a little trouble, keeping Sam in line. My uncle and your dad don't exactly get along."

Michelle stiffened. "Your uncle?" Her voice wavered. "You mean Charlie?"

Danny nodded once.

Jenny exhaled, realization slotting into place. "You helped Charlie blackmail Sam."

Danny's shoulders slumped completely.

Mystery in the Old Quilt

"You helped him?" Michelle's voice cracked, barely above a whisper.

"I didn't understand." Danny's voice was softer now, desperate. "I thought Sam was the bad guy. That he ordered the poisonous mushrooms and he was making Gina sick. I didn't know why. I just knew Charlie wanted me to switch the mushrooms out before deliveries. I didn't think—" He dragged a hand down his face, his eyes glancing at Michelle like he already knew she might never forgive him.

Michelle recoiled. "What? What are you talking about? What poisonous mushrooms?"

Danny pressed his lips together before answering. "The jacks."

Jenny's breath caught in her throat. "The jack-o-lantern mushrooms."

Michelle shook her head sharply. "I don't understand."

Danny glanced at the door and lowered his voice. "I thought your dad was making Gina sick. I thought I needed to keep an eye on him." He swallowed hard. "Jack-o-lantern mushrooms make you sick, not kill you."

If that was true, and it was Charlie who'd orchestrated Danny switching the mushrooms, what happened had been no accident.

"Did you ever do anything with Gina's medication?" Jenny's whisper seemed to hit Danny in the heart.

He shook his head in confusion. "Charlie had some old pill bottles once. He told me Sam had done something with it." His face fell, looking at the floor. "I believed him, because I found a botttle in the food truck."

Charlie had known exactly what he was doing... Gina's heart hadn't stood a chance.

"My dad would never—" Michelle's face crumpled. "Danny, are you saying you killed Gina?"

"No." Danny's head jerked up quickly, eyes wide. "No. Sam did."

Jenny froze.

Michelle's face paled.

"I mean—I *thought* he did." Danny backpedaled. "That's what Charlie said. I thought I was helping."

Footsteps thudded toward them.

"Dad?" Charlie called.

Danny's expression changed in an instant. He shoved Michelle gently back inside.

"Go back in. For a minute. I'll take care of it."

Michelle didn't move. "No. Please. I don't understand."

If Danny was here to turn on Charlie, she had one chance.

Mystery in the Old Quilt

Jenny gripped Michelle's shoulders and softened her voice. "It's okay. I think we can trust him."

Danny met her gaze, understanding the weight of her words. His jaw tightened. Then, with a sharp nod, he shut the pantry door.

A second later, a boot scuffed against the floor outside.

"Danny?" Charlie's tone was too smooth, too careful. "What are you doin' here? Where's Dad?"

Jenny tensed.

"Just picking up the order," Danny said quickly. "Harry had to use the bathroom. Outside. It was weird, but he insisted. He'll be right back."

"The order?" Charlie's voice sharpened. "Sam said you were arrested."

"I was." Danny let out a nervous laugh. "But they didn't have any evidence. So I'm back. Figured I'd help out."

Jenny glanced at Michelle. The pieces were shifting fast.

"What's going on?" Michelle whispered.

Something slammed against the door.

Jenny flinched and they barely had time to react before the door swung open.

"I'd like to know the same thing." Charlie's silhouette filled the space, his face dark with suspicion.

Jenny's pulse pounded as he grabbed Michelle by the hair, yanking her forward.

"Wait!" Jenny lurched toward them.

Michelle cried out.

Smug, triumph hummed in Charlie's voice. "Don't go anywhere." He laughed, tapping the door. "My little girl and I have some catching up to do."

His little girl. He'd said something similar before. She'd suspected he and Gina had a relationship. But how could it be possible that Michelle was their child. Charlie's dark hair and blue eyes matched Michelle's, but she had parents who'd said nothing all this time.

He slammed the pantry door shut. A chair scraped and bumped against it.

"I'm not your girl!" Michelle cried out her voice moving further from the kitchen.

"Come back!" Jenny pounded against the wood, but their footsteps faded. She froze. The door moved.

Her breath caught. She shoved again. It shifted—slightly at first, then more. Something weighed against it. Too heavy for just a chair.

Jenny pushed harder, enough to make a gap she could fit through. On the other side, Danny's body slumped against the chair, blocking the exit.

Mystery in the Old Quilt

"Oh my gosh." Jenny dropped to her knees, pressing her fingers to his neck. A pulse. A shallow breath. Warmth brushed her fingertips. Relief settled through her like a flood.

"Daniel Long. Thank goodness you're still alive." His full name tumbled from her lips in an instinctive rush. Her maternal senses commanding, and grounding. They seemed to steady her racing thoughts.

She glanced around. Charlie had gone toward the living room. Jenny had to move. She had to get Michelle.

She darted forward, only to stumble as the fluffy gray cat from the porch passed under foot and up the stairs. She caught herself against a side table, her heart hammering.

A creak from above made her freeze. Footsteps—slow, deliberate.

Michelle?

Jenny held her breath, ears straining. A muffled voice. Charlie's.

Keeping her weight to the edges of the steps, she climbed carefully, mindful of every creak. A dimly lit hallway stretched ahead, doors standing ajar. One room glowed faintly from a single desk lamp.

Jenny hesitated. This wasn't just a house. It was Charlie's home.

A wingback chair sat near the desk, and draped across it was the Sloane family quilt. Its colors muted in the low light, but unmistakable. The cat lounged luxuriously over the bright links of embroidered fabric.

Jenny moved toward it, beckoning with her fingers. The cat didn't stir. "Here, kitty, kitty. Please?"

Nothing.

"Hey there, sweetheart," she murmured, keeping her tone light, coaxing. The cat pressed into her palm, rubbing its head against her fingers.

A slow blink. A stretch. Still, it didn't move.

"Kitty," she whispered sharply.

With an indignant flick of its tail, the cat leapt onto the small table beside the chair. Jenny exhaled.

A framed piece of embroidery sat perched beside it. Curious, she leaned in, squinting at the delicate stitches.

It was the poem.

> *Love anew has come to me,*
> *New leaves upon a family tree...*

The same words stitched into Gina's quilt, and Loretta's handkerchief. The name at the bottom said Lily Long Millet.

Long? Danny must be related to Charlie through Lily. She thought of Danny slumped over the kitchen

Mystery in the Old Quilt

chair. Jenny couldn't imagine what kind of person could do that to family.

Jenny's mind reeled, piecing together the threads. The quilt. The poem. Gina's secret. Charlie—

A floorboard creaked and Jenny stiffened.

Footsteps moved down the hall.

Charlie was coming.

She tore her gaze from the embroidery and reached for the quilt where the cat had settled. She waved a hand and its tail flicked with mild disinterest.

"Move," she whispered.

It blinked. Stretched. Did not move.

Jenny gritted her teeth.

Charlie was right outside the room.

No time.

Dread sinking in Jenny's chest, she scanned the room and slipped into a closet as the door swung open.

Through the gap, she watched Charlie stride in, phone in hand, his shoulders tense with frustration.

"You don't get to dictate how this goes, Sam," he snapped. "You may take care of her, but I'm her father. I did that. She's mine whether you want her to know, or not. And I know what you did. I'm the one holding the cards now."

Jenny held her breath as he threw the phone onto the desk with a sharp crack.

He really was Michelle's father and Sam... what had he done?

Heat and fear buzzed through Jenny, her questions a tangible force as Charlie dropped his gaze to the chair and he dragged a hand down his face.

On the quilt.

Jenny held her breath.

He stepped closer, staring down at the fabric. His fingers curled, then released, as if warring with himself.

"You always had to be clever, didn't you Gina?" His voice was low, rough. He yanked the quilt off the chair, gripping it in both fists. "Telling Blair how to find the money." He laughed, but there was no humor in it. "The money's in the quilt. That's what I heard anyway. And you made sure I'd never see another penny."

His hands clenched, shaking. "You did this, Gina." His voice cracked. "You forced me into this. I never wanted to hurt you."

Silence.

Pressed against the closet wall, Jenny barely breathed.

Charlie inhaled sharply. "If she could find the money in this quilt, then I can too. I'm not letting anyone else have that piece of you."

Mystery in the Old Quilt

His fingers traced the stitches, searching. Frustration twisted his expression.

Jenny could almost hear the battle in his head.

After a long moment, he let out a furious breath and stormed out, slamming the door behind him.

Jenny waited. One beat. Two.

The closet door eased open and she slipped out.

The quilt lay in disarray across the chair. Beside it, a worn photo lay on the table that hadn't been there before.

She picked it up carefully.

Gina, young and vibrant, smiled out of the image. The edges creased like it had been folded and unfolded a thousand times.

Jenny's heart pounded.

Charlie had been holding on to Gina all this time. Mourning her in his own twisted way.

The cat had returned to the quilt sitting like a sentinel guard. It purred, watching her with lazy disinterest.

Jenny lifted a finger. "Not a sound, you hear me?"

The cat licked its paw.

She nudged it off the chair, clutched the quilt to her chest, and slipped out of the room.

Water groaned through the pipes. Charlie had stopped in the bathroom.

Jenny peeked in the only other open door along the hall. Empty.

She needed to find Michelle.

Gripping the quilt, she hurried down the stairs.

MYSTERY
QUILT BLOCK 1

Clue 6

THE FINAL CUT'S RARELY AN EXPECTED CONTUSION
FOR DEATH, LIKE A QUILT, HOLDS ONE LAST ILLUSION

Clue 6

PUTTING IT ALL TOGETHER

Follow the diagram below to sew the Block Sets together as follows—

- ✓ Row 1 - Block Set 1
- ✓ Row 2 - Block Set 3
- ✓ Row 3 - Block Set 2
- ✓ Row 4 - Block Set 3 (Upside down)
- ✓ Row 5 - Block Set 1

Once the rows are all sewn together, press the block flat, and square to 21" by trimming around all the edges.

Clue 6 – Check the Supplies and Read!

Congratulations! You completed the first mystery quilt block, the Merry-Go-Round block!

Instructions are included to make a full quilt from this pattern after the next chapter.

PART Seven

Nine Patches, Nine Lives

Light footfalls carried Jenny to the bottom of the steps and through the front room.

"Michelle?" she kept her voice low. She couldn't get caught, and she couldn't leave Michelle behind.

Danny lay slumped in the kitchen, but Jenny barely spared him a glance, other than to confirm he was still there and turned down the hall.

The screech of tires peeling into the drive outside sent a spike of panic through her, like someone had jammed the foot pedal of her sewing machine with the speed on its highest setting.

She dashed down the hall, checking rooms as she went. A narrow door stood at the end. The handle rattled loose as she turned it, and fell out in her hand. Light skimmed under the panel and through the hole where the knob had fallen out. There must not be a knob on the other side.

She gripped the handle and pressed it into the metal workings. It caught and she twisted the door open.

Inside, the sloped ceiling led Jenny's gaze down, past shelves to a rickety wooden staircase. Where the shelves ended, stone walls extended into the lower level of the house.

Mildew and dust filled the room with a dimly lit haze.

Jenny hugged the quilt tighter to her chest. "Michelle?"

A whimper came from below, followed by a rustling noise. "Jenny? I'm down here. He tied me to a post."

Relief hit her swift and sharp. Michelle was close and alive. They were going to make it through this. She started down the steps and paused putting the doorknob in her pocket. If it closed while they were inside and she didn't have it, they'd be locked in again.

Damp chill clung to Jenny as she descended

Mystery in the Old Quilt

the stairs, thick with the musty scent of age and neglect.

Moving fast, she kept her breath shallow as she slid past shelves, careful not to brush against the thick layers of grime. Boards sagged under the weight of old canning jars, filled with cloudy liquids and murky, unrecognizable preserves.

At the far end of the room, Michelle sat on the dirt packed floor, bound to a metal post supporting the low ceiling.

Jenny hurried to her side. "Let's get out of here."

Michelle twisted in her bindings, urgency bleeding into her voice. "Hurry. He said he'd be right back."

Jenny nodded.

Fumbling with the bulky quilt, her fingers felt clumsy and awkward, making the knots seem even tighter. She needed somewhere clean to set it down so she could free Michelle.

Her eyes landed on the chest freezer humming in the corner. She didn't have time to think about it. Jenny flipped the lid, shoved the quilt inside, and let the broken hinges clap shut.

Michelle chuckled darkly, "For a second, I was afraid you were gonna find Gina in there."

She cut herself off, sucking in a sharp breath. Blinking rapidly, her brows furrowed in a tangled mix of frustration and fear. "I don't know why I said that."

Jenny knelt beside her again, tugging at the ropes. "Claudia came by this morning, so I wasn't worried about finding her there."

The ropes gave slightly, loosening enough for Jenny to start working them free.

Michelle shook her head, her voice cracking. "Jenny... Charlie said he's my dad. That Gina's my real mother— what do I do?"

A strangled sob bubbled up, choking off the words.

Jenny paused, gripping Michelle's wrists gently around the rope and knots.

Her fingers steadied against Michelle's erratic pulse. Her questions scattered like a quilt needing to be stitched together.

One question. One answer. One seam at a time.

"Nothing, unless you want to." She met Michelle's wide, wet eyes, speaking softly, but firmly.

"You don't have to figure it all out right now." Jenny's hands moved carefully, back to unthreading the knots. "A quilt isn't made all at once. And life is a lot bigger than even this secret."

Silent tears trembled on Michelle's lashes. Jenny held her hands, trying to think and work quickly.

"We'll figure this out. One stitch at a time.

Mystery in the Old Quilt

We'll put it together, or take it apart, until we know what's real."

Michelle's breath hitched. "But I was lied to my whole life. I don't even know Gina, I never got to. My parents—"

"Are still your parents." Jenny confirmed quickly. One of the loops on the rope gave way, and she unthreaded a section of the bonds. "Sam and Claudia chose you forever. That hasn't changed."

Michelle exhaled shakily, eyes darting away. "I didn't even know Gina. And now I can't. Blair is going to hate me."

Jenny stilled. That was what Michelle was afraid of? Not losing parents or having to be connected to Charlie, but how Blair would feel.

Michelle let out a bitter laugh. "My life really was built on a lie. I'm supposed to accept that my real mother gave me away, and Blair . . . she doesn't want a sister. I don't even know if I want a sister. How could they keep this from us?"

Jenny focused on Michelle's wrists, her mind working on a different problem. "Gina didn't chose this. She wouldn't have left all those notes and clues if she didn't want you to know. As I see it, you're the biggest winner in all this. She wanted to tell you. She cared about you, just like Claudia and Sam do."

"I know I have a mother who loves me, but—" Michelle swallowed hard, her eyes shining. "All these years. Why? Did they think there was some kind of shame in having adopted me? What if they didn't adopt me? Because it would leave a papertrail? Surely, I would have seen that."

Jenny took a breath, choosing her words carefully. "All these questions are going to have to wait for your parents. I think Gina did what she thought was best for everyone. For you, for Sam and Claudia, at some level, even for Blair." Jenny's fingers moved swiftly, loosening the last knot. "I don't think I told you, but Bernie knew Gina's mother, Rachel. She sent Gina away when it was time for you to be born. She was trying to protect her daughter."

"I think I understood that better before it was part of my life."

Jenny pulled the knot free, and Michelle sagged away from the post, rubbing the raw lines on her wrists.

"It's going to work out. Once the police catch your crazy father." Jenny sat back.

Michelle cringed. "Too soon."

"Sorry," Jenny bit her lip, moving toward the stairs. "Even broken things can be stitched back together."

Mystery in the Old Quilt

A single beat of silence split the moment before Michelle let out a breathy, half-hearted laugh. "That was better but not good."

Jenny grinned. "Yeah, well. It's what I do."

"If we stitch this back together, Charlie is getting left out of the pattern."

"As he should."

Michelle sniffed. "One stitch at a time, huh?"

Jenny braced Michelle's arm as they hurried up the basement stairs. Voices carried through the door, and Jenny paused, holding a finger to her lips. She quieted their ascent, careful to keep their steps light.

Michelle's voice was raw, barely above a whisper. "Do we run?"

Midway up the stairs, Jenny hesitated. Every instinct screamed, *Yes! Run!* But first, they had to make it through the living room, and she had no idea who was in there.

"Wait here," she whispered. "I'll find out what's happening."

Michelle gave a tiny nod, and Jenny crept up the last few steps, keeping her weight to the edges where the wood was less likely to creak.

At the top, she pressed into the shadows, inching toward the end of the hall. A loud *crash* echoed from the next room. Jenny stiffened.

She couldn't see much through the archway, but she could hear everything.

"You think you can walk in here making demands?" Charlie shouted. "What happened to no complications? Everything was set up, and you send me a note that says you're not gonna pay?"

"You called me!" Sam's voice cut through the house. "You can't believe I was going to follow through with your crazy demands. Danny told me about the mushrooms. You can't blame Gina's death on me anymore. You swapped the chanterelles. You took advantage of the mother of your child."

The door creaked softly behind her. Jenny looked over her shoulder, heart hammering.

Michelle stood in the stairwell, her mouth open in shock. *My dad?* she mouthed.

Jenny nodded but held up a hand. *Wait.*

Charlie cackled from the living room. "You don't have a clue, do you? Gina had a nurse who spent a lot of private time with me. When I became concerned for 'Gina's welfare.'" His voice held a mocking tone that made Jenny's skin crawl. "I convinced her to take home a sample of one of her meals."

There was a brief hesitation and Charlie started again. "Oh! And let's not forget the little surprise waiting in your food truck. A very telling bottle of

Mystery in the Old Quilt

medication, tucked away where no one but the police would ever look. I'd ask why you had a bottle of Gina's medication, but we *both* know you're no criminal mastermind."

Michelle moved closer, hovering behind Jenny.

Everything useful seemed to be out in the middle of the room, where Jenny couldn't get to it. Charlie had taken her phone when he'd locked them in the pantry, so she couldn't call anyone.

The cat lounged in a chair as if the chaos of the house was entirely commonplace.

"You make me sick," Sam sneered. "Where's my daughter? I came for her, not some puffed up presentation on poor Charlie, son of a Mushroom Man's, life." Barely checked fury infused power and aggression into his voice.

It got quiet and Jenny peeked around the corner. A large plant stood against the wall providing vague protection.

Charlie faced Sam moving slowly forward, his expression hardened dangerously. She pulled away hiding pressed against the wall.

Words may be a schoolboy's weapon, but they hit like he'd twisted a deep blade.

"Pathetic," Charlie scoffed. "All this time, I'm the one keeping *your* secret, and you act like I'm the villain." His voice twisted with something close to amusement. "Let's fix that."

There was a shuffling in the room before Sam called out. "Michelle!"

Jenny caught Michelle's arm as she lurched forward. Exposing themselves now would be suicide.

Charlie laughed, his warmth carried the deranged titter of his father.

Jenny edged toward the corner again. Charlie focused on Sam. He didn't even look toward the hallway.

Good.

"You want to know what happened, Sam?"

Sam tried to push past him again, but Charlie shoved him back against the wall, pinning him there.

"I'll tell you," Charlie crooned wickedly. "And when I do, you're going to pay me exactly what I ask—unless you want Michelle to hear the truth about her *daddy* from me."

Michelle's breath quickened, ice cold fingers wrapping Jenny's arm.

"You'd never tell her." Charlie scoffed, voice dripping with derision. "You were always too soft, like Gina. I don't know how you two didn't end up together." His sneer deepened. "Rachel knew, though. She knew exactly how to *handle* a problem like

Gina's." His head tilted, eyes glinting with something dark and knowing.

Sam stiffened, fists curling at his sides. "Rachel helped us adopt a baby. Michelle. *Not* a problem."

Charlie barked a laugh. "Rachel was incredibly helpful! She paid me for years."

"I wouldn't brag about that." Sam exhaled sharply. "Rachel was trying to help Gina. I doubt paying you was her first choice."

Charlie's smirk faltered. "I didn't *want* this. I wanted Gina." His voice turned bitter. "But she wouldn't even *look* at me after Rachel sold her baby to you."

"Sold?" Sam's expression hardened. "That's not what happened, and you know it."

"Please." He exhaled sharply, running a hand through his hair. "I had one more chance when Rachel died. Gina learned about our little *arrangement*. And I was glad. I thought we'd finally get back together, you know? Set things right." Something ugly flickered over his face before it twisted. "Then she decided she was done with me. She cut me off like I was nothing. Like none of it mattered."

"You're disgusting." Sam spat.

"You can't do that to me!" His voice cracked, raw with fury.

Sam grunted as Charlie shoved him harder, pressing him against the wall.

"I *know* you told her what to do," Charlie hissed. "You never thought I was good enough for her! But *I* was the good guy. I paid for everything. *I* was the one who *took care of her.*" His breath turned ragged. "I gave her *weeks*—weeks to fix this, to *fix us*—and all she did was talk to *you.*"

A sick grin curled his lips.

"I had to do something. I *had* to stop her."

Another slam—dust spilled from the wall.

Charlie leaned in, voice dropping to something menacingly soft. "Now it's *your* fault. And now, *you* get to fix this. Or you're going to prison—with or without your daughter."

"He can't do that," Michelle whispered. "Can he? He can't blame all of this on my dad."

"No," Jenny glancing down the hall. "But we need to go. *Now.*" Before Charlie's violence turned on them.

The kitchen door was the closest, but reaching it meant exposing themselves.

Every muscle tightened as she tried to come up with a plan. Michelle could run, but Jenny would never make it. Charlie was bigger and stronger.

"I know what happened." Sam exhaled sharply.

Mystery in the Old Quilt

"You killed Gina, and you've been bleeding my family dry ever since. You're not going to win this."

"I've already won." He growled.

She pressed into the shadows, bumping her pocket against the wall with a metallic thunk.

The cat looked up, its eyes trained on her spot in the hall.

The voices quieted.

Jenny reached into her pocket, fingers closing around the doorknob she'd forgotten was there. She tightened her grip, keeping it from knocking against the wall again, and prayed they wouldn't notice.

It was too quiet in the other room.

Think fast.

She gripped the metal end of the doorknob in her fist and threw it into the room.

The cat leapt from the chair, yowling, and flew toward the men—apparently deciding *they* were the greater danger.

Jenny grabbed Michelle and ran toward the kitchen door.

A siren blared.

Jenny's pulse spiked.

"Dad!" Michelle shouted.

"Chelle!" Sam lunged, shoving Charlie away.

The cat wailed, and Jenny pushed through the room. Sam and Charlie collided with the walls.

Charlie screamed wildly. "You don't get to win, Peters!"

"Freeze!" Officer Wilkins' familiar voice echoed through the house. "Put your hands in the air!"

Danny was gone as they dashed through to the kitchen door. Jenny pulled Michelle with her.

Outside, Blair paced in front of Sam's truck. The moment she saw them, she ran straight for Jenny, catching her in a hug.

Blair's words spilled out in a rush. "What's going on? I called the police. Sam said if he wasn't back in five minutes to call them. Who does that? Was I supposed to? Is everything okay?"

Jenny reassured her, and Blair turned toward Michelle, her eyes glassy with unshed tears.

"I'm so glad you're okay. Where's Sam? Should we go get them?"

Jenny pulled Blair and Michelle toward the car, explaining as much as she could.

Blair's breath hitched. "I can't believe you're my sister!" Tears spilled over as she attempted to wipe them away—then gave up and threw her arms around Michelle. "I almost lost you! I lost my mother, and then I almost lost you!"

Mystery in the Old Quilt

Michelle stiffened in Blair's grip, her worried gaze finding Jenny.

Then, as Blair sobbed against her shoulder, Michelle softened. Her arms slid up, reciprocating the embrace, until both young women were weeping against each other.

Blair pulled back, searching Michelle's face. "You're the secret my mom protected so fiercely. No wonder. You're worth protecting." She exhaled a trembling breath, a wobbly laugh escaping. "Oh my goodness! I did know her secret. Mom used to make these family embroideries with flowers and seashells. There were roses and lilies, for her and grandma, and bluebells, for me, and she always added a seashell. You were the seashell." Blair laughed. "If I'd figured it out sooner I wouldn't have needed the quilt to find you."

Jenny's heart jolted.

The quilt.

How had she forgotten?

"I'll be right back."

She hurried across the lawn to the kitchen door. Even with the police present, she didn't want to cross too close to Charlie.

Danny stood in the living room, speaking quickly as his uncle glared at him.

Officer Wilkins' jaw tensed as she entered. "Jenny?" Frustration flared in his breath. "Why am I not surprised?"

"Sorry," Jenny said, hurrying toward the hall. "I'll be out of your way in a minute."

She reached the basement, lifted the freezer lid, and stared.

Across Grandma Rachel's quilt block was a string of letters and numbers. Jenny's stomach flipped.

Her frozen heart may not provide, but—

"Looks like Michelle wasn't Gina's only secret."

NO ONE UNDERSTOOD AGING quite like a quilter. True value didn't come from the amount of time something existed. But in the stories that gave an heirloom a history. Rips and tears were part of any life. A quilt lasted because of the hands that stitched it, the careful repairs, and the legacy it carried forward.

A patchwork made of history and love.

Families were the same. New pieces were added, old wounds mended, and stitches reinforced. Quilts, like people, could always be repaired.

You just had to keep stitching.

Mystery in the Old Quilt

Jenny leaned against the brick wall at the edge of the food court patio where *In a Nutshell* was serving lunch.

Golden afternoon light warmed the scent of smoked brisket sliders, glazed in Sam's Pecan Molasses BBQ sauce.

They were his latest menu addition now that Sam had officially sworn off mushroom risotto.

Dotty's famous peach cobbler crowned each table, surrounded by plates and bowls of sides passed between friends. It was the kind of easy, familiar rhythm that made Hamilton a home.

Sam stood at the grill, forehead damp from the heat, tossing glances at Michelle across the table, where she idly twirled a fork between her fingers. Dotty and Bernie whispered conspiratorially, their hushed laughter hinting at some scheme in the works.

But it was Blair who Jenny couldn't stop watching.

For the first time since she'd arrived in town, Blair looked like she belonged. She laughed at something Claudia said, her dimples flashing, her eyes bright. It was possible Blair hadn't genuinely relaxed since she'd arrived to care for Gina.

Warmth settled deep in Jenny's chest as a slight shift at the sidewalk caught her attention.

"It's good to see you, Jenny." Loretta stood stiffly near the curb, shifting her purse on her arm as if debating whether she should even be here.

Jenny crossed to greet her. "Loretta! You came."

Loretta lifted her chin slightly. "Well, of course. What kind of person skips a farewell party?"

"Glad you're here." Jenny smiled, choosing warmth over wit. "I'm sure Blair will appreciate getting to say goodbye."

A pained smile hovered on Loretts's lips. "I, uh, wanted to say something."

Jenny raised an eyebrow. "Oh?"

"About the other day," Loretta began, shifting nervously. "I didn't mean to—well, you know—" She swallowed. "I shouldn't have been in your studio that day. I wanted to see the quilt. I was—I missed Gina."

She exhaled sharply, clearly irritated with herself for even attempting this. "Look, I shouldn't have been in your studio. I'm sor—" She hesitated, as if trying to finish but couldn't. Her mouth pressed into a thin line. "I'm glad things worked out."

Jenny bit back a smile. "Me too."

Loretta pursed her lips, a flicker of exasperation crossing her face before smoothing into something more dignified. "Well, there. Are you happy?"

Mystery in the Old Quilt

Jenny bowed her head in mock deference. "Very. It was quite a heartfelt moment."

Loretta rolled her eyes and turned away. "Honestly, I don't know why I bother."

Dotty's voice rang out across the patio. "All right, everyone! We have one last thing to do before Blair leaves."

Jenny nudged Loretta. "Guess that's my cue."

She stepped forward, joining Dotty and Bernie, who held a large bundle behind them.

"Can we have Blair come forward?" Jenny called.

Blair stood wiping her hands on a napkin. "What's going on?"

Holding her hands up Jenny called the group to attention. With an arm around Blair's shoulders warmth filled her chest. Everything was coming full circle. "We'd like to thank you for carrying on a legacy as beautiful as your mother's with a special gift."

Dotty made a grand dun-duh-dun! And Jenny helped Bernie with the dramatic unveiling of their gift.

Blair gasped, her hands flying to her mouth. "Oh my gosh—" She stepped forward, fingertips grazing the familiar fabric. "You fixed it."

Jenny grinned. "The Sloane family quilt, fully restored."

Blair traced the stitches, her breath catching. "You can't even see Grandma Rachel's bank account numbers."

Ron let out a low chuckle. "Are you disappointed?"

Laughter rippled through the group, light and easy.

Bernie leaned close, muttering from the corner of her mouth, "Those heat sensitive pens are amazing. I always wondered if the ink coming back in the cold was a myth."

Jenny chuckled, a smile tugging at her lips. "Lucky for Blair, this one did."

"I have a grandma that hid money in a quilt," Michelle mused.

"It was Grandma Rachel's account, but my mom—uh, Mom—" Blair gave a careful smile before finishing, "is the one who hid it in the quilt."

Michelle laughed. "A family heirloom and a secret savings account? Amazing."

Dotty crossed her arms, grinning. "And *that* is why I check every antique quilt for loose threads."

The whole table broke into laughter. Jenny shook her head. "Remind me not to let you near my throw pillows."

"And here I thought you wanted secret notes and good gossip." Bernie chuckled, patting her sister's shoulder.

Mystery in the Old Quilt

Blair smiled, the quilt held firmly in her grip, then glanced at her packed car. A flicker of hesitation crossed her face.

She looked down at the quilt and, after only a slight pause, turned to Michelle.

"I want you to have this—to remember me."

Michelle's eyes widened. "Blair, no. This is your quilt. Your mom's."

Blair smiled softly. "It's ours. A piece of our family's history, from our mother. One of them, anyway." She hesitated, then smirked. "And let's be honest—I've got about three inches of space left in my car, and this quilt deserves better than being wedged between my vacuum and a stack of shoeboxes."

Michelle let out a teary laugh and accepted the quilt Blair held out to her. "Thank you."

"And there's one more thing," Blair added. "I looked into Grandma Rachel's account. It had very regular payments going out for as far back as I could see... until recently. I couldn't tell who they were going to, but I think we both know what that means."

Michelle lifted her chin and nodded quietly.

"That account was left to protect you." Blair reached into her pocket and pulled out an envelope.

She pressed it into Michelle's hands. "I want you to have what's left."

Michelle's mouth opened and closed, stunned. "Blair, I can't accept this. It's not mine.—"

Blair shook her head, her voice gentle but firm. "The money was there because Grandma Rachel wanted to make sure you had options." She took a breath, steadying herself. "I think that's part of why Mom and Grandma never got alon gvery well, but she tried to help in the only way she knew how. Now the truth is out and we get to decide what it means. We can let it be something good. Think of it as a gift from our grandmother."

Michelle exhaled slowly, her fingers tightening around the envelope. "You don't need it?"

Dabbing at a stray tear, Blair shook her head. "I'll be fine. She didn't leave me with nothing."

Michelle swallowed hard, then looked down as if steadying herself. "Actually . . . I have something for you, too."

She reached into her bag and pulled out a small wooden frame. Inside, delicate stitches formed careful letters on linen.

Blair furrowed her brow. "The poem."

Michelle nodded. "The full poem. I embroidered it for my baby sister."

Mystery in the Old Quilt

Blair's smile lit her eyes as she traced the stitches, her voice barely above a whisper as she read aloud—

> *Love anew has come to me,*
> *New leaves upon a family tree.*
> *In quilted dreams, of starry skies,*
> *A life begins and grows and dies.*
> *Though love is spun in life for thee,*
> *My love again I must set free.*
> — *Lily Millet, grandmother*

"That's us," Michelle said softly. "New leaves on a family tree. And I made one for myself. Now we have a gift from your side of the family tree and mine."

She pointed to the bottom of the embroidery, where she had stitched several sets of names and dates.

"They have our names in the middle with our birthdays, and on one side is your parents, and on the other is mine. We're a little family tree with lots of extra branches."

A slow smile tugged at Jenny's lips. "How did we not know that your birthday was October first?"

Michelle shrugged. "Didn't seem relevant at the time."

Blair let out a half-laugh, half-sob, then launched forward, wrapping Michelle in another fierce hug.

"I'm a little jealous you got Mom's skill with a needle, and I can't even iron. But it's okay, I'm not complaining."

"I learned from my mom." Michelle glanced toward Claudia watching from the tables. "I bet she'd teach you too if you want."

Quiet tears formed and fell over Claudia's cheeks. She nodded to Blair, who gave her a grateful smile.

"Thank you," Blair said through her own tears. "Though if I haven't learned yet, I'm not sure how soon I'll manage it."

Laughter buoyed the two sisters as they clung to each other, years of unspoken words and lost moments mending in the space between them.

One by one, the women who had come to see Blair off joined in the group hug until they couldn't tell whose arms wrapped around whom and whose tears had turned to laughter.

Every quilter worth her pins knew: the older the quilt, the better. But in that moment of family and friendship, it seemed time stitched backward, and a memory wove itself into their hearts.

Ron and Jenny wished Blair well with their friends as she made her way to the car packed with boxes and memories. Standing together, they waved goodbye as she pulled away and slowly, the women around Jenny dispersed. Each carrying a lightness about them that had nothing to do with the approaching golden hour of the day.

"I just witnessed something special, didn't I?" Ron asked.

Jenny nodded, leaning into his shoulder. "You did. We turned an old quilt into a family legacy."

THE END

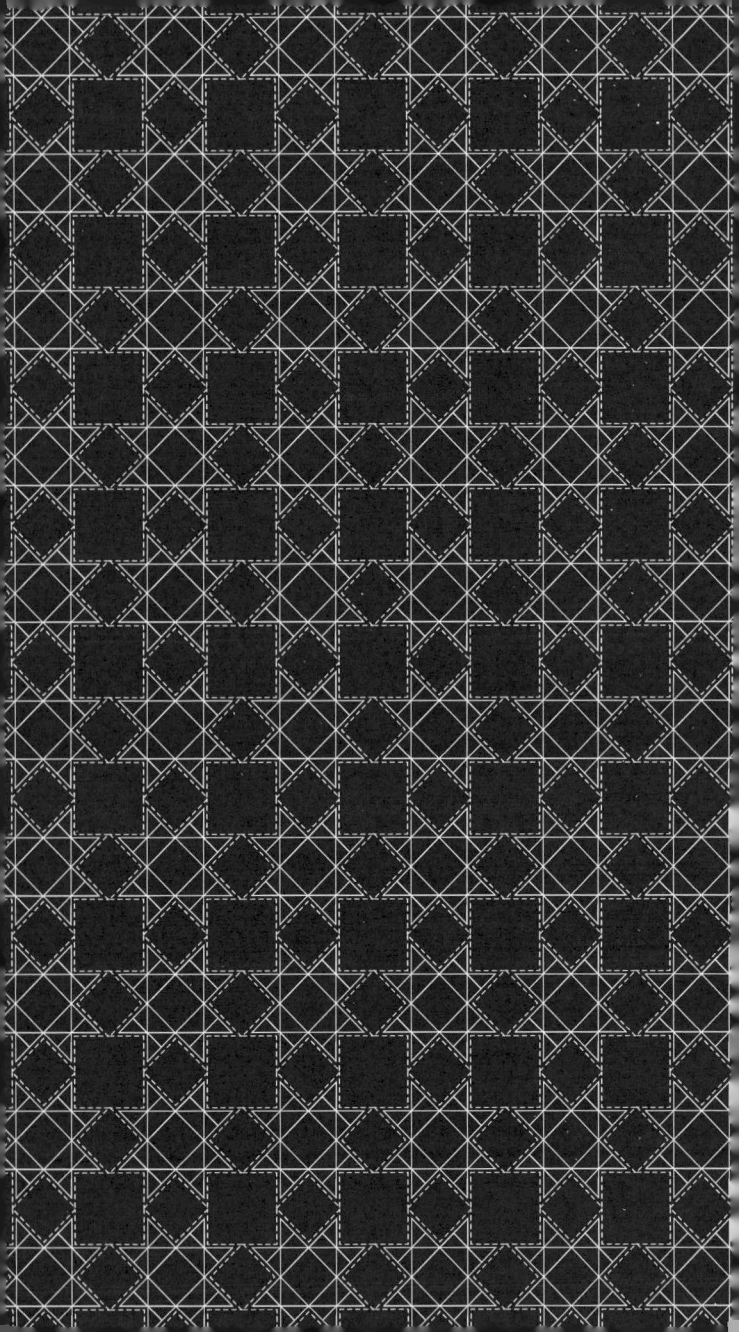

Merry-Go-Round
Full Quilt

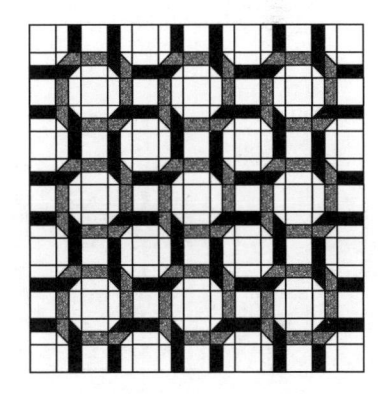

FROM QUILT BLOCK TO QUILT!

Making a full quilt from the Merry-Go-Round quilt pattern is simple and fun. It's made the same as the single block, leaving off the sashing pieces from the bottom and one side. As shown. 👉

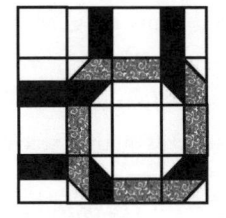

(NOTE: The sashing is the white and print blocks that border the center nine patch.)

Merry-Go-Round Full Quilt Tricks

This creates an 18 ½" square block. When these sections are sewn together, the sashing connects, finishing the linked pattern.

I consider this a self-sashing method. To finish the quilt, make 1 extra sashing strip set for the blocks along the bottom and side of your quilt, as shown.

The example uses a 3 x 3 block layout and would require 6 sashing block sets, PLUS a 5" white (or background) corner square to complete the pattern.

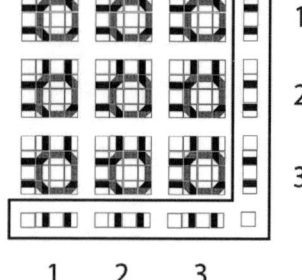

A free tutorial on the Merry-go-Round quilt block with the real Jenny Doan and the Missouri Star Quilt Co. Can be viewed online at www.missouriquiltco.com
Search for this block by name as well as thousands of other tutorials on their teaching page.

(NOTE: The videos may show different sizes and piecing processes due to creating this one as a "mystery" block. Enjoy the techniques and learn something wonderful!)

What You Need to Finish the Quilt!

For each block you'll need –
- ✓ 1 print 10" sq.
- ✓ 1 solid 10" sq.
- ✓ 3 white 10" sqs.

For each border sashing strip, you'll need –
- ✓ 1 solid 5" sq.
- ✓ 3 white 5" sq.

(+ 1 extra white 5" square for the last corner.)

(NOTE: Since this pattern worked strictly with 10" squares, I feel like I should point out the border supplies listed here are in 5" squares. If it's just me, no worries! Keep sewing and ignore my paranoia.

— If you want to continue using 10" squares, you'll need 1/2 a solid 10" square and 1 1/2 white 10" squares for every 2 sashing strips.

— If you're not specifically using 10" squares, it's worth noting that 4 - 10" squares are equal to a 10" strip of yardage fabric. For simplicity, that's approximately 1/3 yard.)

BOUND
IN SECRETS
& LIES

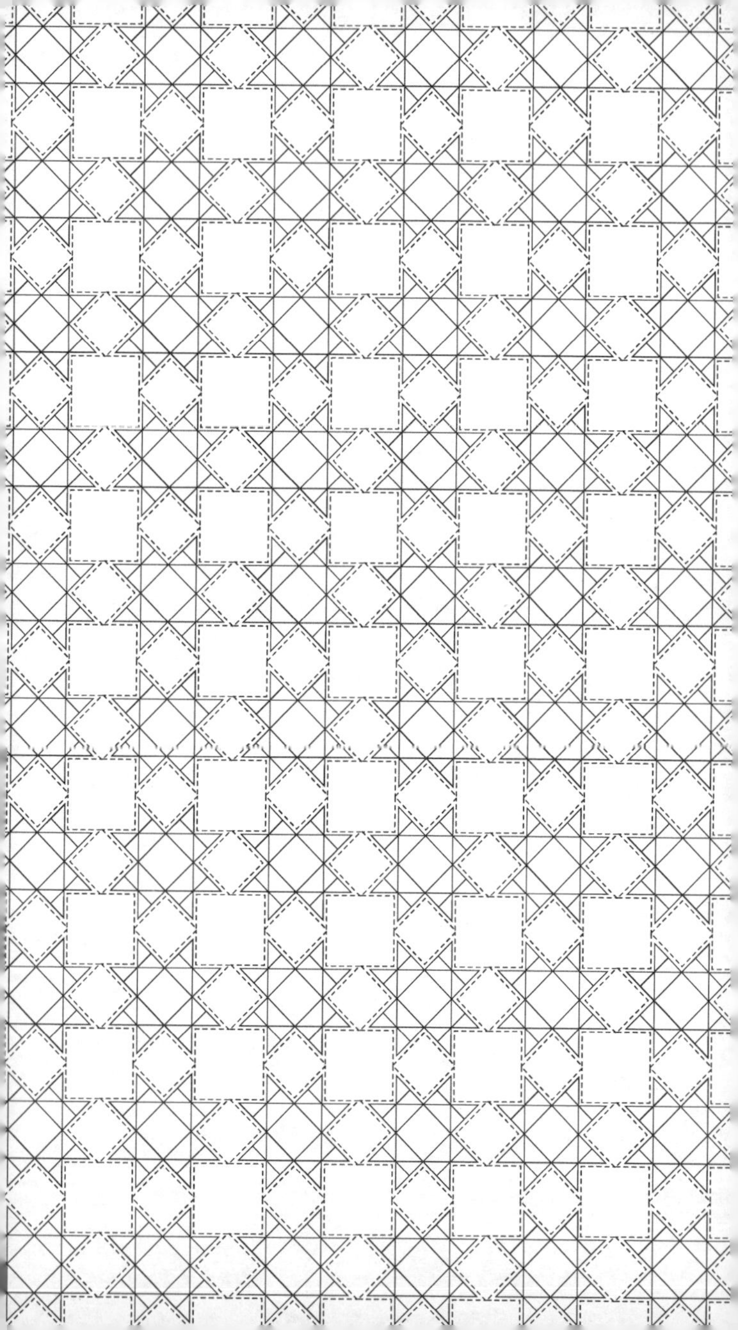

PART One

Cutting Out a Mystery

Finishing a quilt always struck Jenny as the hardest part of the creative process—not for lack of skill, but for the sheer determination it took to stay focused once the initial excitement faded.

Creativity, for Jenny, wasn't limited to quilting. It was the rhythm of life itself, the careful stitching of decisions, connections, and moments into something meaningful. Each stitch transformed fabric into art.

But finishing was another matter. The growing stack of quilt tops waiting for their final binding, proved that well enough.

Bright sunshine and the chatter of her friends at The Antique Barn's monthly sale day was populated with rows of vintage quilts. Each billowed along the weathered boards of the barn with a past stitched into its seams and the bindings already complete.

Running her fingers over a handsewn and mitered binding, Jenny sighed. "I wouldn't mind a few secrets from the quilters who finished these. My pile of binding only ever seems to get taller."

"Not the great Jenny Doan," Bernie teased, nudging her sister Dotty as she dropped a vintage ruler into her basket. "Aren't all your quilts stitched in silver and sprinkled with gold?"

Jenny smirked. "Is that why it takes me forever to finish them?"

Nearby, her new assistant, Cherry Carmine, rummaged through a bin of vintage patterns. Pushing back a wave of strawberry blonde hair. "Let me know if you find any of those secrets." Her southern drawl turned frustration into charm. "My bindings always come out wonky. I don't understand it."

"Unfortunately, the best trick is practice," Jenny's acceptance felt like dissapointment. "And maybe a good tutorial."

"Or really good friends to help out," Bernie added with a wink.

Cherry spontaneously linked her arm through Jenny's, as they started down the next aisle. "Really good friends are essential."

The action surprised Jenny but she welcomed the connection. Cherry seemed like a good fit in her new position. She was organized and very good at knowing what needed doing. But the best part of having Cherry around was that work felt like visiting with a friend, rather than checking off tasks.

As they strolled past a quilt ladder, Jenny kept an eye out for a pre-war sampler she'd been eager to see again—*Echoes of the Hollow*. Grace Day, the owner of The Antique Barn, had shown it to her last week.

Rounding a corner, she spotted the owner adjusting a display. "Grace!" Jenny called. "There you are! What happened to that quilt you showed me? I was hoping for a closer look."

Grace hesitated. "I . . . uh . . . don't have it anymore."

"Did someone buy it?" Jenny frowned. "I shouldn't be surprised. It was in perfect condition."

"No, it's not that." Grace glanced around, a flicker of unease in her voice. "Actually, could I speak with you privately for a moment?"

Dotty and Bernie excused themselves, and Cherry pointed toward a nearby table. "I'll be over there. Don't leave without me."

Weaving between displays, Grace led Jenny past the bustle of shoppers, toward the wide barn entrance.

The Antique Barn shared a yard with Grace's home. The short walk between them was filled with rows of table displays and antiques—all laid out for the monthly sales she held if there was enough inventory to open.

The barn itself seemed saturated with history. Summer heat amplified the rich, musty aroma of the interior under the subtle tang of aged wood and linseed oil.

Grace led Jenny through the narrow aisles divided by mismatched glass cabinets filled with old books, photographs, and vintage fabrics to the storage area. Haphazardly stacked furniture and crates filled the darkened space. A pile of white linen sat on top of a box of beeswax candles and vintage jars.

In the corner, Grace pulled back a heavy canvas cloth. Stacks of carefully folded antique quilts lay hidden in the shadows.

Jenny sucked in a breath. "Oh, Grace. These must be worth a fortune."

A tired laugh, hinted at the dark circles under Grace's eyes. "I hope so. I had set them aside for an auction. I got a notice about some back taxes recently. It turns out, I'm subject to some ridiculous farm-use tax adjustment. I don't even farm. But because the land used to be classified that way, I owe a lump sum. And soon."

Jenny frowned. "Can they do that? They shouldn't be allowed to change the rules like that."

"Apparently, they can. And I can't afford to lose the house over taxes." Her fingers curled against the quilt. "Double H Auctions actually reached out about listing some of my older pieces."

"How did they know?" Surprise threw Jenny's tact out the window. "You didn't agree, did you?"

Double H was the only auction house she'd heard of that had conveniently *lost* valuable heirlooms through their auctions.

"I didn't. But I'm an antique seller." Grace shrugged. "They were just checking in. It was good timing on their part, but I'm not a fan of Double H either," Grace said, interpreting Jenny's shock correctly. "I've always heard they're Horrid Hagglers."

Jenny chuckled. "Really? I heard Double H stood for Heist House."

"Oh," Grace sucked in a breath through her teeth. "Please tell me if I ever get a reputation even close to that."

"I will, but we both know that takes a special kind of business owner. And you're better than that."

"I hope so." Grace gave a weary sigh. "I've started . . . misplacing things. No, that's what Jed, my nephew, said but they're just missing. Anyway, with so many things disappearing, I pulled these pieces out and hid them here."

"Do you have any idea what's happening?"

"I have an idea, but it doesn't matter." Grace scanned the storage area as if expecting someone to jump out and take the quilts right then. "Double H's offer gave me an idea though. I decided to host an auction. I think I can do it myself with less risk and maybe make enough to pay the debt."

"That's a great idea." Jenny's mind started turning with possibilities. "Do you need any help?"

Grace's gaze snapped to Jenny, her eyes wide. "No, I'm fine. I mean, it's all right. I just really hope Jed—er, I hope nothing else disappears before I can make it happen. I've already got bidders on several of the quilts." She traced the faded pattern of a sampler quilt. "This one—*Echoes of the Hollow*—is the quilt I showed you. If you're interested, I'd still sell it to you."

"Oh, I would love that. But the auction sounds exciting. Put me down for a bid on that one." Jenny agreed, heartily. "I hope it goes really well."

"Me too." Grace smiled, tucking the quilt away. Counting softly, she ran a hand along the stack.

Bound in Secrets & Lies

Worry tugged at Jenny's heart. "You really think someone would steal these too? Isn't that why you hid them?"

"Jed knows where they are." She hesitated before turning to face Jenny. "He's the one who's been taking things."

"Your nephew? Isn't he the one you invited to stay with you?"

Grace nodded and Jenny's brows pulled tight with worry.

"Have you told the police?"

"I've only told you." Grace said, her voice firm. "And I won't turn him in. He's my brother's son. He's only here because he has nowhere else to go."

Jenny softened. "I understand. But if he's stealing from you—"

"I can handle it." Grace rubbed her temples. "Jed's made mistakes. But if I call the police, it won't help him. It'll ruin him."

Jenny studied her friend, knowing the conversation wouldn't go any further today.

"Listen," Grace said. "I didn't bring you back here to tell you about Jed." She let the canvas fall in front of the quilts, hiding them in the shadows. "I need your help with something."

Jenny's curiosity piqued. "What is it?"

Grace exhaled. "Something about this whole tax issue feels wrong. Like maybe it's not a coincidence."

"You think it's fake?" Jenny looked around then too, as if maybe there was some trick getting ready to be revealed.

"Not necessarily," Grace pressed her lips into a thin line. "But I've been getting property complaints all year, and I never had before. I don't think the tax change is fake. It's just strange, it's all happening at once. It's almost like someone's trying to get rid of me." The tension in her voice sharpened Jenny's focus. She was about to press further when Grace sighed, rubbing her temples. "Between that and everything with Jed . . . Did I tell you he was in an accident? Barely made it out without jail time."

Jenny frowned. "Jail time? For an accident?"

A hesitation, then Grace murmured, "Well . . . he caused the accident." She gestured for Jenny to follow her out of the storage area as she continued. "It sent Landon Reyes, my neighbor, to the hospital for a couple of nights. Jed's lucky he didn't press charges."

"Was he drinking?" The question came before Jenny could stop herself.

"No, the police didn't find anything like that. But Lanny said he was driving like a maniac. Too fast for a back road. But Jed swears he was driving normally."

A prickle of unease crept along Jenny's spine. "That's strange."

Grace stopped short as they reached the edge of the storage area, her expression darkening. "Yeah. And the part that gets me? It happened out near County Bricks."

The abandoned brickyard was miles out of town. It had shut down several years ago when the last of the brothers who'd owned it died, though no one knew exactly why. There were stories of course, but none of them lined up. "What was he doing out there?"

A slow breath left Grace's lips. "He won't say." Her voice dropped lower. "Anytime I ask, he shuts down. And Lanny hasn't explained either."

"That seems like a lot of secrets for an accident." It was strange. Unless it wasn't an accident.

"And now Jed's here, taking what he wants, acting like nothing happened."

"You should talk to the police," Jenny pressed.

Grace's expression darkened. "I can't. Besides, it wasn't him." Her voice dropped. "He was talking with a woman at the back door that night. I heard him tell her how to get inside."

The words struck sharply, and Jenny's jaw tightened. "Grace, telling someone how to break in is no different than doing it himself."

"You don't understand..." After a moment of struggling for words, Grace abruptly pulled aside the quilt separating the storage area from the main barn. "Thanks for bidding on the quilt. I have to go."

Jenny opened her mouth to protest, but before she could respond, Grace collided with Cherry.

"Grace!" Cherry yelped, her cheeks flaming. "I wasn't listening!" She scrambled back, realizing she'd made it quite obvious she was. A moment later her control burst as if she'd opened the door on an overfilled fabric stash. "Jed's about as dumb as a bag of batting, thinking he can treat you like you're senile!"

Grace recoiled. "Excuse me? You can't talk about him that way, and I am not senile."

"He's taking things and is trying to convince you you're too old or confused to notice." Cherry only softened the edges of her sharp tone. "That's not okay." Arms folded, she radiated annoyed confidence.

Glancing around, Grace lowered her voice. "He's not taking advantage of me."

Jenny met Grace's wary gaze. "You don't have to turn him in," she soothed. "But you need to talk to him. Let him know he's hurting you."

Red hives bloomed along Grace's neck. Fingers twitched near her collarbone. "I'm supposed to meet Mena about... um, a clock. Sorry."

A quick step back, and she tripped over a pale green hutch, before disappearing into the crowd.

Tension absorbed the sound in a false silence, as Jenny and Cherry watched Grace disappear.

"I shouldn't have said anything," Cherry murmured.

"Don't feel bad." Jenny squeezed her arm lightly.

They turned into the barn aisles, the energy of the market shifting around them. They followed the maze of tables on their way to the front passing a larg window on the side wall.

A frustrated voice rang out, sharp with conviction. "This is her last chance to cooperate! Mish doesn't care about that. Why would you?"

Jenny froze. Jed. She'd only met him a few times, but she recognized his voice. And he was mad.

Cherry squinted toward the sunlit opening. "Isn't that Grace's neighbor?"

"It can't be. That's her nephew Jed, and that—" Jenny indicated the dark-haired, olive-skinned middle aged woman, waving a pile of fabric at Jed. "—is not a man."

"Oh, good," Cherry teased. "I thought I needed to call the eye doctor for you."

"I already have glasses," Jenny replied in an intentional monotone.

"But do you wear them?" Cherry whispered without missing a beat. "I met that woman on the way in. She told me she was a neighbor."

"Grace said her neighbor is still recovering from an accident and *his* name—" Jenny shot back. "—is Landon Reyes."

"Reyes? Yes, that's Mena Reyes!" Cherry pointed. "They must be a couple. When we first got here, she accused me of ripping that fabric!"

Jed's voice cut through the crowd. "She listens to me, but I don't know if I can do it—Mish—"

Mena's voice sharpened. "No. I'm telling you, Jed, it's not a good idea. I'll take care of it."

Jenny's pulse quickened. What were they talking about? She was trying to stop Jed—but from what?

Cherry wrinkled her nose. "Her name's not Mish. I know it's Mena. She told me so. Who's Mish?"

Her voice must have been louder than they realized because Mena's gaze snapped to the open window.

Immediately, Cherry dropped to a crouch, and Jenny was left alone. She waved, as Jed's gaze followed Mena's, both setting heavy stares on her.

Hurrying out of view, Jenny stifled a laugh at Cherry's exaggerated tiptoe below the view of the window. "My goodness," she whispered, as she reached Jenny. "My heart is racing!"

"You're fast, I'll have to work on keeping up with you." The words held a playful edge, but the tension in her shoulders never eased.

Mish.

It wasn't even a real name. But the way Jed and Mena talked had made Jenny uneasy.

The thought barely settled before a sharp whistle cut the air.

A megaphone crackled. "This exhibition is being shut down! Return to your cars. No more purchases will be accepted."

Jenny turned to the sound. "What in the world?"

She and Cherry hurried through the barn to the entrance. The crowd already funneling away from the shopping area. At the center of the commotion stood a man with a bullhorn in a perfectly pressed suit.

"Who would want to shut Grace down?" Jenny asked, her earlier joviality was gone.

Cherry squeezed her arm. "Where are Bernie and Dotty?"

"I'm not sure. I'll going to find them," Jenny murmured. "Meet by the house?"

"I'll be there." Cherry nodded.

The bullhorn droned on, commanding people to leave as Jenny pushed through the thinning crowd. Unable to find her friends.

When she'd made it to the house with no luck, she climbed onto the edge of an old well cap near the flower bed. Scanning the sea of people, Bernie and Dotty waved to her near the cars.

A sharp blast assaulted her eardrums and the man with the bullhorn stepped past her directly through Grace's violas.

"Everyone must exit the premises!" His amplified voice drew and smug expression, clashed with the dirt clinging to his expensive shoes.

"Excuse me," Jenny called out. "I'm a friend of the owner. She's been running the Antique Barn for years. Why is she being shut down?"

The man glanced over. "We received a complaint."

Skepticism tainted Jenny's response. "That's all it takes? A complaint?"

"Ma'am, I'm Commissioner Robert Holdin. I oversee city ordinances. I take these matters very seriously." Finally, he met her gaze, tapping a finger on a roll of paper and grinned. He was enjoying himself.

"Too many people in the space, parking violations, land complaints from neighbors," he continued, listing them off like a memorized script. "There are a lot of issues."

Jenny folded her arms. "Funny. This has never been a problem before."

Holdin's smirk deepened, a slow, deliberate shift of expression that left a sour feeling in Jenny's gut. "Things change, Mrs. Doan. This town is growing. Progress is coming. And people like me? We make sure it happens."

Jenny flinched, and the crowd shifted in a subtle wave. People instinctively flowed around the city official with a bullhorn like he was a rock in the river. She clenched her teeth, trying to slow her breathing. A slow unease crept through her.

Then she saw it.

A curl of dark smoke twisted into the air from behind the barn. "What's that?" Jenny asked not trusting her eyes.

"What's what?" Holdin barely turned.

Jenny pointed at the thickening plume of black and gray. "That. Is that smoke?"

Holdin blinked at it once, then gave a low, almost amused murmur. "Oh my."

Jenny shoved past Holdin as people turned to look.

"Fire!" The alarm spread in a fresh wave of panic.

Someone screamed and the world snapped into chaos. The barn doors burst open as people ran for the exit.

Jenny moved upstream toward the barn. It was the last place she'd seen Grace.

At the doors she pushed inside. Thick, suffocating heat surrounded her. Smoke curled in ribbons through the rafters, swallowing the air.

"Grace?" she called, coughing as she moved deeper. "Is anyone still in here?"

A faint sound answered from the haze.

Jed's voice yelled behind her. "Get away from there!"

"Help me!" Jenny called back. "Someone's still in here!"

His expression changed. Shock. Real shock dropped his jaw and drained the blood from his face. "What? No—everyone's out! I already checked!"

Jenny coughed into her sleeve, moving lower. "I heard something."

The sharp perfume of burning wood and dust coated the air, coating her lungs.

Jed stepped back, eyes darting between the smoke and the open door.

"It wasn't supposed to be this big," he muttered. "I just—". His hands curled into fists and he hesitated before calling out. "Fine—your funeral!"

Then, he turned and ran.

Dispelief rang in Jenny's consciousness, before a weak moan found her from deep in the barn.

The sound refocused her on what was actually important. Someone was trapped.

Ducking low, she pushed through the smoke.

Another cough.

"Hello?"

The haze blurred everything. Quilt racks. Wooden chairs. Old display cases turned into burning silhouettes. A bucket of wooden spools clattered across the floor.

And a sneaker.

Someone lay under a collapsed display.

Jenny's stomach lurched. She scrambled forward. "Hang on. I'm gonna get you out of here."

"Jenny?"

Relief crashed through her at the croaked sound of her name.

"Grace!" Jenny crouched beside her, working to move the heavy antiques pinning her leg to the ground.

Flames burned through the rafters, embers raining around them.

"Jenny—" Grace's voice was weak. "The quilts—"

"Quilts?" A sharp pang cut through Jenny's ribs, she must have been trying to save the ones she'd hidden. "Grace we have to get out!"

Another burst of flame roared above them.

They were out of time.

MYSTERY QUILT BLOCK 2

Clue 1

With every measured slice, a secret is revealed
Buried deep, within the truth, a mystery is sealed

Clue 1

GATHER SUPPLIES & PRE-CUT

This block needs four distinct color groups.
A dark background fabric (DK), a light background fabric (LT). A bright pop color *(something to show off in the center)* (POP). And a high contrast color (HC).

Supplies –
- ✓ 2 – DK 10" sqs
- ✓ 2 – LT 10" sqs
- ✓ 2 – HC 10" sqs
- ✓ 1 – POP 10" sq

Now let's prep —
Cut your strips first, then the squares. That's it!

- ✓ 8 – 1.5" DK strips
- ✓ 7 – 1.5" LT strips
- ✓ 4 – 3.5" LT sqs
- ✓ 6 – 3.5" HC sqs
- ✓ 4 – 3" HC sqs
- ✓ 2 – 3.5" POP sqs
- ✓ 4 – 2" POP sqs
- ✓ 1 – 3" POP sq

Clue 1 – Check the Supplies and Read!

(NOTE: Contrast is the name of the game for this block! Your pop and contrast color should coordinate but stand out! And they should be a strong contrast to the background colors, which should also contrast, think black and white differences. Also, a rotating cutting mat is particularly helpful for this block, though not required.)

Your supplies should look something like this —

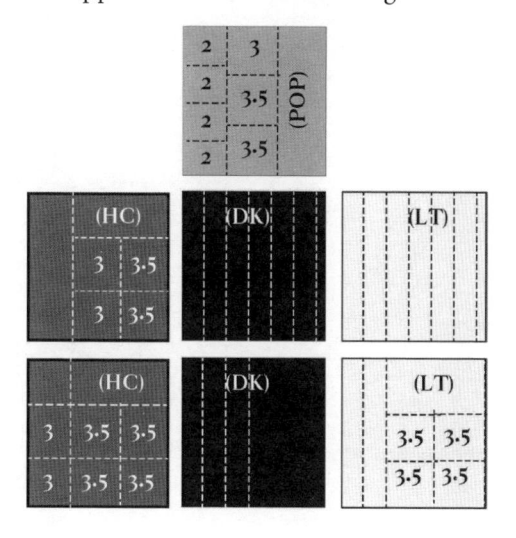

PART Two

A Quarter Inch from Death

Wood splintered as the fire roared, the crack and pop of flames and wood echoing through the barn. Heat pressed in, thick and suffocating, while the acrid haze blurred Jenny's vision. Antiques loomed in large piles around them, a precarious game of Jenga, threatening to collapse with a single wrong move.

A heavy pair of scissors speared deep into the wooden floor too close to Grace's head.

Jenny shuddered. Yanking her collar over her nose, she filtered what little she could of the choking air.

Piece by precious piece, she cleared the wreckage holding Grace. A slow process, until she cleared away enough debris to ease her friend into a sitting position.

Flames crawled the walls, licking over polished antiques and barnwood in an unfinished feast.

They had to get out.

Jenny leaned forward, close to Grace's ear. "Can you breathe through your shirt?"

Slumping against Jenny's shoulder, Grace reached weakly for the neck of her shirt. The collar slipped from her hand as she coughed.

Jenny grabbed a pile of fabric nearby, hoping to filter the smoke for her. The tangle of linen unwound quickly around something solid and heavy. A brick tumbled out, freed from the long cloth strip.

It struck her thigh with a dull, bruising thud before clattering to the floor.

"Of all the vintage insanity—" Jenny muttered rubbing the sting on her leg.

Four linked circles marked the side of the red block. The symbol was familiar but there wasn't time to figure out why. Jenny pressed the rough linen over her friend's face.

"Breathe through this," she said.

Exhausted, Grace sagged against Jenny's arm. Light

streamed through the window at the end of the aisle. It was an open frame without glass. A clear escape.

Turning back to Grace, Jenny jostled her shoulder. "Grace," Jenny urged. "Are you going to wake up for me?"

A flicker of movement. Grace's eyes fluttered open.

Each crackle of fire tightened Jenny's chest. "Grace!" Her voice edged into desperation. "We have to go."

A groan of disapproval from Grace, but she moved.

Jenny kicked aside fallen tools and sewing supplies as they stumbled toward the window. When they reached it at last, Grace sank heavily to the floor.

The window sash was chest high. Jenny slapped the wooden frame in frustration. She wouldn't have the strength to lift, push, or even dump Grace through it.

Jenny gritted her teeth.

Waving wildly through the window, Jenny yelled. "Help us! We're here! Please, someone help us!"

No response.

The crowd had been pushed too far back.

Beyond the property, cars streamed past, leaving the Antique Barn behind. Holdin had done his job well.

"Help," Grace croaked, barely above a whisper.

Jenny's heart clenched and she scanned the room through the smoky haze.

Smoke swirled, engulfing the air. The front. If the fire hadn't yet reached the side of the building, maybe they would be able to make it.

Taking one last breath of clean air, Jenny pulled her collar up and knelt. "We're getting out of here."

One arm under Grace's shoulder, the other bracing her waist. Jenny changed their goal, hauling them toward the front doors. Grace moved stiffly, limping, but moving.

Every step forward felt like a victory.

When they made it, Jenny gasped a laugh of triumph, coughing as she reached for the door. Pushing against the wood panels, she couldn't get them to budge.

She shoved harder. It barely moved.

Something must have fallen on the other side, blocking them in.

Smoke seeped through the cracks, not letting air in. Her eyes burned. Tears? Smoke? It didn't matter.

The window was the only exit left.

Turning, she gripped Grace tighter. Defeat weighed in Jenny's tone. "We have to go back."

Ensuring the cloth still covered her mouth, Jenny coughed, pulling them both forward. The aisles closed in.

Too many shelves.

Too much clutter.

The fire grew louder, snapping and crackling like it wanted to consume them.

Smoke poured out the window as they approached.

"I'm going to help you through there, okay?" Jenny's voice rasped, barely sounding like her own as she shoved a table under the window.

Unable to answer, Grace stumbled forward, feet dragging, she gripped the edge of the table.

Jenny followed, crouching low. "Up you go." One knee bent, she braced herself. "Step here. I'll help you up."

A shove from below and she climbed fully into the window frame. Jenny found a chair for better leverage and climbed up after her.

"What if I fall?" Dread simmered in Grace's voice.

Tight with guilt, Jenny placed a steadying hand at her back. "You can do this. Sit on the ledge and drop onto the grass."

"I can't," Grace whimpered.

"You have to."

"Okay . . ." Grace nodded but didn't move. Then she jumped forward and the window swallowed her.

A soft thud sounded outside, and Jenny scrambled onto the ledge, heart racing. Heat bit her skin, stitched deep in her lungs. She barely noticed. Bracing for the drop, she flung herself off the ledge.

The ground met her hard.

Pain seared through her hip, and she coughed as she pushed up, the sting of smoke clung to her throat like a layer of Velcro.

People shouted. Boots thudded against the grass.

Someone ran toward them. The flash of yellow and red uniforms told her the volunteer fire department had arrived.

"Josh?" Jenny rasped, squinting up. One of the firemen's heads lifted at the sound of his name.

A voice spoke, but she didn't register it.

Then a second firefighter waved someone over.

Footsteps pounded closer. "Mom? Are you okay?"

Her youngest son, Joshua, was there. Jenny nodded weakly, but the fireman beside her answered.

"Nothing appears broken. Can you get her back to the line?"

Josh slid an arm around her, guiding her away from the burning barn. "What were you doing in there?"

Coughs racked her throat. "Helping Grace. Is she okay?"

Josh glanced across the yard, adjusting course. "She's going to be fine." He nodded toward where Grace sat wrapped in a quilt. "I can't believe you jumped from a burning building. They said everyone was out."

"Did Jed not tell anyone? He knew I was there. He knew I was looking for someone." Jenny swung her gaze around the yard.

Jed crossed Grace's front porch. He was still there. Still watching. He pulled the front door open and disappeared inside.

"Thank you," Jenny whispered, letting go of the thought—for now.

Josh hugged her tightly and settled a quilt around her shoulders. The weight and warmth made Jenny realize she was trembling. Even under the summer sun.

"I have to go," Josh said. "Be careful, okay? I don't want you getting hurt."

Jenny took slow breaths, letting the fresh air clean her lungs and settle her heart.

Grace wore a quilt as well, a heavy shawl around her shoulders. Vintage fabric that would have sold for hundreds of dollars, wrapped their sooty shoulders. Huddled in her quilt, she watched with hollow eyes as the flames consumed what remained of the barn.

"You see this?"

Jenny turned, thinking someone had addressed her.

Two firefighters stood nearby, one holding a brick and the linen strip Grace had used as an air filter. The emblem on the side seemed to hold their attention.

"How does a brick from the old place end up here?"

The second firefighter shrugged, handing the brick back.

The four linked circles struck a chord in Jenny's mind again. She didn't know what "the old place" was but it was familiar. She'd have to ask Ron.

"Hang on, is that blood?" One took the linen from the other, examining the fabric.

"Looks like it."

Her lungs squeezed as she sucked in air and coughed. The firefighter glanced in her direction, but she kept her head lowered, watching under her lashes.

"She get hurt?" he asked, pointing to Grace.

"Yeah, got knocked with in the head. She's pretty lucky."

"I'm not sure this is lucky. Seems like the old brickyard really is cursed."

A dry chuckle. "Wonder what she did to upset the ghosts of County Bricks?"

Their voices trailed off as they moved away.

County Bricks. That was where the logo was from. Four linked circles. It originally stood for the four brothers that started the company.

Now it marked each brother that had died there.

Jed had been in an accident near County Bricks.

Bound in Secrets & Lies

Her skin prickled with jittery apprehension, and she edged closer to Grace.

"How are you doing?" Jenny murmured, not really expecting an answer.

"They're gone." Grace's eyes glistened. "What am I going to do about the auction? My quilts are gone."

The quilts. Grace's treasured antiques.

The back corner of the barn was a blaze of ruin. Regret washed through her. All that history, gone.

Sympathy squeezed around Jenny's chest. "Oh, Grace. I'm so sorry."

She shook her head. "No. This is my fault."

"You didn't light your own business on fire." Jenny frowned, moving closer.

"I didn't. But—that's where I kept all my storage." Grace's voice carried an undertone of mourning. "The quilts, furniture, and other things like polish and beeswax candles."

"Of course you did," Jenny said softly. "It was your inventory." She'd seen a box of those candles. Stacked with other decorations and fabric. It was to be expected in an antiques business.

"The furniture polish and beeswax are, apparently, a fire accelerant."

"They told you that?"

Grace nodded. "The firemen asked what I kept

back there, and it popped into my head. It burned so fast. They said something had to be feeding it."

Compassion pinched Jenny's heart. "It was still an accident. Even if you stored supplies there."

"I suppose." Grace shook her head. "I don't remember what happened." She hesitated. "I was checking on a clock for Mena when I heard Jed. But I don't know why he was there."

"You heard him?"

"Yes." Her lips twitched, chin quivering as her hand drifted to the back of her head and she winced.

Blood. The firemen had mentioned blood on the linen. Jenny hadn't noticed but if Jed had been there...

"Did Jed hit you?"

The question seemed to shake Grace.

Finally, she nodded. "I think so." Tears clung to her lashes. "I was waiting for Mena and—" She pulled her quilt tighter and gave a tiny, pained shrug. "I heard Jed. Mena was still there. But I know I heard him. He said, 'Don't die on me, Grace.' That's when Mena nodded and walked away and—everything went black."

The words sent a shiver through Jenny. A cold realization ran down her spine.

Mena had been carrying a pile of linen during that argument. Linen Jenny had seen sitting on the box of candles... and that she had unwrapped from around the brick Grace had been hit with.

The brick tumbling from the tangled fabric replayed in her mind.

The blood. The dirt. The impact. The fire.

Mena had been there before the fire just like Jed. Jenny thought back to what she knew about them.

It didn't take long.

She didn't know Mena at all. And Jed had only been staying with Grace for a few months or so, and she hadn't gotten to know him. The argument she'd overheard earlier was more than she'd known about either one.

Jed had been involved in all of it, but so had Mena, or Mish.

Jenny didn't dismiss the name now. But it still didn't explain anything. She glanced over at the house where Jed had disappeared.

"Grace." Jenny squeezed her friend's shoulder, speaking gently. "The firefighters are busy. So, I'm going to find a first aid kit and get you cleaned up."

A small nod. Grace pulled her quilt tighter. "Thank you."

Jenny crossed the grass toward Grace's home, hoping she'd find more than the first aid kit inside. If Jed were still there, she would have questions for him.

At the front porch she let herself in, closing the door softly behind her. Stillness settled over the old farmhouse, a quiet so thick it made her breathing feel like a siren, calling out her presence.

Furniture scraped over the wood floor in one of the back rooms accompanied by low voices.

Careful steps carried her slowly through the house. Faded floral wallpaper and pale chair railings lined the halls until she reached Grace's bedroom.

The door stood slightly ajar, giving her enough space to see Jed standing at Grace's desk, pushing it back against the wall.

He wasn't alone.

A man opposite him, leaned slightly on a cane.

Jenny eased the door closed, enough to stay hidden.

"If we need it," Jed murmured, sliding a file across the desk. "These are like the others."

The man picked it up, flipping it open and nodded.

"Things went well today." His gaze flicked up to Jed and toward the door, a quick, nervous check before he turned away. "This looks good, too. Well done, Jed. Mish will be pleased, so far."

Steady tapping filled the room as he moved toward the French doors leading to Grace's private garden.

"Lanny?" Jed called him back softly and he turned.

Recognition clicked into place as he turned back.

Lanny Reyes. Grace's injured neighbor. The two were working together, tangled in Jed's bad decisions.

Jed cleared his throat. "We're not going to need it . . . are we?"

Lanny raised an eyebrow. "That's not our decision." He paused, reached into his coat pocket, and pulled out a folded slip of paper. "The auction is set. You did good."

Lanny's tone was casual as he held the paper out. But the words sent a ripple of unease through her.

Jed hesitated before he took it, unfolding the note. "The quilt's in place." He dropped the tiny message in the trash. "That's it?

Jenny's breath stuck in her throat. She wondered the same thing.

What quilt and where?

And what was in that file?

"Trust us. Just a little longer." Lanny turned slowly towards him. "You're doing the right thing, Jed."

His jaw clenched. "Why doesn't it feel like it?"

"Grace needs this, right?" Lanny exhaled, voice soft but firm. "You care about her. All of this is to help her not be burdened by a failing business. Her debts. That's why Mish got involved. He wants to help. Or do you want to back out? Leave Grace to the wolves. We can only help if you let us."

Jenny's pulse hammered in her ears.

It sounded like a script. Lanny was saying the right words, but he didn't sound convinced.

But Jed bought it.

His head lowered slightly, shoulders slumping as Lanny's cane tapped away. Jed cursed and shoved the desk, crossing to the hall where Jenny waited.

Her pulse quickened. Body frozen in the doorway. A moment later it opened, and she was caught.

"Jed!" she gasped, forcing herself into the entryway like she'd meant to be there all along.

His eyes narrowed.

Jenny forced a smile. "Oh, I'm so glad it's you! I heard a noise. Are you getting something for Grace? I was looking for a first aid kit."

Jed didn't answer immediately.

His mouth curved slightly in an amused smirk. "You need a first aid kit? Guess the fire was more dangerous than you thought." Jed gestured toward the hall. "It's in the kitchen."

The tone put Jenny on edge. "Maybe if you'd mentioned I was in there to the firefighters that danger could have been tempered."

"Should've left when I told you to." He turned back to the desk, shifting a few things, stacking a book beside a jar of pencils, as if trying to look busy.

Bound in Secrets & Lies

Jenny didn't move. "The first aid kit is for Grace. Did you want her to get hurt?"

The shift in his posture was subtle but unmistakable. "What happened?"

Jenny scoffed, studying him carefully. "She was hit in the head and trapped in a burning barn."

"I thought it was just a bump?" The question was measured, testing her before he reacted. "I mean, you're looking for a first aid kit. So, she's fine, right?"

Jenny tilted her head and frowned. "She'll make it. But she was hit over the head—with a *brick*."

"It was wrapped in fabric," he blurted out, fast and defensive.

A breath stretched between them as the words settled. "How would you know that?"

"I didn't. I don't." A flicker of alarm crossed his face. The denial was embarrassing.

Jenny arched a brow. "You did." Her voice softened. "Grace heard you warn her, Jed. She says you didn't want to, but she knows you were there."

"No." He rocked back. "I'd never hurt her."

"Maybe not, but you did." Jenny held his gaze. "You hurt her and left her in a burning barn."

"It was just supposed to get smoky. It was going to scare her, not kill her." Doubt darkened his expression. "Will she tell the police?"

Jenny hesitated. "She should." Then, softer. "But no."

Relief flickered across his face. "She's a good person," he muttered, looking toward the desk. "Tell her to be careful. And keep her documents put away."

That was an odd request... "What documents? Why?"

Jed changed course, ignoring her question. "I'm trying to help, but she's making it really difficult. She needs to quit fighting everything."

Jenny's pulse pounded. That sounded very much like what Lanny had said about helping Grace. "Burning her business isn't helping."

"I didn't have a choice. Mish—" He clamped his jaw shut so fast Jenny saw his Adam's Apple bob.

Mish—what? Mish told him to? Mish set it up? "Tell Grace to listen." Jed turned toward the French doors. "Her time's up. And this is bigger than you know."

Then he was gone.

Jenny rushed across the room, but it was too late.

The desk loomed beside her. Various jars of pencils and notecards littered the surface. Jenny moved things around, but nothing noteworthy appeared. A Victorian era book sat on a stack of papers. She opened the book, flipping through the pages curiously. A bookmark stopped her on a blank page.

She pulled out the page holder and found a full sheet of paper with a bullet point list.

Star of the Prairie.

Moonlit Mist.

Grandmother's legacy.

Echoes of the Hollow — Jenny stopped reading when she saw it. These were quilt names.

She didn't know all Grace's quilts, but she knew that one.

It read like an inventory list.

"Grace's auction." Jenny muttered. Except, Double H Auctions was printed in the timestamp at the bottom of the page. Her stomach dropped. "Oh, no."

It had been printed days ago. But Grace had told them she didn't want to sell her quilts through them.

Jenny glanced at the trash. The note Jed had dropped in the wastebasket was right on top. She pulled it out.

Meet by the clock. The quilts in place.
Don't wait. – Mish

A chill slid down her spine. This wasn't random.

She reread the note. The clock. The quilt . . . No, it said *quilts* plural.

When Jed had read it, she thought he'd meant one quilt. It could be bad grammar but that almost made it more confusing. Where would they have taken a lot of quilts? The only ones she'd seen were in the barn. And those were gone.

Before the fire, Grace had met with Mena to show her a clock. However she'd gotten the name, it had to be her. Mena was Mish.

Had she moved the quilts?

Or was this about something more?

Jenny shoved the note in her pocket and gripped the inventory list. She needed to talk to Grace.

She rummaged in the kitchen until she found a washcloth and a bandage, then hurried out to help her friend. Scanning the yard for Grace Jenny stepped off the porch.

The large yard was still artfully arranged with table displays and shelves of antiques. It was familiar and out of place set against the backdrop of firemen and a smoldering building.

Grace crossed the grass in her direction, meeting Jenny only steps away from the house. In a rush, Grace pulled Jenny into a fierce hug. "Thank you," she whispered. Then, stronger, "I didn't really get a chance to tell you before." Her voice cracked. "You saved my life twice today."

Tears burned behind Jenny's eyes, threatening to break free.

"If you hadn't been there—" Grace let the sentence hang, unfinished.

The grip around Jenny's shoulders tightened, and for a brief moment, she felt the suffocating press of smoke again, the searing heat, the helplessness. The moment when she wasn't sure they'd make it.

Grace tensed, pulling away enough to look at her. "I need something, Jenny."

A new heaviness settled over them.

"The police were asking about Jed. I need someone to help me find him."

"I saw him." The words came too quickly, too much like a confession.

Grace's eyes went wide. "He's not still here, is he? I need him to stay safe."

"Grace—" Jenny exhaled. "He said you're in danger."

"No. It's not me. It's Jed." Tension returned to Grace's shoulders. "He's tangled up in something dangerous."

Jenny hesitated before responding. "Okay, I'll help if I can. But I need to ask you something first."

She unfolded the auction inventory list and held it between them. "Do you recognize this?"

Grace frowned. "These are my quilts." Her eyes drifted over the page. "Where did you get this?"

"Jed had it on your desk while I was looking for the first aid kit. It's from Double H Auctions."

Grace paled. "Did Jed send them information on my quilts?"

Dread settled in Jenny's stomach. "I don't know, but he's tangled up in some bad decisions. I think we're going to need to do more than just find him."

Grace's face fell as a scream shattered the air.

Her heartrate skyrocketed and Jenny spun toward the sound.

Cherry stood only a few paces away, the only barrier between them and a massive blue truck barreling across the gravel.

All three women stared as the mechanical monster headed for them, with no one in the driver's seat.

MYSTERY QUILT BLOCK 2

Clue 2

Sewn in death, truth makes a perfect deception
For knotted threads lie in a quilted confession

Clue 2

SEW CLASSIC

Let's shake things up by sewing a classic quilt block.

Place your 3" sq of POP color RST with a 1.5" LT fabric strip.

Stitch down the long edge, trim the fabric to the length of the block, and press open.

Turn the block so the most recently added fabric is at the top. Add another strip of LT fabric to the right side, trim the excess fabric length, and press open. *(Don't discard the ends of your strips if it's long enough to cover the next side, use it! Most strips will need to be used for more than one side.)*

Repeat with the DK strips, adding DK strips to two sides of the block.

This completes the first round. Press open and square the block. (approx. 5" sq).

Repeat two more rounds with DK and LT fabric. Round 3 finishes approx. 9" sq.

Clue 2 – Check the Supplies and Read!

(TIPS & TRICKS: It helps me to always turn my blocks, so that the newest fabric is at the top. That way I don't lose my place. Another help is after the first round you'll always be adding a strip to the side of the block with the most exposed seams!)

Congratulations! You made the first three rounds of a Log Cabin Block! Quick! Read the next section to find out what's next!

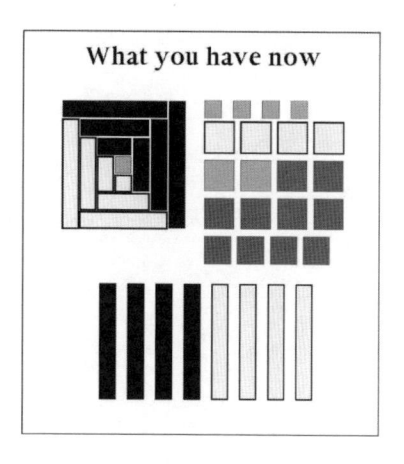

PART Three

Bordered in Deception

Chaos filled the air. A maddening buzz of voices, shouting to run or watch out. Cherry's scream hung above it all, transforming the other sounds into high-pitched white noise.

Officer Wilkins' hand shot out, crying out for everyone to stop. For a split second, time obeyed.

The world stilled. The speeding truck became a documentary in slow motion on the trajectory of spitting gravel.

A heavy clunk rattled as the truck reached the lawn, bounced onto the grass, and kept rolling forward.

No one moved.

No one tried to help.

The realization hit Jenny like an unfinished quilt.

If she wanted to save them, she'd have to do it herself.

Lunging for Grace, Jenny seized her friend's arm, yanking her to safety and shoving Cherry with them as the truck careened past. It slammed into the gnarled oak that had stood for decades by Grace's porch.

The impact sent a shudder through the truck frame. A cloud of dust settled around them, and for a moment, everything was eerily silent.

Jenny clung to her friends as the crowd surged around them. Like carefully laid out quilt blocks, they were surrounded by a patchwork of frightened faces, protective officers, and the echo of a changed day—and Grace.

Officer Wilkins helped Grace to her feet, trembling with every move.

Jenny stepped back, needing a moment to collect her thoughts. They rearranged themselves, centering around Grace—accidents, people, and events all orbiting her.

Small groups of onlookers lingered across the yard, despite Mr. Holdin's forceful demands for everyone to leave. From a shaded spot on Grace's porch, the city commissioner watched the crowd, glowering as though counting every face that lingered.

Logging complaints, or taking inventory . . . What was he waiting for?

Nearby, a second set of police officers catalogued the damage from, and to, the truck. Jenny circled the vehicle, careful to stay out of the way. Steam billowed from the crumpled radiator.

Standing face-to-face with the wreckage, Jenny's heart tightened. She'd been the only thing between her friends and irreparable harm.

The Antique Barn logo was painted across the truck doors. There couldn't be many vehicles associated with Grace's business.

As the officers moved on, Jenny lingered, staring at the driverless vehicle. Hadn't Jed been using this truck? If Grace mentioned her nephew's involvement, Jenny was sure it would help. No one had been inside the truck when it crashed—telling them Jed had access wouldn't convict him.

Soft giggles and the creak of metal drew Jenny's attention.

The door had swung open, seemingly on its own. Two little heads bobbed near the open cab. Fiery red curls crowned a girl tiptoeing to peer inside, while pale blond waves bent over something near the pedals.

Jenny frowned. "Are your parents here?"

Both of them spun around.

"Are you supposed to be here?" Jenny asked.

The girl had an impish grin—not guilty, but amused. The boy hid his hands behind his back.

"We wanted to see the ghost truck," the girl announced matter-of-factly.

"That's silly," Jenny teased, as a cold ripple crawled down her spine. "Trucks can't drive themselves."

"This one did." The girl pointed. "It was moving before it hit the tree."

The boy nudged her arm. "The lady talked to the ghost and she started it."

The girl rolled her eyes. "But she didn't drive. The ghost did that."

Jenny's pulse ticked up.

"You saw a lady?"

He nodded. "She made it go. She said after it stopped, the ghost would turn into a brick!"

Jenny's stomach dropped. A brick.

She peered over the children's heads to the interior of the truck cab. A key was plugged into the ignition. A fine dusting of red powder coated the floorboards and gas pedal. A brick partially hidden under the seat.

The girl huffed at the boy. "You're not supposed to tell that part."

"Why not?" Jenny kept her voice light. "Did she tell you not to?" Her heart pounded as she pulled her attention from the cab. A glint of silver embedded in the seat cushion caught her eye.

A small hoop earring? That wasn't Jed's.

"I'm not supposed ta say." His lip pushed out in an impressive pout for such a little face. "If I say, she said I couldn't keep the ghost."

"When it turns into a brick you mean?" Jenny smiled warmly. And the little boy nodded. "That's so exciting. Did you find the ghost?"

The girl jumped in before the boy could say anything. "She said it was an old truck." Tugging at a curl, she paused and nodded. "—And old trucks have ghosts. Yeah."

"Yeah." The little boy agreed.

He shifted something behind his back, beaming at the girl after she remembered their cover story.

Someone had counted on the kids spreading a rumor instead of asking questions.

Jenny crouched beside them. "What else did she say?"

The girl squirmed. "That we should go before we got blamed for the mess."

Before they got blamed. The mess—the truck, the crash . . .

Jenny's gaze swept down.

Behind the boy's back, a brick peeked out as he leaned over, whispering to the girl, "Don't forget your ghost!"

A breath caught in Jenny's throat.

"So you did find the ghost!" Jenny crouched lower, trying to create a conspiratorial feel. "Where was it?"

The blond rolled his eyes. "On the pedals, of course. Everyone knows you press the pedals when you drive."

It confirmed what she'd suspected. The bricks had been used to weigh down the pedals after the woman had started the car.

She had one more question.

"Do you see the lady now?" Jenny asked. "Maybe she can find more ghosts."

The boy's eyes widened, and both children looked around. "No," he said. "She's gone."

"Can you tell me what she looked like?"

The girl shifted, her attention looking everywhere but at Jenny. "She had black hair and a little heart on her neck."

Jenny moved a little closer. "Like a necklace?"

"Uh-uh." The little boy inched away, caught between Jenny and the truck door. "Just a heart. On her neck."

He dashed to the side, and Jenny reached out. "You can't take that," she said. "The ghosts have to stay here."

Even cute little boys weren't allowed to tamper with evidence. By some stroke of quilter's luck, the little boy listened. He stopped and released the brick before running away.

Through the window of the open door, Cherry crossed the grass toward them and behind her was Officer Dunn.

Suddenly, Jenny's quilter's luck made more sense. Even cute little boys knew if they'd get in trouble.

Jenny picked up the brick, returning it to the truck. Red dust gathered on her fingers. The tiny silver hoop winked at her from the fabric of the driver's seat.

The truck may have traveled across the lot without a driver, but someone other than Jed had been in this seat not long ago.

"Jenny, Officer Wilkins wants to talk to you." Cherry had reached the truck and stood behind her.

Jenny looked around. It was Officer Dunn, not Wilkins who was behind Cherry. Wilkins was across the yard talking to Grace. He looked up and nodded at her in the distance. As he did, a familiar blond head dashed in, grabbed the brick with both hands, swung around, and tried to run off.

Cherry quickly seized the tow-headed scamp by the shoulders, and Jenny reclaimed the brick.

"You can't steal a ghost if it doesn't belong to you," Jenny called after him. "It'll haunt you."

"Oh, my stars!" Cherry exclaimed.

Officer Dunn tipped his sunglasses down as he approached, glancing between them. "What's the problem ladies?"

Jenny handed him the brick. "Is someone watching the truck? Kids have been trying to take things."

"It's fine. Shut the door." Officer Dunn shrugged and set the brick in the vehicle. "Cherry Carmine? I have a few questions for you. Will you join me over here?"

"Me? But I already talked with Tyler." Confusion swirled in Cherry's eyes like blooming tea. "Oh look, there's Bernie. I think she saw who started the truck."

"She did?" Officer Dunn turned excitedly and hurried off.

Cherry rolled her eyes. "Poor Bernie. I just couldn't handle him asking me out again."

Jenny chuckled softly as Cherry's phone rang.

"I'll be back," she said, stepping away. "Once you talk with Officer Wilkins, I think we can go."

Jenny sucked in a breath, and headed toward Grace, conveniently finishing up with the officer she was supposed to see next.

Cherry might be ready to go, but Jenny had more questions.

"Make yourself at home." Grace shot Robert Holdin a steely look as she passed him. "You always do. Even when it's not your home."

He grumbled something under his breath as she opened her door, and Jenny followed Grace inside.

"Do you think he'll leave?" Jenny asked as the door shut. "I'm pretty sure Cherry and I could get rid of him."

"It's fine. He's never been a man who had enough. Now with his little bit of power." Grace shook her head. "I wouldn't put up with him if he hadn't been friends with my brother. Sometimes I think I've lived in this town too long." She pulled the quilt from her shoulders, folding it carefully before setting it on the couch.

"Is everything all right?" Jenny's breath caught on her nerves, like she'd threaded a sewing machine with the tension all the way up.

Grace swallowed hard, shaking her head. "I just can't believe Jed would do this to me. Could someone be trying to frame him? Maybe he got in with the wrong people."

"Well," Jenny considered it. "You said Jed knew where you kept the quilts? Did anyone else know?"

"No. But he may have told someone." Grace looked almost hopeful. Then she hesitated as if something had just occurred to her. "I guess I showed Mena, too. And you. But that's all."

Jenny stiffened. "When did she see them?"

"I showed her just before the fire. She came to see a clock and was asking questions about my collection of quilts. I didn't want her to worry when the auction happened." She exhaled sharply. "It's strange, isn't it? My business never troubled anyone until Landon and Mena moved in. But—they've always seemed so nice."

Too nice. Of course, Mena would be charming even if she were up to something sneaky. It made Jenny rethink her impression of the delicate woman. Unassuming—until she wasn't. "What do you know about her and Lanny?"

"They love it here," Grace murmured, though doubt flickered in her voice. "They wanted to buy my house before they bought the one next door. They told me if I ever wanted to sell, they'd happily pay top dollar for it. They'd never hurt it."

"Unless you're taking too long to sell it to them." Jenny's pulse quickened. That was motive.

Ruining Grace's business and the tax debt were both things that would eventually push her to move.

"I'm not going anywhere. Only, without the auction quilts—" determination faded from her voice as Grace moved through the thought process. "I could have a little trouble paying the back taxes."

"You need to be careful," she warned. "They may not be what they seem, and someone is trying to hurt you," Jenny said.

Grace bit her lip. "I can't be afraid of my neighbors. Neighbors care about each other—we watch out for one another. They don't steal or burn down each other's barns."

"I'm not sure the title 'neighbor' comes with an automatic trustworthy card." Jenny paused and said the next part slowly, watching Grace. "If it's not them, it makes Jed the main suspect again."

Color drained from Grace's face, her breath growing shallow. "You promised not to turn Jed over to the police."

"Don't worry," Jenny said, softening the blow of her statement. "They might want to talk to him, but for now, there's plenty for them to think about."

Grace nodded gratefully, but Jenny couldn't keep her questions from circling.

She went to the kitchen, returning with water for

herself and tea for Grace. "When I was here this afternoon with Jed, he seemed to be looking for something in your room." Jenny tread carefully, she felt like a pincushion in a party store, balloons pressing in as she tried not to explode anything. "Do you think there's anything he might want in there? Maybe something in your desk?"

Grace's gaze darted toward the desk, then away. "Jed would never hurt me. That's what I've been telling you. He's a good kid at heart—I know he is."

Jenny exhaled slowly, her eyes drifting toward the barn. "I'm sure he is, but he's not himself right now."

"I give him whatever he wants," she said. Tears warped Grace's expression as she whimpered.

"He's stealing for no reason—and none of it is worth hurting people over." Jenny mused tracing the edge of her teacup.

"That's right." Grace sat up straight, suddenly hopeful. "So, it's not him—Jed wouldn't—"

"Except," Jenny interjected, "The same bricks were in the truck as the one he used to knock you out in the barn. He might be doing it for someone else."

In the silence that followed Grace's small nod felt like a physical wound.

Picking up a spool of thread from the counter, Jenny unrolled a length of the blue string. Jed's earlier comment that this was bigger than they realized seemed stitched across her mind. He talked about things as if he were warning them. If he didn't want this, then who did? Who wanted Grace out of the way?

"What about those complaints?" she asked. "The ones the commissioner was yelling about this morning?"

"Oh, I've been getting complaints for months—I'm not even sure who they're from," Grace replied.

"That's going to make it hard to get to the bottom of things," Jenny murmured.

A knock on the front door pulled their attention.

"I'll get it." Jenny stood and motioned for Grace to stay where she was.

A firefighter stood on the porch, asking about an outdoor water line. Jenny checked with Grace and gave directions.

She lingered on the porch as he left. Holdin had disappeared after Grace's chilly greeting, and Jenny relaxed, searching for a moment of peace.

Leaning against the railing, Jenny's mind spun faster than a rogue rotary cutter.

Stragglers were finally clearing out. The police officers huddled together near the barn. Thankfully, the truck sat alone, no more kids trying to steal evidence.

A voice—low and clipped—drifted from the side of the house. "—the auction is moving forward."

The voice paused and the hair on the back of her neck rose.

"Yes, yes. The quilts are in place. Payments are secure."

The quilts? Payments? Jenny's pulse ticked up. She kept trying to hear Jed's voice in the tone of the caller, but it wasn't him.

The voice came from the side of the wrap-around porch. Jenny followed the sound, pausing at the corner. She couldn't see much. If she was lucky, they would reveal a little more before they left.

"No. The land won't be a problem. Jed says he can get the information. It won't be long. Merkel will get what they need."

Who was Merkel?

"Looks like Day is coming to a close." A dark chuckle came from around the corner.

Did they mean Grace?

Goosebumps chilled Jenny's skin. Her fingers curled against the wall of the house. She needed to relax. They would come around the corner of the porch soon and she didn't want them to know she'd heard their conversation. She leaned casually against the railing, because apparently it was impossible to eavesdrop while leaning against porch rails.

Giving up the façade, she sat down and waited, like

a normal person. Floorboards creaked, but no one appeared.

Edging around the corner, a figure in a short coat slipped through the hedges, away from the porch and into the side garden.

Jenny crossed the porch. The stranger ducked around trees and dashed over the path. Then, at the end of the garden, the silhouette stopped.

Her breathing was too loud as she followed. She slowed, trying to listen to the voice she'd heard.

"—I fixed it," someone whispered.

She wasn't sure whether it was the same person or not. Branches blocked her view as she shifted closer. A crackle of sticks startled her. Jenny held her breath. It could have been her, or the person ahead of her, who'd made the noise.

Heart hammering, she waited.

There was more shuffling and hushed voices before the footsteps moved quickly away. She picked up her pace, moving beyond the wild garden plants and skidded to a stop.

Mena Reyes was half a dozen yards ahead of her. She couldn't have been the one on the call.

Behind her she couldn't make out any specific sounds, but the garden gate swung as it stretched around the other side of the house.

Jenny let out a frustrated breath. She'd followed the wrong person.

As Mena strode away at a brisk, purposeful pace, Jenny fell into step behind her. She may have seen the person from the porch. Maybe she could still help Jenny get some answers.

When they reached the Reyeses' back porch steps, she paused and spun around.

"What do you want?" Mena asked sharply. Her voice was harsh and low.

That was unexpected. Maybe she had been the one on the call. "Hi. I'm Jenny. I thought I heard something just a moment ago. By Grace's house. Did you see anyone come out the back of the garden?"

"I wasn't doing anything." Mena snapped. "Leave me alone."

"I didn't say you were." Jenny softened her tone. "I don't mean to bother you, but I saw you walking home, and someone was having an odd conversation at Grace's. And with the fire. I just thought I should ask. You're Grace's neighbor, right?"

Mena hesitated at the steps, her fingers curling over the railing. "I didn't see anything."

"Really? That's too bad." Jenny moved closer. "Maybe you didn't see anything, but did you hear anything? Were you there when the truck crashed?"

"I wasn't paying attention to some truck," she said too quickly. A silver earring glinted in the sunlight and when she looked away, one was missing.

Jenny leaned in, studying her.

"What are you doing?" Mena asked as Jenny got close enough to step on the porch with her.

A small heart tattoo was inked on her neck just below her ear.

Keeping her expression neutral. Jenny moved a step closer. "Grace is shaken up over all this. And out by the truck, a couple of kids said they saw someone." She tilted her head and swirled a finger toward Mena's hair and face. "They described her just like you. A woman with black hair. A little heart-shaped mark on her neck."

Mena's hand came up to her neck. "I'll keep my eyes open for a lady cupid."

Jenny held her gaze. "You don't care that Grace could've been killed?"

"Accidents happen." Mena's fingers twitched at her side, and she took a step closer to the back door. "Anyway, I wasn't there. They're just kids and I'm not the only one with dark hair."

Jenny exhaled, letting a beat of silence pass. "Yeah, but this woman, is also missing an earring that looks just like yours. It's stuck in the driver's seat."

Mena reached up, finding her empty earlobe and took a step back. Fear creeping into her eyes.

"You were there." Jenny pressed forward spitting facts like truth serum. If Mena saw how much she knew maybe she'd come clean. She wanted Mena to come clean. "You started the truck. Then let it run into the tree, hoping it would hit Grace on the way."

"No." Mena shook her head reaching back for the door handle.

"Then why would you do it? And why does Jed call you Mish? What is all this about?"

Mena stopped cold.

Jenny barely had time to register the reaction before Mena spun, grabbing her arm in a crushing grip.

Yanked inside, the door slammed behind them. Furniture crowded the tiny space, and Jenny stumbled past an armchair as Mena backed her toward the wall. Before letting go, she pressed a forearm to Jenny's collarbone, shrinking the dark room around them.

Her voice turned sharp. "Where did you hear that name?"

MYSTERY QUILT BLOCK 2

Clue 3

Stitches lost in agony make enemies of strangers
As needle slips & secrets lie in border to a danger

Clue 3

QUARTER SAWN LOGS

10" strips, can only take a log cabin so far. For the next step, cut your whole log cabin block in quarters!

You'll have 4 - 4.5" sqs.

Use your remaining 1.5" strips to add one more round to the outside of each corner.

Add a 4.5" LT or DK strip to the side of each block as shown.

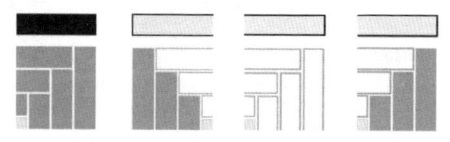

Add a 5.5" LT or DK strip to the remaining side of

each block as shown.

Each quarter will end up approximately 5.5" sq.

Clue 3 – Check the Supplies and Read!

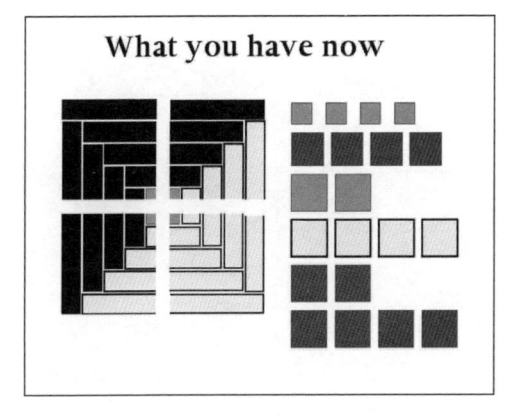

What you have now

PART Four

Truth on the Bias

Fury scorched deep shadows in Mena's eyes, fraying the edges of Jenny's confidence.

"No one is supposed to know about that." Mena's voice laced rage with terror. Hot breath hit Jenny's cheek as she echoed her previous question. "Where did you hear it?"

Jenny turned away, willing herself to stay calm. A dozen sharp retorts bubbled up. "I only share secrets on quilt tutorials."

Mena's lip hitched up in a snarl.

This was not the time for sarcasm. She scrambled

for a careful answer, but the truth slipped out first. "Jed."

She felt the mistake the moment she'd said his name. If she thought Jed had told her outright, they were both in trouble.

"I mean, I heard him call you that. When you were arguing outside the barn," Jenny said carefully. "Aren't you Mish?"

Mena let out a sharp laugh. A mocking sound that curled inside Jenny like fabric held too long under a hot iron. Then, slowly, she smiled. Not the kind that softened a face, but one that carved sharp edges into it.

"You think I'm Mish?" she asked. "Should I take that as a compliment?"

Jenny couldn't answer. Doubt had stitched a new pattern in her gut.

"You can't keep doing this," Jenny said, pushing into the wall as far as she could. It did little to relieve the pressure.

Mena's expression barely flickered. "Why not?"

There was no reason. Jenny forced her voice to stay even. "Grace isn't hurting anyone. She won't give up because someone tried to scare her and ruin her business."

"The fire?" Mena's voice turned mocking. "That's why you think I'm Mish?"

"And the thefts," Jenny added. She swallowed, her throat dry. "And the truck."

"Hey, babe?" A man's voice. Smooth. Even. Measured. "Is that you?"

Mena twitched, her gaze shot toward the hallway. "Yeah, Lanny, I'm home. I have a . . . guest."

"I need some help." The voice called again. "Will you—"

"I'll be right there." Mena cut him off sharply but didn't leave. "You don't know anything," Mena said to Jenny. She pressed harder. Waiting. Testing.

Alarm trembled in Jenny's logic, unsure what she'd said that had exposed her. Air fought through her pinched throat in a fit of coughing.

Shoving against her collarbone a last time, Mena released her and backed away.

Even after Mena let her go, Jenny felt the bite of pressure at her throat. She resisted the urge to rub the hot impressions left on her skin. "Grace has lived in that house forever. She won't let you take it."

Mena hesitated near the hallway. "I don't want Grace's house," she scoffed, not quite able to shed the biting tone. "I don't even like it. I can barely stand living in this tiny town. All I want is to get out."

"Then why—?" Jenny hadn't expected to question her intentions.

Mena hesitated, jaw tightening. "Mish has plans." She shot a glance at the desk in the corner. "And I don't get to decide what he wants."

Jenny studied her.

"Mena?" Lanny called.

The young woman pulled her shoulders back, inhaled and fixed her eyes on Jenny. "Don't touch anything. I'll be right back."

Mena disappeared down the hall.

She took in the room. It wasn't what she'd expected an evil villain's lair to look like.

Floral artwork. A plush couch. Dainty china tea cups resting on smooth wooden shelves.

Nothing about it fit.

The room was pristine. Cozy, even.

Her mind spun. Either Mena was a criminal mastermind who terrified full-grown men, or she was a pawn in someone else's game.

She turned toward the desk in the corner.

Opening the drawers, one by one, Jenny found tape, notepads, pens and even tiny bowls of straight pins. The lower drawers were filing cabinets.

Jenny skimmed quickly over names she didn't recognize.

Grace's name wasn't there.

She slid the drawer halfway closed and stopped.

Her name might not be there—but her address was.

Jenny glanced over her shoulder, straining to hear anything. She split the file open and peered inside.

Pictures of Grace's house. Aerial shots of the property.

Jenny's pulse spiked.

The other files were labeled with more street names, containing more property images of homes and land.

Each file carried a small pile of information and most had a claim deed marked in the front. Grace's file was the size of three of the others.

If Mena wasn't interested in the neighboring home, then why was there so much information on it?

Her fingers flipped through the pages. Property values. Parcel numbers. A notice of complaint. And another, and another.

Jenny's stomach sank. Notice of delinquent taxes on property—This is what Grace had received from the city. The last page held an acquisition notice. A pending transfer request, by Hamish Holdings. The closing date was only a few days away.

Whoever that was, they wanted Grace's house—and they would be getting it soon.

Dim light filled the hall. Mena was still somewhere at the end. As she turned to leave Jenny glanced into the kitchen. Brightly lit and against the far wall, a neat stack of folded quilts sat atop a table.

Jenny's breath caught.

Moving cautiously through the kitchen entrance, a familiar pattern peeked from the bottom of the pile. She lifted the folds of fabric, sliding the quilt of faded blues and gold out of the stack. Intricate hand-stitched quilting and appliqué, worked beside Log Cabin and Flying Geese blocks.

Jenny's heart lurched.

Grace's pre-war antique sampler quilt.

Without thinking, Jenny grabbed the quilt, stacked the file on top, and turned for the door.

Two steps through the arch, she stopped. Her breath hitched. Across the hall a door hung slightly open. Inside, a bed was piled with more quilts. Stacks of them.

These were the pieces Grace had assumed were kindling in the barn fire.

Not destroyed. Not burned.

They had been here the whole time. She'd suspected someone had taken them. Now she knew.

Mena and Lanny were thieves and criminals.

Tucking Grace's file into her waistband, Jenny kept watch on the hallway. She'd need both hands if she were going to carry more of the stolen quilts.

Passing a decorative table, Jenny felt something scrape the wood and shift. She instinctively reached out, to steady whatever it was and knocked a lamp completely sideways.

It toppled with a crash.

Footsteps pounded down the hall, fast and heavy.

"What are you doing?" Mena's voice hit like a whip.

Stumbling backward, Jenny hugged the quilt to her chest.

Pressure pulsed through the room as Mena bolted across the floor.

Twisting away, Jenny clutched the quilt tighter. "This isn't yours," she said firmly.

"Of course, it's mine," Mena insisted. "Why else would I have it?" Tension pulled Mena's body taut, poised to spring. Fear battled in her gaze, eyes locked on the quilt. As if seeing it in Jenny's arms was worse than losing it altogether.

"Why don't we ask Grace? It was at her place this morning," Jenny countered, her tone unyielding. She couldn't even pretend to believe the lie.

"You think Grace is so desperate for a quilt that she'd steal ours?" Tension tainted Mena's voice. "It's a family quilt—on my husband's side. I tore it. See?" Frantically, she pulled at the binding, showing Jenny a white patch, an incomplete repair. "That's why Jed gave me the fabric."

The patch was made of linen, the same kind that wrapped the bricks. It was completely out of place.

Mena wasn't calculating anymore. She was scared. Her gaze flicked toward the quilt, fingers curling around the side.

"This is Grace's quilt," Jenny insisted.

She held tight to the delicate fabric, while Mena clutched its edge. Fighting to keep hold, without damaging the brittle material, it was the weakest game of tug-of-war she'd ever played.

With the highest stakes.

A paper worked out of the patch on the binding, sticking out of the pale fabric. *Payment Secured* was stamped in bold below a string of numbers and other text. It ended with a #401MK. Mena twitched trying to grab it and it slipped out and fluttered to the ground.

Payment secured. That's what the stranger had said on the phone call. Jenny's gaze shot to Mena's. "What are you doing with these?"

Dropping the quilt entirely, Mena lunged for the paper, and Jenny tightened her hold on the quilt.

"Put it down, Mrs. Doan." The voice sliced through the air, firm and controlled.

Jenny tensed, turning sharply.

Lanny Reyes stepped into view, leaning on his cane like a scepter. There was something too smooth about the way he moved. For a man supposedly recovering from an accident, he seemed far from fragile.

"Lanny." Mena shot him a worried glance, torn between keeping an eye on Jenny and helping him. "You should be resting."

"I'm fine." His gaze never left Jenny as he took another slow step forward, shifting his weight from the cane. "Unlike some people, I know how to stay out of trouble."

Jenny exhaled sharply, trying to read the layers beneath his words. Fabric moved in her tightening grip, comforting and old. She still held the quilt.

"Mrs. Doan, you will kindly put our belongings back and leave this house."

Lanny slid his cane between them, not in a show of force, but as if marking a line she'd already crossed.

His gaze drifted lazily toward Mena, then back to Jenny. "You should stick to quilting, Mrs. Doan. People like you don't do well in games like this."

"What kind of game are we playing?" The air suddenly felt heavy.

"A game where no one wins." He leaned forward. "You need to let this go. Mena may not be Mish, but I know who is, and he won't take kindly to you sticking your nose where it doesn't belong." He spoke about Mish as if he were a looming storm beyond the horizon. Not a guess, a certainty.

She'd been so focused on Mena, on Jed, on Grace—she'd overlooked the man standing right in front of her.

Lanny.

Blood drained from her face, pooling at her fingertips. "Mish?"

Lanny barely reacted, watching Jenny with unsettling calm as he adjusted his grip on the cane.

The quilt slipped from her hands as if weighted with lead. Mena snatched it up. "If I were Mish, you'd be dead right now." Something anxious flickered in her gaze. "Jed should never have told you about him."

It wasn't a denial. It was a warning.

Jenny drooped under the realization of what she had done. Her friends were in danger because she couldn't hold her tongue.

"Jed," Lanny repeated. He shook his head as if the name itself was a disappointment. "That boy doesn't know half of what he's gotten himself into."

Jenny steadied herself. "He said Grace was in danger."

He leaned slightly on his cane, watching her. Studying. Then, exhaling through his nose, Lanny nodded. "Grace has problems, sure. But not the kind Jed thinks."

Jenny glanced at the door, mentally weighing her options.

"Don't worry, Mrs. Doan. You'll leave here just fine. But you should be a lot more careful." His voice softened. "Even famous quilter's go missing. After a while, people just forget."

Tension curled around Jenny's ribs. "What does that mean?"

"It means you can be replaced."

THERE WAS NO QUILT to give back when Jenny left the Reyeses' home, just more questions. Grace had plenty of those with the police and firefighters still working on things. So, Jenny climbed in Cherry's convertible and went home.

The phone call they'd had lasted over an hour. The shock of discovering so many documents in her neighbor's possession had worn off quickly. None of the information was new, but there was no clear reason why Mena or Lanny would have property maps and back-tax documents related to Grace's home.

The tax paperwork had unsettled Grace the most. Not because it was unexpected, but because she didn't know what to do about it. She had so much information in front of her and no solutions.

It didn't translate well to an evening at home watching television and sewing.

And yet, here she was.

"Found it!" Ron called as he pulled the remote from between the couch cushions, lifting in the air like a trophy.

He made a grand flourish before clicking the power button and the TV flickered to life. The jingle of an evening news segment filled the living room.

"—a record-breaking night at a local auction house." The announcement came from an onsite news reporter standing in the middle of a large quilt display.

"I thought Grace canceled her auction?" Ron asked, his triumphant tone becoming puzzlement.

"She did," Jenny said. As unlikely as it was, she couldn't help watching for a familiar pattern, but *Echoes of the Hollow* wasn't in the quilts they showed.

"Too bad," Ron muttered. "After the barn fire, Grace could've used a big sale like that."

A row of quilts panned across the screen, draping over a pole and table assembly. It wasn't the most elegant display, but it showed off the fabrics. The camera bumped slightly as a quilt slipped and caught, a spot of white flashing between the bindings.

"They're keeping someone on their toes." Ron chuckled.

In a quick recovery, they transitioned to a closeup of the reporter, releasing Jenny from the spell of the vintage quilts.

"We'll be bobbin' along shortly to show you which quilts had the seams and stitches to be sold for thousands at auction tonight." The reporter grinned, clearly pleased with her wordplay.

"Thousands?" Ron lifted an eyebrow and lowered the volume. "That's impressive."

Jenny shook her head. Gathering her binding , she settled into her chair. A thread of unease spooled at the back of her mind. "Do you know where Double H hosts their auctions?"

"Is that who this is?" A frown tugged at the corners of his lips. "I haven't paid any attention in so long, I've forgotten. Is she using them? Maybe they're not as terrible as we thought."

"I don't know." Jenny said. "This does seem like too good a sale, to be one of theirs."

"Maybe they have a list of collectors." Ron handed her the remote and turned toward the stairs. "If you get the show ready, I'll get the cake."

"Mmm, cake." She winked at him, earning a chuckle.

The music of the commercial faded into the background as Ron headed downstairs.

Gripping her quilt needle between her lips, Jenny worked her needle into several stitches before pulling it through the fabric. It didn't take long before the commercials ended, and the news story returned to the screen in her periphery. Grabbing the remote, Jenny tapped up the volume button. The camera zoomed in showcasing the delicate craftsmanship of one of the quilts on display.

"Sales are all sewn up for some of the county's most beautiful art pieces!" The reporter announced with overdone pleasantry. "After a tragic morning, when a massive fire consumed the antique business and inventory of Grace Day, owner of The Antique Barn in Hamilton, Missouri, we've been told many bidders, and even Ms. Day herself, didn't know if the auction would happen."

"It didn't!" Jenny's shock glued her to the chair as the reporter smiled through talk of a literal fire sale and donations from good people around the county.

The camera man made several passes over the same quilt display as before, pausing on two men engaged in a hearty handshake.

Bound in Secrets & Lies

The quilt in the background grazed a memory. No one had fixed the spacing where a short edge of white divided two otherwise beautiful quilts. She squinted, pulling at threads of memory.

Mena's repair popped into her mind. The white space wasn't a gap, it was a patch on the binding.

But that wasn't *Echoes of the Hollow*. The patch showed up on several of the quilts, almost like a label.

Wishing she'd paid more attention to the quilts at Grace's and Mena's, Jenny moved closer to the screen.

The next shot cut to a nervous-looking man beside a table of flyers. A large quilt was displayed in the background. Awkward and shifting around, he glanced toward someone off-camera before his gaze snapped back to the front.

"We at Double H Auctions want to express our sincere . . . uh, sincerest condolences for what happened to a fellow cure—ay—" He squinted as if reading cue cards before forcing a smile. "Curator of anti—quities."

Double H? Jenny was stunned. It couldn't be them. She scanned the screen with greater intent. It changed from the confused man to the reporter, catching her mid-gesture, waving desparately at the cameraman before slipping on a mask of smiles. Rapid-fire chatter buzzed in the background as the reporter filled the space with over done praise.

"Is everything all right?" Ron asked, carrying two plates of cake and a worried expression.

She closed her mouth, realizing it was hanging open . . . and she'd lost her sewing needle. "Sorry, yes." She searched her lap, following the thin grey thread to the silver needle at the end. "I feel as awkward as that man from the auction house."

She shook her head glancing back at the screen as Mena Reyes appeared. "—Ms. Michelle Bricklan, a local friend of Ms. Day, and one of the benefactors of the auction donated dozens of quilts."

"No," Mena cried out, throwing her hands up and trying to hide. "I can't, I don't do cameras." She dashed away, followed by the film crew, into half a section of empty chairs.

As the image pulled back, it wasn't just half the room, or low attendance. Every seat was empty.

The chatter in the background had sounded like a full house. "Where are the bidders?"

"Did they stage the auction?" Ron handed Jenny her plate.

"Why would they stage a quilt auction?" Jenny asked.

"Well!" The reporter jumped in front of the camera. "Ms. Bricklan must want to stay anonymous, but we won't tell—will we?" She gave a dramatic wink to the camera and laughed brightly. "Thanks to anonymous donors with deep pockets and help from Double H Auctions and Hamish Holdings this charitable evening was a success."

"Is that what Double H actually stands for?" Jenny asked.

"Hamish Holdings?" Ron's lips turned down thoughtfully. "Could be. It fits. Maybe they're sister companies. Or Hamish Holdings decided they needed an auction house."

Jenny nodded, making a mental note to check out this alternate name.

Tension rolled off the reporter in a tiny repeating single shoulder shrug. She walked past a white wall, moving toward the table display where the Double H representative had fumbled through his comments.

Splotches of red dotted the reporter's neck like an illness had sprung upon her to go with her developing shoulder tick. Stopping at the edge of the display, the camera took in a wider shot of the quilts. The reporter held a hand up to the quilt behind her.

Jenny caught her breath.

A handmade, pre-war, heirloom quilt that she knew belonged to Grace.

Echoes of the Hollow.

Jenny pressed the remote repeatedly, trying to pause or save the news show. A large black box popped onto the screen, notifying her that the live channel didn't allow that feature. The reporter kept talking under the box till it finally vanished.

"Don't be surprised if you weren't on the list to hear about these auctions," the anchor continued. "Hosted by Hamish Holdings, the creators of this exclusive event only sent out invitations today. Or maybe we were just last on the list. But thanks to an inside tip from a devoted fan," the reporter said, clearly relishing the chance to flaunt her exclusive access. "We got this amazing chance to see the charitable heart of quilt country in action!"

"Exclusive invites? That's ridiculous." At some point Jenny had gotten out of her seat, the quilt she'd been working on slumped to the floor at her feet. "Exclusive invites to an event no one knows about are about as meaningful as a VIP pass to an empty room. This whole thing is a scam!"

Mena didn't have dozens of quilts to donate. Those quilts belonged to Grace.

"And who are these people anyway. If Mena—excuse me, *Mrs. Bricklan* is on their invite list, maybe Hamish Holdings is her secret boss!" Jenny's breathing turned shallow. "Mish."

Bound in Secrets & Lies

The reporter laughed at some punny joke and grinned at the screen. "—living in quilt country has taught me many things, but I'm particularly grateful to know that we have the benefit of being part of a community *bound* in caring. This is Fawna Stringer, signing off."

Her smile dropped half a second too soon, nostrils flaring. She shot a glare past the camera as they cut to the final image.

The television screen showed a large brick building with a curved roof and a barren parking lot.

"I told you Hamish Holdings wasn't worth it—" the voice of the reporter carried through the film of the building. "Never take story tips from someone's neighbor! What is this? Are we passing out free publicity any time a house burns down—What!" There was a pause and a crackle. "Well, shut it—"

The sound cut off and a laugh bubbled from Jenny, while Ron chuckled, his eyebrows lifted to the top of his balding forehead. "Well, at least we know Grace's house didn't really burn down."

New pieces of the puzzle whirled in her mind.

Hamish Holdings.

Jenny sat up straight. "I know where I've heard of that company."

She jumped out of her chair as Ron groaned.

"They can't be serious," he complained.

"Is something wrong?" Jenny paused, looking back at the television. The image panned out from the building, past an old door with four linked circles burned into its old wood panels.

"It's County Bricks?" Jenny recognized the symbol that had shown up over and over that morning.

"No." Ron thrust a hand toward the screen, all good humor stifled. "Apparently it's Merkel Fabrication & Processing now."

The circles had triggered her brain before the name. Large letters spelled out Merkel Fabrications below the logo. As the image morphed on the screen Jenny could hear the voice of the mystery phone caller. *Merkel will get what they need.* Jenny shivered. These companies were connected deeper than she'd realized.

The company name warmed to a friendly orange, centering the name on overlapping discs in shades of ocean blue. It was bold and almost cheery ... if it weren't for Ron's grumbling beside her.

"They can't think taking over a respectable business is going to change anything." Ron took a large bite of cake and glared at the screen.

"What do you mean?" Jenny asked.

"They're an animal processing plant. They wanted to bring hog farms and processing plants into the county a few years ago, remember? We voted them out, but they keep hanging around. And knocking 'processing' off their name doesn't mean they aren't the same company."

She remembered the uproar they'd caused trying to buy up land in the area. Jenny frowned at the screen. "That's quite a rebranding."

"Now that Merkel has taken over County Bricks, they'll probably claim they 'saved' a local business and try again." Ron stuffed a piece of cake in his mouth.

"They may not need to." Jenny glanced at Ron. "I'll be right back."

The file she'd brought home lay spread across her bed. Jenny dug through the pages looking for one name. And there it was.

Tax payment transfer request, to Hamish Holdings.

She'd never seen a document like this before, but when someone owed back taxes, she had heard people could come in, pay the tax debt, and the house could be transferred to their ownership.

Hamish Holdings must be trying to do that to Grace. Her home and antiques inventory were being stolen by people capable of auctioning them to the highest bidder.

And if they'd done it with other homes or land parcels, Hamish Holdings and possibly Merkel

Fabrication would have the land they needed to bring anything they wanted to town, without a single vote.

Including, hazardous land developments.

Too many unsettling threads dangled across her mind. And now they'd begun to fall, disrupting everything she thought she knew.

MYSTERY
QUILT BLOCK 2

Clue 4

Fabric draped fear can hide all distortions
But truth cuts a lie in biased proportion

Clue 4

HALF TRUTHS AND TRIANGLES

Place 4 sets of a LT and a HC 3.5" sq RST and sew around all the sides.

Repeat with 2 sets of a POP and HC 3.5" sq.

For each block set, cut diagonally both directions into 4 triangles.

Press open and you have 4 half square triangles.

Trim all the HSTs to 2" sq.

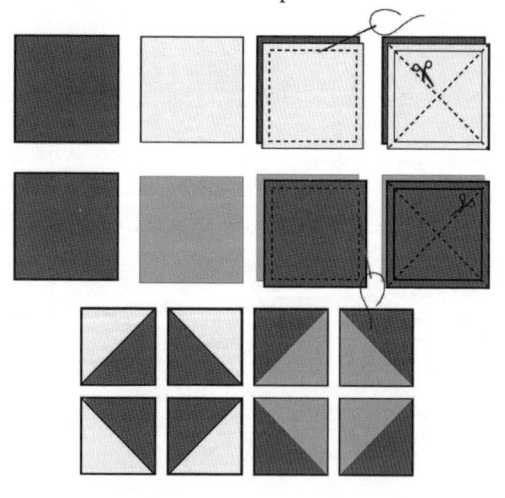

Clue 4 – Check the Supplies and Read!

Here's what you've made in this step —

- ✓ 16 - LT & HC half sq triangles
- ✓ 8 - POP & HC half sq triangles

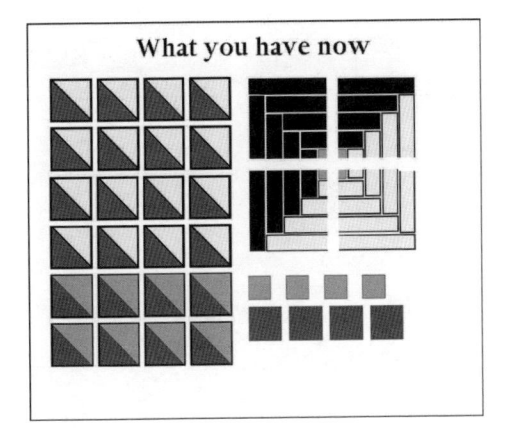

What you have now

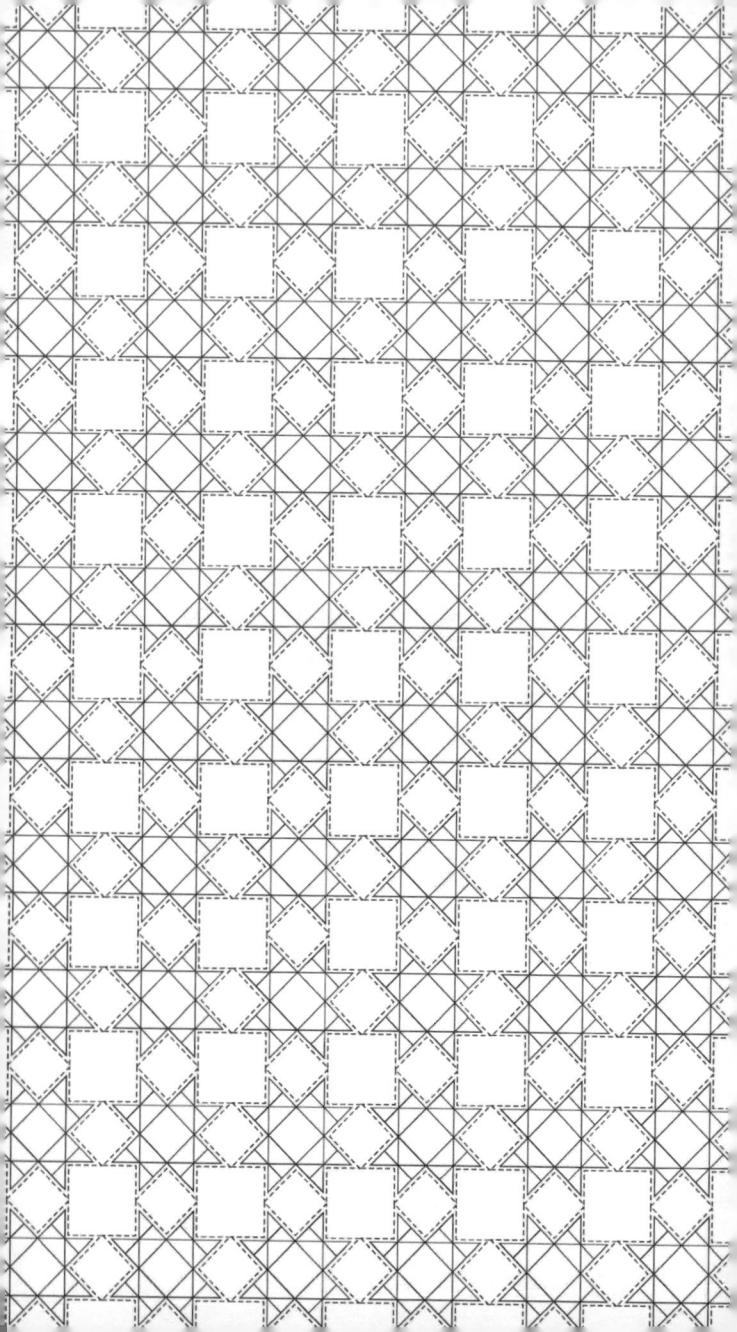

PART Five

Pressing out Secrets

GLASS SHATTERED UNDER THE MORNING SUN. The sound of tiny crackling blades moved through her like a symphony of crystalline destruction.

From Jenny's back porch, the crash had come from somewhere far too close.

Heart racing, she abandoned her breakfast and hurried to the front of the house, looking for the source of the accident.

Beyond the neighbor's hedge, she caught a glimpse of someone sprinting past.

They were too fast. Too far away.

"Ron!" she yelled, forcing herself to move again.

The glint of broken glass scattered across the pavement. She sucked in a breath as she reached the end of the driveway where she could see the wreckage that had been dealt to her car.

The windshield curved the wrong direction, caved in on itself like a shimmering, broken hammock. A fabric-wrapped brick lounged in the center. Jenny couldn't see the four linked circles, but she knew they were there.

"Is that . . . blood?" Ron asked from beside her. She hadn't heard his footsteps, but his labored breathing told her he'd come running.

Jenny nodded slowly, taking in the color that had saturated the fabric in batik style streaks from pale salmon to a deep velvety red. The torn edges hung limp from the knot tying the cloth wrapped around the brick.

"I think so," she said.

The fabric wasn't thick, but it was soaked. This hadn't come from a finger prick. Or a shallow cut.

This would have taken a lot of blood.

Ron reached for Jenny's hand, and she took it. The phone call to the police was brief. They stood in tense silence until Wilkins arrived, his cruiser pulling up with a low rumble.

"I see," Wilkins said, gesturing to his partner before making some phone calls and pulling out a camera.

Officer Dunn slipped on gloves and removed the crude weapon from the windshield.

"Is there something written on there?" Wilkins asked, stopping Dunn and aiming the camera toward the wrapped block.

Thin, black streaks arched over the folds in the fabric, she hadn't noticed it before thanks to the destruction.

Wilkins took the brick and carefully unwrapped it. The imprint of four linked circles pressed into the side of the brick as she'd suspected. The logo of County Bricks had burned into her mind.

The fabric hung heavy over Wilkins' hands his fingertips having quickly marred with red. Narrowing eyes darkened his expression as he scanned the words and held the message out for Officer Dunn.

Quilts burn—so can you.

"Short and to the point," Dunn said, "That mean anything to you Mrs. Doan?"

"It seems like a reference to Grace's barn." Her pulse hammered as Officer Wilkins folded the fabric, so the message lay flat across the top before closing it in a plastic sleeve.

"I agree," he said and turned to look at her. "But it makes me wonder... why are you getting threats connected to the barn fire?"

Jenny swallowed hard. She'd forgotten that he didn't know Grace had asked for her help. "I couldn't say." She shrugged and leaned toward the evidence bag. A scrawl of dark lines smudged and faded near the bottom of the fabric. "Is that another message?"

Wilkins raised an eyebrow and glanced, then did a double take, spotting the secondary message. He shifted the plastic sleeve to see it more clearly and read aloud—

Grace is mine. Police, stay out of it.

"That's not what it says." Jenny tilted her head trying to see the words. "Mine and police aren't even readable. There's a dark spot here, like it was a taller letter." Jenny hesitated, if it was connected to Grace and the barn, it had probably come from Jed.

Jenny looked at the line again. "I think he wrote, Grace is fine. Please, stay out of it. That's not a threat. I think it's a warning."

Wilkins' brows pulled together. "You said he. Do you know who did this?"

The bloody fabric slipped between her fingers. "Not for sure." She flipped through information as she tried to figure out what she could tell them, and what they needed to know. "What do you know about Double H auctions or Hamish Holdings?"

Wilkins stiffened, crossing his arms. "What do *you* know about them?"

"Not much. I saw a news piece about a quilt auction they put on last night, after the fire. Mena Reyes was there. She had Grace's antique quilts. I think they were stolen before the barn burned down."

Dunn turned his attention to her, taking a similar wide stance as Officer Wilkins. At least, Dunn's glare hid behind his sunglasses.

"Stolen. That would give someone else reason to burn down the barn."

"It's a hunch," Jenny said quickly. "I'm guessing. Same as you."

"We don't guess," Dunn snapped. "We are trained police officers."

Wilkins shifted moving slightly in front of Dunn. "I take it, you don't think Grace started her own barn on fire destroying her inventory and business by herself?"

"No." Jenny raised a skeptical eyebrow. "Do you?"

Dunn gave an indignant sniff and walked away.

Wilkins hesitated briefly. "No." He relaxed slightly but kept Jenny in his gaze. "But Grace won't give us any other explanation. I haven't finalized anything, but she's going to be looking at insurance fraud when I do."

"I don't know who did this," Jenny said. "But Mena was at the auction with Grace's quilts, and it looked like they had staged the event. Reporting record sales, but there were no bidders. Crediting an auction house that has notoriously terrible sales. It just didn't make sense."

"That doesn't explain why you're getting threats."

She inhaled deeply. "After the incident with the truck, I heard someone talking about an auction. When I tried to figure out who it was, I found Mena there too. She had stacks of quilts at her house and was sewing white strips on the binding that held little papers." Jenny hesitated. "I don't know what they were, but they marked payments and had numbers and details... almost like a receipt. I tried to take the quilt back I knew belonged to Grace, it didn't go well."

"So, you're meddling." Dunn chortled. "No wonder you're getting threats."

"That's the thing," she said, skimming her fingers across the plastic layer protecting the bloodstained cloth. "I don't think this is a threat."

Dunn raised a skeptical brow. "Why not?"

His tone was anything but cooperative. He was testing her.

"The main message is bold and unmistakable, this one feels different."

"I'm gonna need more than *feelings*." Dunn growled. "Like I said, I don't work on hunches."

"It's not like I'm here on a job interview," she muttered. "But that says *please*, not *police*. If it was meant for the police, it would've gone through one of your windshields."

Wilkins chuckled, worry lines creasing his brow as he glanced back at the wreckage.

"Please?" Dunn crossed his arms and glared. "What criminal says please when he's threatening someone?"

"Exactly." Jenny lifted the fabric indicating the bottom line. "This part isn't a threat. It's a warning."

"Threat, warning—what's the difference?" Dunn scoffed. "Both are dipped in blood." His fiery gaze burned through her.

"Only one will kill you," Wilkins retorted.

Dunn grumbled quietly, while Wilkins studied her for a long moment, then nodded slightly. "Go on."

Jenny swallowed, pointing to the first line. "Whoever wrote the first message had some knowledge of working with fabric—or at least marking it. This had to be prepared and given time to set into the fabric." She tapped the smudged lower line. "But they rushed this one. The ink bled."

"It didn't have time to dry."

"Basically, yes. To set, it needs time and usually heat. So, it seems like the second message was added at the last minute."

"Like someone was sneaking in a warning." Wilkins nodded and took the fabric back, turning it over and reading the message again.

Dunn snorted. "I always throw bricks into the windshields of the people I want to keep safe."

"Ignore him." Wilkins lifted an eyebrow toward his partner. "Cherry shut him down, when he asked her out yesterday."

Wilkins peered at the fabric closely. "The handwriting's definitely different. One person could have prepped it, and the other added a note before delivering it. Maybe we can compare it to Mena's handwriting. If she really warned you—" he shook his head. "I'm surprised she got away with adding the note."

"That's a lot of blood," Dunn said, taking the evidence bag. "I'm not so sure she did."

A chill ran through Jenny. Someone had been hurt. Badly.

If Jed had gone against Mish, this blood could be his. Worry thickened in her chest. She had promised to help keep him safe. "Maybe you should check in with Grace and Jed too. Mena has fabric knowledge. But after trying to take the quilt back, I'm not sure she'd warn me of anything."

"But she might throw a brick through your window." Wilkins clenched his jaw, removing his gloves. "This isn't an idle threat, Mrs. Doan. I appreciate hearing what you know. We'll figure this out. Be careful."

ASH AND SOOT COATED the charred remains of the barn. Jenny shook a layer of dust off a collection of thimbles and dropped them in the "to be saved" basket.

The smell of carbon filled her lungs, dragging her back to the memory of flames and the frantic moments helping Grace through the smoky barn.

"I've been looking into the tax notice," Grace said, brushing off the stained-glass shade of a floor lamp.

A cloud of charcoal powder drifted to the ground around them.

Jenny coughed. She'd known it would be hard to work in the sooty barn, but she wasn't about to let

Grace do it alone. Lifting the collar of her shirt, she waved a hand to clear the air.

"It's some kind of back tax on a rezoning issue that wasn't communicated," Grace continued. "I think I'm going to be able to get it revoked." She waited for the dust to settle and when it didn't clear fast enough, she moved down the row to keep working.

Jenny followed. "Are you sure?" She didn't want to deny a bit of hope, but she'd seen something different. "The paperwork in the files said it had a transfer date and everything. Can you check, and see? If they came and paid the debt first—"

"Don't worry." Grace dismissed her concern with a wave of her hand. "I've gotten something like that a few times recently. Jed says it's a scam. And I only heard about the tax issue a little over a week ago." She paused, tapping her finger in the air as if retracing a timeline. "Maybe several weeks ago . . . recently," she added with a smile before turning away to blow the carbon dust off a container of miniature pincushions, another toxic cloud forming in its wake.

She held her breath for a moment, then skirted the ashen mist to try and keep up. "Will you double-check? For me?" Jenny pressed. "There were signatures, and the dates were coming up soon." She hesitated, wanting to believe she was wrong or had misread something. "Just check," she finally said. "At least call City Hall."

"I'll call. It's been a while since I've chatted with Gretchen anyway." A cough rattled in Grace's chest as she shook the dust from a stack of antique photos. Charcoal smeared the melted images, so the subjects were barely identifiable. "These always make me sad. They're someone's family. I had hoped I'd see them returned home." She sighed and dropped the thick slab of photo paper into the trash bag.

"This property has been in my family for three generations," Grace murmured. "My parents built the house, and my grandparents built this barn. I worried there might be electrical or code issues with the house, but I never anticipated this." Her chest lifted in a deep breath that fell with her countenance. "I don't know what I'll do If I lose it."

"You're not going to lose your home," Jenny assured her.

Grace glanced up and gave a sad smile. "I heard Robert talking with the fire chief. He mentioned that because of the accelerant at the—fire starting point, flash... whatever it's called—that it looked intentional."

Officer Wilkins' comment about insurance fraud resonated deeper than before. Jenny's lungs burned.

"But you didn't start it."

"Well, I won't tell them it was Jed." Grace laughed softly, picking up a tiny dust broom. She used the antique to clean off a shelf of glass and metal flower figurines. "And insurance companies don't like it when you destroy your own property."

"Right." Jenny bit her tongue, fighting the urge to argue. Protecting people from consequences was complicated. "And you'd rather they blame you than him."

Grace didn't reply. She didn't need to.

Jenny righted a small table. The leg crumbled beneath it, toppling the small antique to the ground. "Well," she said, smiling. "I guess we won't worry about that then. Where's Jed? I haven't seen him today."

"He stayed with a friend." Grace moved on to the next table, dropping a cracked jar into her basket. Then, realizing she'd made a mistake, took it back out. "I'm supposed to take care of him. My brother disappeared and—" She stopped mid-sentence, brushing at the corner of the table with her little broom. "I have to keep Jed safe till his dad gets back. He's never been gone this long."

She hadn't thought much about Grace's brother not being around. "How long has he been gone?"

Grace stilled, but didn't look up. "Almost six years."

Jenny straightened. "Six *years*?" Questions percolated as little bubbles of thought shifted hidden truths.

A touch of a smile returned to Grace's face. "He always took care of the business side of the family property. It hasn't been a true farm for a long time, but I'm sure that's how all this mess started. Something, I didn't know I had to do, got missed."

The table hadn't been cleared of antiques yet, but Grace moved further down the row.

Jenny followed. "How long was he supposed to be gone?"

"He wasn't supposed to go at all. He was just gone one day. Like he went on vacation and decided he liked it so well he didn't come back." Grace sighed. "We waited too long to file any legal paperwork and there wasn't much they could do. Judy, his wife, uh... didn't handle it well. She spiraled pretty bad and a couple of months ago, she ended up in a care facility. That's when I invited Jed to stay with me. I know he's an adult, but I didn't want him to be alone."

"Grace, I had no idea you were going through all this. Have you heard anything? Is someone looking for him."

"No. We filed several missing person reports but couldn't afford an investigator. I always assumed his leaving had to do with County Bricks. He was working there at the time. The company named him as trustee of some legacy property clause— but it was never supposed to be necessary. When the owners passed away, and it went into effect, he brought me a box of things to keep track of for him. He said if anything happened, I would need them." Her voice softened. "Then he disappeared and never came back."

Jenny's breath stilled.

Grace exhaled slowly. "I never even went through the box. Except for the quilts. *Echoes of the Hollow* was in there. Judy was a quilter before things went downhill, and it was one of her family quilts." Grace's smile vanished, tears filling her eyes. "I never wanted to sell it. Mitch told me it was valuable. After the tax issues, I thought... this could be what he meant, when he said I might need it. But it's gone too. Jed keeps looking for some letter, and it's not here."

"Your brother's name is Mitch?" Jenny asked.

Grace nodded.

Dark shadows swirled around the name. Mitch or Mish? It wasn't the same, but it was close. And he was connected to everything. County Bricks, the quilts, and even Grace's property.

"I've never met your brother," Jenny said slowly. "You said he was older, right? So how did you end up with the family home?"

"He got married and I didn't. I lived here till Mama and Daddy died. He asked if I wanted it, and he never seemed to mind that I stayed." Grace sniffled, wiping her eyes with the back of her hand. "Mitch and Judy lived north of here. But he would never stay gone like this. I keep hoping he's going to show up and help me figure it all out." She let out a short, sad laugh, sending the tears hovering on her lashes tumbling down her cheeks. "I guess it's time to let that idea go, huh?"

She picked up a charred rolling pin beside the broken jar and put it in her basket without caring what it was.

"I'm going to go put this away." Her voice was thick with emotion. Wiping her eyes again, she left battle scars of dark charcoal across her cheeks.

The dim barn shrouded Jenny in empty darkness, as Grace's steps faded. Her lungs burned, and suddenly the sense of smoke gnawed at her throat.

She couldn't stay here alone.

Jenny crossed the barn toward the exit as a text pinged on her phone. She dusted her hands off and checked the message.

Cherry: Hey, I heard you were cleaning up at Grace's. I'm on my way to join you!

She tapped the screen and sent a quick reply.

Jenny: Would you mind helping me run an errand instead?

CHERRY'S RED CONVERTIBLE TOOTLED through Hamilton at a pace that tested Jenny's patience. She tapped her fingers. "I know County Bricks doesn't have business hours anymore, but I'd planned to get there before sunset."

Wrapped in a cheery headscarf, Cherry only smiled. The fabric apparently did more than protect her hair, muffling the sound of wind . . . and conversation.

Jenny sighed. It was fine. She could be patient. For now.

At the town's only traffic light, Cherry slowed to a stop. Jenny glanced out and caught sight of a red barn logo on a white truck door—Grace must have more than one. As she looked at the driver she started. Jed Day sat behind the wheel.

"Turn here," she said, grabbing Cherry's arm. "Now!"

Cherry jumped, slammed the gas, and lurched forward before stalling. "Sorry!" she muttered, restarting the car. "You scared me."

She tucked her scarf back so she could hear, and Jenny pointed. "That's Jed! I need to talk to him."

There was barely time to take the corner before the truck slowed and turned into the back parking lot of City Hall.

The entire lot was empty as Cherry pulled into an outside spot. Jed shot them a glance, climbing out of the car, a fistful of papers in hand.

"Well, that was subtle," Jenny teased.

"Now you ask for subtle." Cherry scoffed. "Maybe next time give me more than point-two seconds' notice that we're tailing someone."

They sat staring at the back of City Hall—a one-story beige box, formerly the old firehouse. No grand brick courthouse or clock tower here.

Cherry tapped the wheel. "So . . . are we going in?"

"Yes—maybe." Jenny frowned. "Why would he go in the back?"

Cherry shrugged and hopped out, tucking her scarf into the glove box. "Let's find out."

Jenny led the way, grabbing the back door handle. Locked.

She tugged at the handle again.

Cherry scanned the lot. "Well, now what? I hear there's a new lunch place in Gallatin."

Determination spurred Jenny forward. "How about after? While we're here, I want to see why the commissioner shut down Grace's business."

Cherry coughed. "It's almost like you planned this."

"I may have a list." Jenny slowed as Cherry's heels clicked behind her.

"I'm coming," Cherry said, picking up pace. "I may not have your stride, but I won't slow you down." She clipped across the pavement in electric-blue heels, completely unbothered.

As they reached the front entrance, Cherry paused, smoothing her colorful measuring-tape print capris. "Whatever you're looking for, Gretchen can help. She knows everything."

Jenny hesitated. "How do you know Gretchen?"

Cherry flipped her strawberry-blonde hair and looked casually away. "Oh, I make it my business to know everyone who's anyone."

Jenny chuckled. "Really? And Gretchen's one of those people?"

"Mmhmm," Cherry whispered, nodding toward the desk. A crown of short pale curls peeked over the counter like a blonde floral arrangement.

"Have you asked her about how to make sure you're getting the best deli meat from the butcher?"

Jenny raised an eyebrow. "Didn't know I needed to."

"Oh, you do." Cherry grinned. "That woman knows things that'd scare the pins off a pincushion."

Jenny laughed. "Now I'm concerned."

Cherry leaned in. "Gretchen."

The friendly face popped up, smiling as she adjusted her crazy-quilt vest in pinks, greens, and purples. "Cherry! And Jenny! What brings you in today?"

"Well," Cherry said lightly, "we ran into Jed this morning, and he suggested we see you. We're helping Grace with some things, right Jenny?"

Jenny stepped forward. "Right. Grace has gotten some alarming tax notices recently, and I wanted to find out when the land was rezoned or what caused it."

"Oh," Gretchen whispered, glancing over her shoulder. "She must be part of the commercial farming project Commissioner Holdin's pushing." She leaned forward. "I've had complaints. He's not the most popular person right now."

Jenny smirked. "With that bullhorn of his I can't imagine he ever was."

Cherry arched a brow before Gretchen giggled.

"Give me a sec," Gretchen said, typing rapidly. "I'll pull everything you need."

"You're amazing," Cherry said. "And don't forget you promised to tell me where you found all that Anna James fabric. I'm on the lookout for a few more yards."

Gretchen's smile ticked up. "I don't know if I can reveal all my sources." Her soft chuckle quieted, pulling down at the corner of her lips as something flashed onto the computer screen. "That's odd."

"Odd how?" Jenny leaned forward, unable to help herself from trying to see what had bothered Gretchen.

"Well," Gretchen nodded. "Normally, tax liens follow a structured timeline of warnings, opportunities to pay, and a required period before foreclosure or transfer. But . . ." She tapped a few more keys. "Grace's case moved really fast."

Jenny and Cherry exchanged a glance.

"Fast, like it shouldn't have gone through yet?" Jenny asked carefully.

"Not if you ask me." Gretchen shook her head. "I can get you the rezoning information but I'm not sure it'll help. Oh . . ." Her voice trailed off as she clicked to another screen. "I'm so sorry. The lien is already being transferred to Hamish Holdings."

A chill crawled down Jenny's spine.

Cherry shifted closer. "Wait—Hamish Holdings? Is that the company you said held the quilt auction?"

Gretchen glanced up in surprise. "Grace's auction? I heard about that! If that was Hamish Holdings, they couldn't be that bad. Let me look at something just— right— quick. There. I'll be right back." Gretchen got up, headed toward the back room. The door swung open, revealing Jed standing there.

"Jed!" Gretchen grabbed his hand, squeezing it. "I didn't know you were here! Jenny and Cherry just came in with some excellent questions. Great job getting them in here and teaching our community about local government." She pumped a fist enthusiastically as she bustled past.

Jed's grin faltered as his gaze locked on Jenny. He hesitated, then called out as the door swung shut. "Have a good day, ladies."

Jenny only paused a beat.

"I'll be right back."

She dashed out, reaching the back parking lot as Jed climbed into his truck.

"Jed!"

He fumbled with the keys.

When Jenny reached the cab, the engine roared to life, and she yanked open the passenger door and slid in. "Maybe lock your door next time."

He sighed heavily. "What do you want, Jenny? I told you to stay out of it."

Jenny smiled sweetly. "Ah, so it was you that left that carefully crafted insurance claim on my windshield."

"Sorry," he muttered. "I didn't have a choice. Grace is all I have left. I have to take care of her."

"If that's the case you need to take a long, hard look at your life, Jed. You can't take care of Grace from a jail cell."

His eyes darkened. "She'll break if she finds out the truth." He gripped the steering wheel and shook his head. "I'm saving her."

Images from the past couple of days flashed in Jenny's mind; Jed's argument with Mena, her argument with Mena, Lanny's desk, Jed asking Lanny if they'd really need the documents he'd provided. The auction at County Bricks.

Tell Grace . . . this is bigger than any of you know.

"You're not saving her," Jenny whispered. "You're handing her over."

Jed's jaw tightened.

He pulled a stack of papers. "It's too late. The fire sealed it, there's no going back after that. And she signed everything away weeks ago. These finalize her tax default."

Jenny glanced down at the paperwork spread between them. Bold headers stating Tax Default, and Legacy Property Sales clause, and one document identical to the tax lien Transfer of Title page she'd found in the Reyeses' filing cabinet. All approved and signed by Grace and H.R. Holdin, city commissioner. "No. She didn't sign anything. You told her it was all fake, and she believed you."

"Thank goodness." His voice wavered. "I told you. I won't let them hurt her. I have to go. I've got to get these to Lanny. In a couple of days, it will be over."

A couple of days.

Jenny shook her head. "You don't believe that. Do you? You really think you'll be allowed to walk away?"

Jed hesitated. "Lanny's helping. We'll all get out together."

Jenny stared at him.

"Like I said," Jed whispered. "Grace is fine. Please, stay out of it."

Jenny got out of the truck, stepping onto the pavement as the engine revved and Jed's truck disappeared down the road.

Cherry met her with a stack of papers twice as thick as Grace's file. Large packets of stapled documents, contracts, forms, and legal jargon Jenny wouldn't understand without an interpreter.

"These—" Cherry handed it over, "—are the rezoning requests and tax sales ... all tied to Hamish Holdings."

Jenny's jaw dropped. "All of them?" she asked taking the file and flipping through the pages. "How many are there?"

"I don't know." Cherry inhaled deeply shaking her head at the amount of paperwork Gretchen had unearthed. "Unsurprisingly, Grace's address is at the top but look at this."

Flipping through pages of familiar homes, Jenny's stomach dropped a little more with each one. When she stopped, Cherry tapped a page with the image of a large brick building. "They tried to acquire County Bricks at one point."

Jenny blinked, looking over the page. "You said tried?"

Cherry nodded slowly, brow furrowed. "Yeah, it was never completed. There was something about illegal dumping accusations and a legacy clause got triggered. The original owners wanted it to be maintained as a family business, so selling created all kinds of legal hoops to jump through."

"Grace mentioned her brother was part of a legacy clause while he worked there." Jenny flipped through the pages and looked up at Cherry with admiration.

"You learned all that from Gretchen? I might need to come to City Hall more often."

Cherry bit her lip. "Actually, only the sale part. The accusations were online in some old news articles. I got bored after you left and started digging around."

"Wow." Jenny's grip tightened on the papers.

"Oh," Cherry jumped as she remembered something and tugged the last sheet off the stack. "Gretchen did find this."

The header read: Hamish Holdings — Property Management Entity; Landon Reyes.

Cherry bit her lip. "It was filed six months ago."

Jenny's stomach tightened and she turned toward the car. "We might need to pay a visit to the Reyeses."

Cherry raised a brow. "So . . . no County Bricks?"

"Not yet." Jenny shook her head as Cherry tied her scarf on and pulled out her sunglasses.

They moved through town faster than before. As they approached the Antique Barn, a police car sat on the street between Grace and the Reyeses' homes.

Cherry pulled off to the side of the road. "Do you still want to go in?"

Jenny tensed, shifting her gaze from the police cruiser to the Reyeses' home. "We probably should."

Officers Wilkins and Dunn stood at the front door waiting. Jed's truck was in the driveway.

"Good morning, Wilkins, Dunn." Jenny greeted them as they crossed the street, and Mena rounded the corner from the backyard.

Officer Wilkins nodded to Jenny but turned his attention to Mena. "Good morning, Ms. Reyes. We were hoping to talk with you and your husband for a few minutes."

"Is there a problem?" Mena asked.

"I hope not." Wilkins cleared his throat, throwing a glance at Jenny and Cherry. "We were at Grace's house and wanted to follow up on some questions."

"Well, come inside." Mena flinched but gestured toward the house. "I'm sure this won't take long."

Jenny shrugged to Cherry and turned to leave as Mena opened the door and stepped inside.

"We can come back when they're done." Jenny murmured on their way back across the yard.

A scream stung the air. The sharp sound rocketed through both women. Cherry spun around and stared, as Jenny dashed to the house and ran up the steps.

She flung the door open wide and found both officers with their guns drawn. Jed held his hands in the air in meager defense, gripping a bloody knife and towering over the scene below.

At his feet, Mena had collapsed, sobbing over Lanny's lifeless body.

MYSTERY QUILT BLOCK 2

Clue 5

Under hot irons, faint wrinkles and folds reveal all their secrets steamed bare & untold

Clue 5

SEW THE STRIPS

We left you with a pile of half sq triangles and nowhere to go. Let's make some strip sets!

Stack 4 sets of 1 POP & 2 LT HSTs with the angles faced as shown in the diagram. ☞

Repeat making 4 more strip sets with 1 POP & 2 LT HSTs with the HSTs facing the *OPPOSITE DIRECTION* as shown. ☞

Add a 2" POP sq to the bottom of these 4 strip sets only.

You've made 8 strip sets after this step.
- ✓ 4 – Short strip sets
    (1 POP HST & 2 LT HST)
- ✓ 4 – Long strip sets
    (1 POP HST; 2 LT HSTs; 1 POP sq)

Clue 5 – Check the Supplies and Read!

Border each Log Cabin corner as shown below, placing a short HST strip to the cut side of each block with the HC fabric on the side of the strip against the Log Cabin block.

Add the longer block set to the bottom of each block with the POP sq meeting in the corner of the strip sets.

That's it! See you after the next chapter!

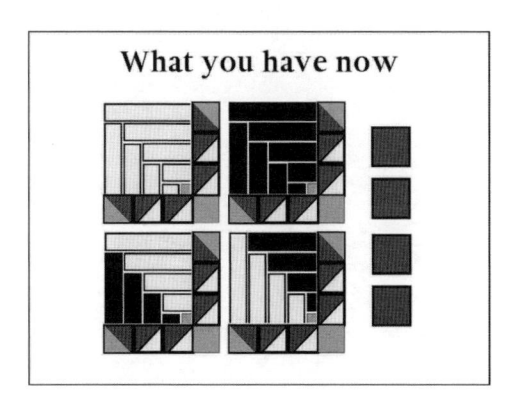

What you have now

PART Six

Sashing the Suspects

BLOOD SPILLED AROUND LANNY'S CORPSE, seeping into the grooves of the worn floorboards. The knife lay beside him, where it had fallen as Officer Dunn tackled Jed away from the body.

Sound and activity were everywhere, Jed arguing at the back of the house, Mena thrashing as Officer Wilkins struggled to pull her away from her husband's body.

"Let me go!" she begged. "He's not—he's not dead!" Blood smeared her hands and Wilkins arms as she fought. "He was fine this morning. He was fine!"

"There's nothing you can do." Wilkins gritted his teeth, trying to keep hold of her.

"I know what it looks like, but I didn't kill him!" Jed begged innocence, but finding him like that, it didn't matter how much Jenny wished she could help. He had a lot to prove.

"Wilkins?" Officer Dunn called, mid struggle. "Are you calling this in? I want to tell Cass I got this one—"

A crash sounded at the back of the house as Jed slammed out the back door.

"Hey!" Officer Dunn shouted, rushing after him.

Wilkins let Mena go and took a step toward the exit. Mena fell over her husband's body, gripping his shirt with renewed tears.

Still moving forward, the officer reached for the door with one hand, the other extended, palm out behind him as if he could manage to be in both places at once.

"Stay," he said, darting a sharp gaze from the exit to Jenny. "Stay right here."

She barely nodded before Wilkins tore out the door, chasing after Dunn.

Jenny and Mena were alone with Lanny's body.

Cherry had decided to wait at Grace's. Since the police officers had told her she couldn't stay, and Jenny refused to leave.

For a moment, Jenny looked at the room beyond the body. A struggle had taken place. The end table was overturned, a chair had deep scratches in the finish, and in the midst of it all—a streak of red smeared the front of the bookcase.

Lanny's? Or Jed's?

"This wasn't supposed to happen." Mena's voice cracked through her tears. "He was getting out. *We* were getting out."

The words hit deep. Jed had said the same thing. "You mean Mish and his organization?"

"He told me. We were leaving after this—" Mena's breath caught in a fresh wave of sobs. "We had a plan. We were going to have a baby." She let out a wretched moan, fingers smoothing back Lanny's hair with blood smeared fingertips, in a rhythm Jenny suspected had once been comforting.

"Mena, you need to breathe. Look at me." Jenny's voice was firm but gentle. "I need you to think. Who would do this? Who were Lanny's enemies?"

Squeezing her eyes shut, Mena rocked back and forth. "I don't know. I don't know."

Jenny knelt, taking the woman's hands, ignoring the blood, slick across her own fingers. Her gaze flicked to Jenny but darted away just as fast, like she was afraid to look away from Lanny or he would really be gone.

"Mena, if Jed did this, I—" Even saying the words gave her pause, torn between protecting Grace and Jed and trying to find the truth. Her throat tightened, and she leaned forward. For her, the truth always won. "I want to find the person who killed Lanny."

Her hands tightened around her husband's shirt. "It wasn't Jed. He's not a killer. They were friends. He tried to be what Mish wanted but . . ." Mena exhaled shakily. "He never could."

It was a relief to hear her say Jed was innocent but there was so much more. "Who was Mish? Who did you work with? You can't want this to keep going."

Mena's lip trembled. "You think I wanted this?"

"No." That hadn't gone the way she meant. "I'm sure this isn't what you want. But—" Jenny struggled finding the words to convince Mena to talk to her. Coming up empty, she defaulted to blunt honesty. "You don't know me. I'm just a friend of a neighbor you're manipulating, but I want to help." Jenny's transparency seemed jarring to Mena's emotions.

She flinched, her breath shuddering. "All this stuff with Grace," Mena said, shaking her head. "It's not the way we work. Usually, it's sending a note, or complaint. Lanny filed paperwork. We've never had to steal or threaten people. Grace—and the auction—" Mena bowed her head as if she couldn't go on.

"I saw the news spot on the auction. Was it you or Lanny that told the media about it."

Mena cringed. "How did you know that?"

Jenny gave her a sympathetic look. "The reporter said it on the air."

"I wonder if—" Mena sucked in a breath, looking down at her husband's body. "That's why he was killed. Retaliation."

Silence gathered between them as she held his hand and wept. Jenny's heart ached for this young woman caught in a trap of bad decisions. Before she could figure out if she should offer comfort, apologize, or just leave, Mena turned and walked to the couch.

"I called them," she said. "Lanny had been holding onto information. Mish always wanted a paper trail, to show that things had been handled in the system, skipping the illegal parts. So, if anyone questioned him it was documented, and things appeared in order. Lanny wanted to wait, but I was so tired of it all. I thought if Mish knew we could expose his lies, he'd think twice about hurting people. And if the public knew about him auctioning Grace's quilts, then maybe she would actually get something out of it."

"But the auction was staged." Jenny prodded. "I saw the empty chairs. If he wanted to sell the quilts, wouldn't he need bidders?"

Her brow furrowed. "I don't know all the details, but it was never about the value of the quilts. They didn't need the auction at all. The bidding was done proxy, by a shell corporation. The payments were secured before it ever happened. The quilts were essentially receipts for the land sales."

"Receipts? Was that what you were sewing into the quilts at your house?"

A resigned sigh fell from Mena, and she dropped her voice. "Yeah. We'd send complaints or tax concerns for properties and Mish worked it so there was some kind of land seizure. The quilts were 'auctioned' and mailed off. The receipts let them look up documentation." Mena bit her lip. "Then something changed. Jed got involved and Mish started getting more quilts than land. Half the time I was sewing receipts into quilts and the other half I'd find them destroyed in the warehouse."

Jenny's pulse jumped. "What warehouse? Are they still there?"

"I don't know if it's still there. I only went once. During the auction, when we had to get rid of Grace's quilts," she said softly. "They're at County Bricks." Mena let out a shuddering, painful breath, her whole-body trembling. "There's a meeting there. Tonight."

"What kind of meeting?"

Mena shook her head. "I don't know, just that there's a meeting. Mish was always in the shadows for me. I was just trying to help Lanny and Jed stay out of trouble." Mena's eyes shone with something between guilt and certainty. "But he did this. I know it. By his hand or another's—Mish did this."

Jenny's breath caught in her throat. Mena's conviction had reached into her heart jumpstarting an intensity they now shared. Emotion spun threads of determination through her as Mena took her hand.

"If you really want to find who killed Lanny, you need to be at that meeting. I can't let him win."

"Did you die before you got here?" Cherry looked her over before letting Jenny into Grace's kitchen.

"No." Jenny crossed to the sink and turned on the water. She was more of a mess than she realized. After the police sent her home, she hugged Mena, transferring blood from her hands to . . . everywhere else. "You're lucky Grace was close by, or I'd be getting in your car like this."

"No, you wouldn't!" Cherry's shock was instantaneous. "I don't care if someone died. He did—I mean—but it's blood. And I don't—not that I wouldn't—It's vintage white interior." Cherry's logic train had broken, her words tangled in each other.

Jenny nodded understandingly, then reached for her with a bloody hand.

Cherry shrieked and jumped back.

With a smirk Jenny stuck her hands in the water. It ran red as she cleaned away the blood. "What are you doing later?"

The scoff Cherry gave was mostly confusion, until Jenny raised an eyebrow waiting for an answer.

"Oh, you're serious." Cherry coughed. "Well, I guess nothing. Why?"

"I might need to get in your car one more time."

"I assumed so. We have to go home . . ."

There was a sound on the porch and Cherry turned to look. "Hang on," she said. "Grace is out there."

Jenny dried her hands and followed Cherry to the front room.

On the porch, Grace stood rigid, her voice raw with emotion. "You can't take my home."

Across from her, Robert Holdin exhaled sharply, exasperation crackling off him like a live wire. "I don't know what to tell you. The papers are complete, I tried to make sure you knew. It seemed like things moved quickly but you missed your deadlines. The county is processing the sale. What do you want me to do?"

Jenny's stomach tightened. This wasn't just a threat anymore, it was happening.

Cherry stepped in. "Well, it's not done yet." She crossed her arms, blocking Holdin's view of Grace. "So, you can go now."

Jenny climbed onto the porch, gaze steely and unyielding. "When, exactly, did you let Grace know about the sale? She had the right to dispute this. You should have given her options before you allowed a transfer."

"I tried." His defensive tone burned. "The county followed procedure. Ms. Day received all the notices. She was given time to respond, and she ignored them."

Jenny clenched her jaw. "She didn't ignore them—she didn't know what she was looking at. There was no explanation, and no reason for them."

"The numbers don't lie." Holdin exhaled, pretending patience. "She owed the money. She didn't pay. The tax lien transferred, and the sale is final." He shook his head, dismissing her. "Look, I'm not here to argue. I need to find Jed."

Jenny stepped closer. "That's not possible," she said coolly. "He's not here."

Holdin's eyes narrowed, flicking between them before he huffed and turned toward his car.

Jenny and Cherry shadowed his steps, guiding him down the porch. Only when his car disappeared down the road did Grace crumble. "Oh girls," she whispered, voice trembling. "What am I going to do? He's really going to take my home."

Jenny tightened her grip on Grace's arm. "If he does, we'll find another. You won't be homeless."

Cherry squeezed Grace's other hand. "And that's the worst-case scenario. It's not over."

Grace swallowed hard, nodding. "You're sweet. But if the sale is processing, that means it's done."

Jenny shook her head. "Not if we fight it. This whole thing is shady. There's something we're missing."

She pushed the front door open as something crashed inside.

A loud thump. A growl.

Jenny's stomach twisted as a chair scraped violently across the floor inside.

"Where is it?" Jed's voice was raw with frustration. "You told me you had Dad's things, Grace. Where are they?"

Grace's face paled. "What are you doing here?"

"Jed?" Jenny asked, her brows pinching a crease in her forehead, pushing inside, Cherry followed. "The police are still looking for you."

"That's why I'm here. I have to find it. We're out of time!" Desperate and searching, Jed shoved furniture aside, and emptied drawers onto the floor surrounded by the wreckage of the living room. "Where is it?" he growled.

Jenny stepped forward, heart pounding. "What are you looking for?"

"The letter!" He whipped toward Grace, wild-eyed and panicked, as if Jenny and Cherry weren't even in the room. "Dad gave you a box of stuff before he left," he snapped. "I need to find it. If I don't, it's over."

"I don't know what you mean." Grace stared, frozen in the entry. "There's a box of stuff, but there were only a couple of quilts, and random belongings. The only letter was to me—And the quilts were lost in the fire or—" her eyes darted between them, landing on Jed. "—stolen."

"No, the meeting is tonight," he snarled, yanking open drawers, papers flying. "If I don't have it. We're done. Everything is over."

"It's a meeting," Cherry muttered. "It's not the end of the world."

"I have to find them!" Jed tore through the room. "He left you a letter. Grace! You told me he did. It must say where the rest of the quilts are. Where did it go? Where are they?"

"Jed, stop." Grace threw her hands up. "They're not here. Please, give me a second. I moved them!" Grace backed away while Jed slammed drawers, fists shaking. His rage and terror flung into the living room.

"Mena said something about a meeting too. It sounded important." Jenny's mouth hung open, as Grace disappeared down the hall.

Jed barked a laugh and spun around. Gripping the back of the couch, he leaned forward on locked elbows. "There's some kind of legacy documentation in my dad's things. He was the trustee for County Bricks after the owners died. And he's not here so I'm the trustee's heir or something—" he paused, breathing heavily, as if the weight of responsibility and loss had slammed into him. "If I don't find what Mish wants . . . he'll kill Grace."

Jenny's skin prickled from a thousand points, her body a pincushion to fear.

"You know he'll do it." Jed shot a look out the window. "You've already seen it. I don't know if what happened to Lanny was Mish or Merkel or —God! I was told to go clean up the mess and look at what that got me." He looked between both women. "I'm a fugitive with a death sentence!"

She caught her breath. It was the first time she'd heard Merkel and Mish mentioned together. Jenny grabbed at a button, feeling for the string that had been stuck there for a while now.

"But you don't even know what you're looking for," Jenny muttered softly.

Jed shook his head like that shouldn't even be a concern. "Grace will die tonight if I don't find the quilt... or letter or whatever the key is to selling County Bricks."

"Selling County Bricks?" Cherry asked sounding more confused than ever. "What is your boss now? A realtor? And he'd kill someone over the sale of a property?"

Jed shook the back of the couch and stormed past, stopping in front of the window. He pulled back watching briefly then turned to the hall. "Grace!"

She returned, holding a cardboard box labeled '*for Grace*' in thick, fading ink.

Jed snatched it from her hands and upended the entire thing.

Grace cried out, as if he'd torn out several essential organs. "Wait, —those are all I have left of Mitch. Jed, please, be careful!"

"I don't have time to be careful!" he tossed things aside, shaking out stacks of papers and grabbing up an envelope. "Is this it?"

Jenny peered over his shoulder.

The paper he pulled out was handwritten, the ink smudged on warped, off-white pages.

Dear Gracie,

If you're reading this, then something has happened to me, and you need to understand what's at stake.

Jed moved the page as he scanned it. and Jenny lost her place, catching only a few more words. —*Keep it safe*— and —*there are echoes about County Bricks.* — and further down a line stood out, as if written in bold.

If Hamish was willing to erase his own family, then I had no reason to believe he would stop there.

The words hit her like a slap.

Hamish? As in Hamish Holdings? And if so, where was he now? This shadowy character had lived like a ghost in her own corner of the world.

"This is it." Jed's voice was hoarse. "This is what I need."

He folded the letter and stuffed it in his jacket pocket, locking his jaw in neutral and keeping his expression unreadable.

He wasn't going to tell them what it meant.

Jenny grabbed his arm, hoping he'd prove her wrong. "What does it say?"

"I have to go." Jed barely heard her. "If I don't do this, none of it will matter." His voice was tight with finality. "Stay out of it, Jenny."

"We can't let him run off like this." Grace's hands shook as she ran them behind her neck, pinching the pressure points.

Jenny took a deep breath, straightening. "We won't." She glanced at Cherry. "We need to go talk to the police."

Grace stood in stunned silence, finally nodding as Cherry pulled Jenny toward the door. "We'd better hurry. I saw lights headed down the road a couple minutes ago."

Jenny squeezed Grace's hand and followed Cherry onto the porch.

The younger woman crossed the yard faster than Jenny, even in her delicate footwear, and Jenny had to climb into the car as it was already starting. They didn't pull forward though. Holding a finger up for patience, Cherry pointed ahead of them.

An old sedan waited in front of Grace's yard, right across from the convertible. Beside it, Jed's truck idled. His silhouette leaned toward the passenger window.

When he pulled forward, Cherry gave him a

moment to get rolling before she pulled out too. "Call the police," she said, her voice cold with resolve.

As Jenny made the call, telling the desk agent what they'd seen. Jed pulled ahead and turned a corner. Once on the main road he hit the gas speeding out of town.

"Don't lose him." Jenny gasped, gripping the edge of the seat.

Cherry's fingers tightened on the wheel. "I don't plan on it."

HIDDEN IN THE MOONLIGHT, potholes littered the abandoned highway. Jed's truck lit the road ahead, guiding them to a place that should have been forgotten.

"You called the police, right?" Cherry asked as the car ahead of them pulled off the road.

Jenny nodded, but her mind was on the looming brick building rising from behind a vine-covered wall. Atop the arched gate, four linked, cast-iron circles gleamed faintly. It was a symbol Jenny had seen before.

Killing the headlights, Cherry slowed to a stop. And waited as Jed parked.

Even craning her neck, Jenny couldn't see inside the compound. Not without standing in the convertible. Which she could do, but she wasn't ready to risk getting caught or hurt.

"Hang on," Cherry whispered. "I'm waiting till I hear them go inside."

Fascination spun briefly in Jenny's mind for this woman she'd only begun to know. "I missed where you listed stealthy driving skills on your resume."

Cherry gave a soft snort of laughter. "I'll remember that if I need a new job after tonight. Wait," she said and narrowed her eyes at Jenny. "I won't lose my job for this, will I?"

"Are you kidding?" Jenny murmured, her eye shifting to the gate as a car door slammed. "Getaway driver skills make you an even more valuable asset."

Voices grumbled in the distance followed by a heavy creak, then silence.

The car rolled forward, crawling past the gate. It was the first full view of the building Jenny had seen in years. "It's creepier than I remember."

The main door sat on the other side of a gravel parking lot, raised by several steps to a porch lit with the murky light of a single bulb. The structure's curved metal roof reflected the moonlight across outlying sections of the property. Piles of bricks scattered along the barren ground. A reminder of what had once been the life blood of the business.

Immense oaks and wild hickory trees made up the tree line bordering the property. Posed with thick armed branches flung skyward, it was as if they'd cried out in panic and frozen mid wail. Their silhouettes followed the outer wall, meeting the edge of the crumbling brick edifice.

It was a life-sized diorama made of black damask and hung from the stars. Unsettled by the macabre monochrome Jenny shivered.

"County Bricks," Cherry announced in a breathy, haunted tone. Then, added a weak, "ta-da." She exhaled, gripping the wheel. "Didn't someone die out here?"

"I wouldn't be surprised," Jenny whispered. "If we see any ghosts, you can ask."

"So," Cherry's voice rattled slightly. "We called the police. Can we go home now?"

Jenny hesitated. "Almost. Park over there. It's dark so we'll be hidden. I'll call the police, and we can wait there till they come."

"You haven't called them yet?" Cherry's question dragged through a minefield of agitation.

"I did, but that was back in town. If we want help, I'll have to do it again."

"Fine," Cherry said and pulled to the other side of the lot. "Call them. Then we go home."

Shadows sprawled through the warm night air. The car door creaked as Jenny opened it.

"No. Don't get out!" Alarm climbed through Cherry's voice as she followed Jenny from the car. "We're waiting here."

An owl hooted and Cherry ducked, the hair on the back of Jenny's neck prickled. "We will." She gripped the edge of the car door. Her knees seemed to have forgotten how to balance. "But we should at least look around."

Cherry turned to her, incredulous. "I am not going in there. I just moved here and started over with a job I love, thank you. Have you seen that place? It would look haunted in the daylight."

"Okay, not inside." Jenny nodded toward the fence. "We'll start over there. Be careful. No one has been taking care of things, and an old brickyard isn't really made for heels.

"Don't doubt me." Cherry pursed her lips, but after a moment, she glanced at Jenny. "If we get eaten by feral raccoons, I'm haunting you."

Jenny smirked and led the way, Cherry following. They stepped carefully over cracked pavement and patches of wild grass. Then the smell hit.

Cherry gagged.

Jenny covered her mouth and nose. "What is that?"

"I was about to ask you the same thing." It wasn't dirt, or rust, or mildew from an old factory rotting into the landscape. It was something worse—thick, pungent, unnatural.

"Maybe those rumors about illegal dumping weren't rumors." Jenny crouched, reaching for something protruding from the shadowed ground.

Cherry yanked her back. "Don't touch that!" she commanded, voice muffled by the hand still clamped over her mouth. "You'll come home with extra body parts growing out your ears."

Jenny shook her head at the exaggeration but followed Cherry's lead, picking her way past what had at first looked like piles of discarded bricks.

Dark sludge pooled in the low areas, coagulating in thick puddles around lumpy masses of earth and debris. Something had eaten away at the soil, warping the ground beneath.

Acid burned inside Jenny's throat as her body recoiled. "This has to be illegal. How can they sell a property with something like that out back?"

Cherry shook her head and turned in a slow circle, scanning the trees bordering the property.

A low rumble echoed down the road.

Jenny's head snapped up. The distant glow of headlights flared against the tree line.

"Someone's coming."

Cherry's breath hitched. "I told you we should've stayed in the car."

"Well, I don't want to get caught here." Jenny grabbed her wrist. "Come on."

They darted toward the side of the building, slipping into the shadows. Dust and stale air made the room heavy and dark as they crept through an unlocked side door into the warehouse.

Jenny pressed her back to the wall, breathing hard. Outside, an engine idled.

Cherry peeked through a grimy window. "Whoever it is, they're not getting out yet."

The cavernous space stretched before them, high ceilings lost in darkness.

Across the room, a row of small offices lined the far wall. A single bulb cast dim light into one of the windows.

Jenny nodded toward the room. "Let's move. Jed's here somewhere. If we find him, maybe we can figure out where the meeting is."

"You're not planning to stick around, are you?" Cherry's face pinched in confusion.

Jenny shrugged. "I guess not. But if he's here for

that, we should at least figure out what to avoid before the police get here."

"I'm guessing *everything* is off the table." Cherry muttered and followed Jenny across the room to the open office door.

"Jed?" Jenny called inside.

The room sat empty, except for a single desk cluttered with papers and an old filing cabinet stuffed into the corner.

The desk lamp shone a circle of light on a page, separated from the others.

"What are you doing?" Cherry hovered behind her. "We're supposed to hide."

"So shut the door," Jenny whispered.

Grumbling, Cherry checked the main room, then closed the door.

Jenny stared at the document centered under the circle of light. "*County Bricks Family Business; Sale Stipulations, Legacy Property Clause.*"

"Maybe you *can* believe everything you read on the internet." Cherry said, disbelief thick in her voice.

Jenny slid the paper toward her. "Jed mentioned a legacy clause too, didn't he? Do you think this is what he was looking for?"

"Maybe." Paper shushed over paper as Cherry flipped through the pages. "It lists County Bricks as a fourth-generation homestead, protected under a legacy trust set up by . . . Judy Holdin." She lifted her gaze, questions glowing in her eyes. "That's not the same Holdin as Robert, is it?"

Jenny bit the inside of her cheek lightly, shaking her head. "I'm not sure."

A voice cut through the stillness. "I told you to stay out of it."

Both women's heads snapped up.

Jed stood, hunched in the doorway.

Before Jenny could process his presence, he crossed the room and took the papers from Cherry.

"You should have stayed with Grace," he whispered, looking over the document, then lifted his dark gaze to hers.

Jenny squared her shoulders. "What's going on Jed? This all feels so cloak-and-dagger. Is someone trying to sell this place? Or steal it?"

"It's not like that." His voice dropped lower. He shot a glance over his shoulder toward the closed door. "The Holdins owned County Bricks. I told you. They named my dad as trustee of the legacy clause. It's my job to figure out how to bypass it. I'm almost there."

"For what? Jed, you don't have to do this. Getting caught up in illegal activities won't help Grace."

"At least she'll be alive."

Jenny's tone sharpened. "Alive to worry about you."

Frustration flickered across his face. "I don't know what's going on yet, but someone died tonight. I won't let that happen to anyone else." A door slammed and Jed's face drained of color. "You can't be here."

He darted a look around the room.

Jenny pressed her palms against the air, in a calming gesture. "It's okay. We'll hide."

"It's too late for that." He stuffed the papers into his jacket and snatched a key off the desk. "Stay quiet. I'll keep him busy."

"Wait," Jenny thrust a hand forward. "Where are you going?"

The door shut and the lock clicked into place.

Cherry's voice shook. "Did he lock us in?"

Voices rang through the open warehouse.

"Jed! Are we ready?" The deep voice was gruff. Expectant.

Low anxiety answered in Jed's tone. It was easy to tell who would command the conversation.

Ducking behind the desk, Jenny crouched, barely making it below the window as voices moved past. From this angle, she was nearly eye-level with the scattered documents. One name jumped out at her.

Jenny put a hand on Cherry's shoulder. "Did you say Judy Holdin filed the legacy clause?"

Cherry nodded, keeping her gaze locked on the door. "Why?"

The name peeked out from under another sheet. Shifting the page, Jenny let out a soft breath. "Clarence and Judy Holdin filed a Cease and Desist; for illegal dumping activities against Merkel Fabrication & Processing, in connection with Hamish Robert Holdin, of Hamish Holdings." Jenny went still. Her whisper barely formed words. "Hamish Robert."

The pieces crashed together.

The tax lien. The foreclosure. The stolen quilts. The illegal sale of County Bricks.

Cherry flipped to another page. "Contamination Reports. Environmental Hazard. Failure to Meet Safety Standards." Her voice lowered, heavy with surprise and disbelief. "Hamish has gotten himself into a little bit of trouble."

"Mish." Jenny swallowed hard.

Robert was Mish.

There was still a question, since she'd been sure before, but the pieces were finally starting to fit.

A sharp voice rang through the warehouse. "You've had plenty of time!"

Something slammed against the wall.

Footsteps echoed, pausing as a shadow filled the window.

Jenny's breath caught. She gripped the edge of the desk, heart pounding.

They were trapped.

MYSTERY QUILT BLOCK 2

Clue 6

VILLAINS & VICTIMS ARE SASHED IN THE SEAMS
WHEN BOTH HAVE A MOTIVE AND EVERYONE SCHEMES

Clue 6

ONE LAST PIECE

Using a 3" square of HC fabric "snowball" the corner of each log cabin block by sewing the square corner to corner over the POP color fabric that connects the half square triangle blocks.

Trim the excess fabric and press the snowball open. *(A small corner of POP color should show.)*

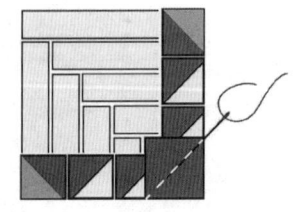

Swap the solid color log cabin quarters and sew the pieces together as shown.

Clue 6 – Check the Supplies and Read!

14.5" Unfinished Block

Flyaway Home Block

PART Seven

A Template for Murder

EVERY QUILT BEGAN WITH AN IDEA, A SPARK OF creativity. Watching it glow into existence, catch fire, and send life into the world was breathtaking.

Even a spark of light couldn't exist without a shadow, a moment of fear.

Fear that the pieces wouldn't fit, that the vision would unravel, that all the careful work would be lost.

Moments of fear were unavoidable. But the test wasn't in avoiding the shadows— it was in pushing through, trusting the stitches would hold, believing the pattern would come together.

Hiding under the desk of a killer, Jenny crouched in thick shadows of unescapable fear. How had she gotten here? Had she made the right choices? Or had her efforts to help instead unraveled lives, piecing together a quilt she hadn't intended to make?

The lock on the door clicked. The handle jiggled. Jenny's options lay out before her, clear as quilt blocks. Sew them together or scrap the whole thing.

She slunk lower behind the desk, grip tightening on Cherry's arm, holding a finger to her lips. The pattern was there, tangled but unmistakable. Mish was knotted in the final design, but Jenny had the needles now. And she was ready to pull the threads tight.

Cherry stared toward the door as if she could see through the wall of the desk drawer. When it creaked open, she breathed in, slow and deep, darting a glance at Jenny.

"Actually, I wanted to show you what I found in the quilt room," Jed said, his voice too bright, too eager.

Mish hadn't seen them. Jenny was sure of it. She pulled her legs in tightly as footsteps crossed the threshold and stopped.

"Did we get a last-minute batch of quilts?"

"No," Jed's voice quieted.

Bound in Secrets & Lies

"I didn't think so." Papers shuffled over Jenny's head. A low noise—half growl, half sigh—scraped against the walls. "You're wasting my time."

"I don't think so," Jed insisted. "You need to see—"

A sharp thud rattled the desk. Jenny flinched.

"You must like being stupid." Mish's voice sent ice down her spine.

"No, sir."

"Really?" A pause. "Because I've been through every quilt in that room. The only thing they have in them are payment details for land seizures."

Cherry squeezed a hand over Jenny's. *Land seizures?*

Jenny nodded, taking in the details, as her back pressed painfully against the leg of the desk, like she was trying to bond her spine with the metal rod.

"But I thought—"

"If I wanted to know what you thought, I'd stick my head in a microwave."

Papers hit the floor in a flurry and Jed yelped.

"One of us is going home in a body bag tonight, and it's not going to be me. So, tell me one more time . . . do you like being stupid?"

Silence. Then, "No, —"

"Uh-uh." The false sweetness in Mish's tone sent nausea curling through Jenny's gut. "You like it. You like it so much you'd risk your aunt's life just to keep being an idiot. Say it, Jed. Do you like being stupid?"

Jed's swallow was audible. "Ye—yes."

"Yes, what?"

"Yes, sir." His voice cracked, but then something changed. A shift. A decision. "Yes, sir, *Mish*." He emphasized the name, as if confirming it for Jenny. "I like being stupid."

Silence.

Mish exhaled sharply. "That's what I thought. Isn't it easier when you admit it?" His voice took on a quiet, almost soothing quality. "Honesty is important, boy. Never forget that."

Footsteps. A pause.

"Come here. No, it's okay, come here."

More movement.

A sharp crack and a choked groan.

Jenny squeezed her eyes shut.

Mish's voice dropped to a mutter. "You're lucky I have a backup plan."

The door slammed.

Silence stretched, thick as batting until Jenny scrambled from behind the desk. "Jed?"

He lay on the floor, rolling to his side with a groan. No blood, but color spread across his cheekbones, a swelling bloom that darkened toward his temple.

Jenny dropped to her knees, pulse pounding. "Come on, Jed, we need to get out of here."

He winced, one eye squeezed shut, his breath coming in short, sharp bursts.

"Can you sit up?" She reached for his arm, careful to keep her voice steady.

He let out a shuddering exhale and pushed himself up with a groan. "I'm fine."

"That was not fine," Cherry muttered, rubbing her shins where they'd been tucked under the drawer. "That was horrifying. He really commits to the villain act, doesn't he?"

Jed let out a breathless chuckle, then flinched as pain caught up with him. "He's had practice."

Jenny studied him, frowning. "You didn't have to do that, you know."

"I thought I could stall him long enough for ... I don't know," Jed sighed. "Something."

Jenny exchanged a glance with Cherry. "Why is Mish meeting with Merkel?"

His body sagged. He traced an invisible line across the floor before finally looking up to meet her eye. "You don't want to know."

"Jed." She held his gaze until he looked away.

He sighed again, running a hand over his face. "Mish is trying to get rid of County Bricks."

"But why? If he could get killed for it, why not walk away?" She helped Jed to his feet. He bit back a groan, still stiff from Mish's beating.

"They won't let him. You heard what he said to me. They won't risk anyone else getting ahold of their mistakes. Mish wanted to sell years ago and let them dump excess waste. Then he found out his parents set up legal trusts to keep the property in the family. And he couldn't sell it. Merkel is trying to cover their tracks, and Mish wants the problem to go away. In the meantime, Merkel is still dumping animal byproduct here, like it's a butcher house bathroom."

"I still don't understand," Cherry said. "He wants to sell. They want to buy. What's so hard about that?"

"My dad put all the information in a quilt. But no one knows which one." Jed turned, glancing out the door. "Mish is right outside." He beckoned them closer, pointing through the window to the back of the main room. "We don't have much time. The quilt room is through that door at the back. If we hurry, we can hide there and get out the fire door."

Watching him, Cherry crossed her arms. "I feel like I should be excited about somewhere called a quilt room, but you act like it could hurt us."

Cherry pulled the chain on the desk lamp and joined Jed.

He patted his pocket where Jenny knew he'd stored his father's letter and the legacy clause.

"So, we run, right?" Cherry asked.

Jenny nodded. "Let's go."

Jed pulled the door handle.

Locked.

Frustration clunked against the door as Jed dropped his forehead against it. "He took the keys."

Jenny tried the knob herself, rattling it in frustration. "He locked us in?"

Jed's face drained of color. "He would do that." He staggered back, his fingers curling into fists. "He *knew* I was lying."

"This is bad." Cherry exhaled through clenched teeth.

"Now what?" Jenny scanned the space. The tension in the air behind them was thick, the voices too close.

A low murmur carried from the front of the building. Mish's voice, and he wasn't alone.

"What are we waiting for, Commissioner?"

Jed went rigid. His head snapped up, eyes wide. "That's them," he whispered. "Merkel's people are here. He's meeting with them now."

Jenny barely had time to move before the tension in the room snapped tight.

Heavy footsteps echoed across the cavernous space stopping outside their door. Mish's profile appeared through the window and Jenny pulled back into the darkness.

"Thank you for meeting me. Apologies for the delay. We had a few—interruptions." Mish carried his usual smugness in his tone. "But I'm anxious to move forward, given our history with the property."

His gaze flicked toward the office door and Jenny ducked instinctively.

Behind them, Mish launched into a smooth sales pitch. "You know I always deliver. And I have everything we need to complete the deal tonight."

The woman scoffed. "Do you?"

Mish had taken on his commissioner's tone, with something tighter in it, more forced. "Everything's in place. I'm just finalizing the details like we talked—"

One of the men from Merkel cut him off. "You mean, you still don't have what we asked for."

Silence. "It's difficult to prepare all the pieces, when you don't know what's needed because the Trustee of the account was *silenced*."

A laugh—dark, amused, and dripping with condescension sounded outside the office. "Are you under the impression I should feel bad about killing Mitch Day?"

"I'd never dream that you might feel guilt over murder." His harsh tone mirrored the woman's, only he shifted awkwardly, sending another glance toward Jed.

"He was keeping us from closing a deal." There was a dark chuckle before Mish spoke up.

"And how much longer is it taking now." He sounded like he was questioning their methods, and Jenny suspected you didn't do that with these people. "I'm not sure you know what good decisions are."

"Don't worry. We have strict instructions not to kill anyone tonight." She glanced at one of the men who grinned.

"We had to come up with *alternative* plans should any punishment become necessary." Merkel's main enforcer, a broad-shouldered man in a sleek black jacket, pulled out a gun.

"You really thought you could string us along forever?" she asked.

"Now, hold on—" Mish lifted his hands.

"Hold on?" The man smirked. "We know how to take care of problems, Holdin. And right now, you're a problem."

Mish stiffened. "We can still—"

The woman turned to him, unimpressed. "You used Ms. Bricklan's name at the auction. That was not supposed to happen."

Mish's expression faltered. "It wasn't. The woman who used it was bidding for you. The news crew wasn't supposed to be there."

"Someone called them," she finished flatly. "We know about that, too. They were dealt with. But Ms. Bricklan's not happy."

Jenny's pulse pounded. This wasn't a business deal going south. This was a death spiral. It seemed like they wanted to kill someone.

"I'm very sorry. It won't happen again." He stood, moving toward the door. "But I've got someone who wants to talk to you."

Jed looked at Jenny. *Hide*, he mouthed.

Jenny hurried back to the desk bumping into Cherry on the way.

Behind her the door opened. "Jed is the Trustee's heir, and we've confirmed he can legally be positioned to—" Mish's spiel stopped.

Jenny froze.

For a split second, nothing happened. The entire room seemed to inhale at once, the tension snapping so tight it hummed in the air.

Mish stepped into the room. His breath hitched—a fraction of a second too late to hide the shock.

Then, something dark crept in. His expression sharpened. Fury burned slow and hot behind forced composure. He looked over each of their faces, not with anger but something worse... calculating recognition.

"Well, well," he drawled, stepping forward. "Isn't this a surprise?" He turned to Merkel's people, spreading his hands like he was in on a joke. "Ladies and gentlemen, it seems we have a little... unexpected company."

The woman narrowed her eyes. "Who are they?"

Mish laughed lightly. "A nuisance," he muttered. "But don't worry, I'll handle it."

Jenny held his gaze, refusing to back down.

Merkel's enforcer glanced between them. "You two know each other?"

Mish's lips parted, but for the first time tonight, he hesitated.

Jenny saw it. So did the woman.

The enforcer chuckled. "This keeps getting more interesting."

Mish clenched his fists, forcing a strained smile. "Like I said, nothing to worry about. I'll handle it."

"See that you do," the woman replied coolly.

Mish nodded, but his gaze stayed locked on Jenny. Barely contained rage flickered behind his eyes.

He wasn't just angry.

He was unraveling. "Jed," he snapped. "Tell the representatives what you were telling me earlier."

Jed's eyes widened and he shook his head. "I don't know what you—" he stopped himself as Mish's neck started to turn red.

"About the quilt room. You were thinking something today."

Petrification is a process that normally takes years. Jed managed it in less than thirty seconds.

Mish glared at him, before turning back to the Merkel team and smiling like a toothpaste salesman. "Jed is my secret weapon. He's replacing his father so not only will the property be yours, but there will be no legal ramifications or inquiries."

"But that isn't a solution." The woman stepped forward pressing clawed fingernails onto the surface of the desk. She appeared to be the main Merkel representative. "Where are the documents? The legacy clause? The authenticated land claim deed? The original and heritage surveys?"

Mish tried to swallow, choking on the attempt. "You know that's all a bunch of historical garbage right. Jed convinced me he could find them. That didn't work out. I'll have verifiable forgeries next—"

"Hasn't worked out," The woman repeated, cutting him off. "That's disappointing."

With a nod to the man at her side.

A gun fired and Jed jerked back.

Bound in Secrets & Lies

A strangled sound escaped his throat as blood spread over his shoulder into the fabric of his shirt.

Cherry gasped, covering her mouth.

Jenny surged forward, catching him before he hit the ground.

Mish turned back to Merkel's people. "Now, hang on! We still have options!"

"You're right. It was not our preferred plan." The taller man sighed, adjusting his cuff. "Make the call."

The other man nodded and made a few taps on his phone.

The tall man whispered something to the woman. "You're lucky we're not allowed to kill anyone tonight," she said. "I think we're done here."

The short man hung up the phone and nodded, "You can expect a police officer at your door by morning. It's your choice whether you're going to be there or not. But all evidence of your illegal activities running the now defunct Merkel Fabrications over the past six years is being sent to the authorities."

Mish's face drained of color. "Wait—"

All three turned in unison and walked away.

"What do you mean?" Mish trailed after them. "I never did that. We have a plan. I can get you the deeds. I will make this happen. Tell Ms. Bricklan I'm ready to close the deal."

Jenny shut out the sounds, pressing her hands against Jed's wound. "Are you okay?"

He grimaced, then moved her hands from off his shoulder. "Run."

"No." She hesitated. "Why didn't you give them the letter?"

Jed hesitated. "I couldn't." A shaky breath. "I never cared about any of this. Not really. But tonight, when they talked about my dad—" His breath shuddered as he looked up, something raw in his eyes. "They killed him. And they'd do it again. I don't want to be part of this."

The shift in his reasoning struck Jenny. Grace needed someone who cared enough to care for both of them. Not the self-sacrificial nonsense that had them in this mess.

A pause. Then he shoved Jenny toward Cherry. "This is your chance. Go. The quilt room has a back exit." His voice dropped. "Get her out."

Jenny didn't have a chance to ask any more questions.

Cherry took her charge seriously. Grabbing Jenny's hand, she flew out the door.

The front door slammed, as they exited the little office. The Merkel representatives were gone but Holdin was still there.

"Back door," Cherry muttered. There were a couple along the furthest wall of the warehouse. She ran straight to the largest one.

The heavy panel caught as Cherry pulled against it. Jenny grabbed the long handle to pull with her. Footsteps pounded as Holdin ran across the floor toward them. When the door released, they slid inside a room at least as large as the one they'd left.

"What's all this?" Cherry's question pulled Jenny around and she gasped, the air scooped from her lungs.

Each side of the room held half a dozen pallets piled with quilts. On one side they were in pristine condition and on the other, they were shredded.

Batting and fabric lay in clumps strewn through the chunks of broken bricks and dust that covered the floors. Pieced and appliqued blocks lay torn, ruined badly enough they'd never go back together.

Jenny couldn't imagine how many quilts had been destroyed for Robert Holdin's random search.

Old pulleys hung from the wall to the ceiling, a row of light switches littered the wall in various stages of repair, and Jenny's eye fell back to the quilts.

There must have been hundreds.

"Mena said he was looking for something. Jed had talked about documents, but I never expected this."

An ache grew in her chest, pain that it was a possibility to be so casual with someone's legacy.

"They're not really all what did he say? Land payments?" Cherry shook her head as Jenny stepped over the crumbling pieces of brick littering the floor.

"Not if they're doing that to them?" she whispered.

A door opened a little way down the wall and Mish walked in. The door clapped shut. Mish came into the room scanning till he found her.

"You," he whispered. Unfiltered rage twisted his expression. He moved toward her slowly, eyes burning, chest heaving. This wasn't just about Merkel now. This was personal.

"You ruined everything," he spat. "You cost me everything!"

"You're giving me way too much credit." Jenny steadied herself, keeping her voice level. "You managed that on your own."

His hand darted into his pocket, raising a knife in his hand.

Jenny moved. The quilt stack behind her toppled, fabric spilling in a colorful cascade.

"They will ruin me. And it's your fault." He pointed his knife at Jenny as a chunk of brick hit his shoulder and the knife slipped from his hand.

"You shouldn't hurt people," Cherry yelled, another chunk of brick in her hand.

"No," Jenny gasped. She took a step forward at the same time Mish did.

Cherry threw the brick, but this time he knew it was coming, and he dodged.

Jenny grabbed the nearest quilt and flung it at him. A heavy, well-stitched bundle of fabric slammed into his chest. He stumbled, cursing.

The motion ripped another quilt from the pile—Echoes of the Hollow.

Jenny staggered. The tie she'd developed with that quilt gave her an inability to hurt it.

Mish seemed to recognize her debate and lunged. His knife hit the fabric, splitting it open with a laugh.

"Oops," he said, slicing through it the other direction till the hilt tore the fabric.

A flurry of pages erupted from inside. Yellowed paper and hand drawn lines over surveyor marks. *Holdin Family Farms – 1803,* was written in bold on one of the pages.

His fingers twitched. He'd recognized them the same time Jenny had.

Historic deeds. Ownership documents. The key to everything he had been searching for.

Mish let out a guttural scream. "No! That's not possible."

Jenny scrambled back, grabbing Cherry. The pages fluttered around them, proof of everything Mish had never been able to find. Proof that he could have won.

Mish's eyes snapped to Jenny. "You!" he roared.

He charged, nostrils flaring, and launched a chunk of brick at Jenny. It missed, shattering in a gut-wrenching crash, shards of hardened clay flying in all directions.

Jenny shrieked, her breath shaky. She backed up as Mish picked up another brick, eyes brimming with rage. She had to find a way to defend herself.

He barged forward, as Cherry leapt out from behind a stack of quilts, arms flailing in Robert's face. The brick flew hitting Cherry in the ribs.

She pitched back, tripped over the corner of the quilt pallet, and landed on the floor. Scissors clattered to the floor. Jenny grabbed them, grateful she finally had a weapon to defend herself with.

Aiming their sharp points at the commissioner, Jenny searched for her next step. She wouldn't intentionally hurt anyone, but she had to make him think she would.

"Watch out, Mish." Her voice wavered despite her attempt to sound confident.

"What are you going to do with those?" Mish taunted, "Shorten my sleeves?"

"I'm more capable than that." Jenny's threat was hollow. She tugged another quilt free and threw it at him.

Mish stumbled around it. "I'm tired of games. Your time's up. Take your best shot and let's go." He picked up a large chunk of brick, tossing it in the air.

Jenny jabbed, plunging forward a half step. Mish jerked back reflexively. Then she turned and stumbled over the brick strewn floor to the nearest wall.

"There's nowhere to hide," Robert called after her.

A chunk of brick hit her shoulder blade and pain shocked her system. She ignored it pulling at the rotting rope attached to one of the pulleys.

Jenny grabbed a brick and tossed it behind her. The commissioner jumped but it didn't stop him. She followed the line of the pulley and raised her scissors, cutting the already shredded fibers holding the rope together.

Another brick clattered but Robert was the one who grunted at the impact.

"Hey Mish!" Cherry called out, while Jenny's scissors sliced through the last of the rope.

She spun around as the rope released and a pulley tumbled from the ceiling, swung in the gears, and caught Robert on the side of the head.

He let out a yowl as he went down, eyes closed. He didn't move, but Jenny had no way of knowing how long he'd be out.

Jenny stepped toward him, scissors at the ready. "Cherry! I need a quilt."

Cherry scrambled over the bricks and discarded fabric, grabbing the first thing she could.

Handing it over, Jenny took the heavy scissors and sliced them into the fabric. Cherry gasped, and Jenny pointed to the floor where the first strip was falling.

"Grab those quick." She cut long slices of fabric, as fast as she could. "We'll need a several long strips, sturdy ones, that will keep him down until the police get here."

Cherry held his arms steady as Jenny tied a knot to secure his wrists behind his back. Wrapping a strip of fabric around his legs several times, they tied it off there as well, securing it with a knot.

Robert lay face down on the filthy ground as Jenny and Cherry collapsed against the wall. Brick dust blew around them in displaced movement.

"Did that just happen?" Cherry held her side breathing heavily.

Jenny slid an arm around her shoulder. "I won't get to keep you after this, will I?"

"I don't know." Cherry lowered one brow as she eyed the commissioner. "I hear people do a lot of bonding in prison cells."

"Prison? We're the heroes. He's the one getting locked up." Jenny's breath heaved from her chest as she looked at Cherry. "Speaking of. Were you calling the police? Because if not. We should do that."

"Weren't you going to call them?" Cherry laughed, her expression shifting quickly to one of pain. "Don't worry, they're on the way."

Jenny exhaled, exhaustion creeping in. "You are going to make an excellent assistant."

Cherry groaned. "Let's survive the paperwork first."

A QUILT WORTH STARTING was a quilt worth finishing. It took effort and dedication. The extra care taken to complete each project determined whether the seams held fast or unraveled.

From the idea to the final binding. Every stitch mattered. The binding was what gave a quilt its strength, its lasting shape. The last step was where the maker's hands lingered longest.

The beauty of the binding wasn't in a two-inch strip of folded fabric, but in what they held together.

Without bindings, quilts frayed, seams pulled apart, and all that effort unraveled into nothing.

When a quilt was bound, it held a lot more than fabric inside. The quilts in Jenny's home held family, healed hearts, old wounds, and new love.

Echoes of the Hollow had held the truth. But in the end the truth only mattered to the ones it saved.

Alongside the Antique Barn, a new collection of quilts hung billowing in the breeze, their bindings strong and whole. The display fluttered as Jenny and Cherry strolled past. Sunlight danced over the spread of vintage china sets, weathered books, and delicate lace gloves. The usual signs of life had returned, filling the space with color and history.

But when the wind shifted, Jenny caught it—the faint, lingering scent of smoke. It only reached them when they passed the burned corner of the barn, where blackened beams stood like scars against the sky.

Construction crews were already at work. A fresh framework rose beside the damaged section, sturdy and new, a quiet promise that some things could be rebuilt ever stronger.

Jenny's gaze flicked to the quilts on the line, their bindings neat and strong.

No trace of the white patches that Mena had sewn onto so many. The police were working on matching

Bound in Secrets & Lies

the names to the purchase amounts to find the fraudulent buyers who'd worked with Mish.

Cherry opened a set of collapsible opera glasses, and held them to the ridge of her nose, turning to peer at Jenny.

"Wilkins!" Cherry yelped, pulling the miniature glasses away and flipping the robotic movement closed. "I didn't know I'd see you at the Antique Barn every time they had a sale."

Officer Tyler Wilkins stood in full uniform, near the porch, arms crossed stoically. Beneath his watchful eyes, a quirky grin had softened the hard angles of his face.

Cherry set the spy glasses down and swept her hair back. "Expecting trouble?"

"I'm here as a precaution." Officer Wilkins shook his head. "Mish is out of the picture, but the feds are still piecing together the full extent of his operation."

Cherry leaned toward Wilkins. "So, is Mish gone for good?"

Wilkins crossed his arms. "He's facing enough federal charges to keep him locked up for a long time. Between fraud, money laundering, and attempted murder? Yeah. He's not walking away from this one."

Jenny exhaled, letting the weight of those words settle. "Good."

Mish was gone.

After all they'd been through... Hamish Robert Holdin would face charges that ensured he wouldn't see freedom again.

"I heard some of the affected families might be getting their homes back. Is that true?" Cherry asked.

Wilkins' grin flattened in a thoughtful nod. "Takes time," he said. "But it looks hopeful."

"Better than nothing," Jenny muttered. At least some wrongs could be set right.

His confirmation eased some of the worry in Jenny's chest.

His jaw shifted as he turned to her, one eye narrowing cautiously. "One of these days, Mrs. Doan, you're going to need to stop running headfirst into trouble."

Cherry's laugh popped the tension like a shimmering soap bubble.

Jenny chuckled to herself and held out a hand to the officer. "One of these days." Jenny grinned.

Silent laughter shook Wilkins' shoulders as he turned his attention back to the group, leaving the rest of them to their morning.

"So, Sherlock." Cherry picked up a mint green pie pan, looking it over. "You really think you'll be able to keep from tripping over another mystery?"

"With a little help." Jenny winked.

"Me?" Cherry asked wide-eyed. "Not even I'm that good."

A metal rack of vintage clothes squealed past, Grace pushing it into place at the edge of the display tables.

"How about I keep you out of trouble," Cherry said, her eye on the bright fabrics. "And you keep me from buying all Grace's vintage dresses."

Cherry walked away before Jenny could respond, passing Grace with a smile.

"Things are finally settling back into place," Grace said, dusting her hands on her apron. "It almost feels normal again."

"Hamilton wouldn't be the same without you." Jenny glanced at the barn. "I'm so glad you decided to have a sale today, even if it's a pop-up, in the middle of repairs. So many people want to support you."

Grace followed her gaze. "I'm not the kind of girl to get knocked down by a little fire. We're still standing. That's what matters."

Jenny smiled, but something tugged at her thoughts. The last loose thread. "Jed never told me what was in his dad's letter."

"Actually," Grace's expression softened. "I wanted to share that with you." She reached into her apron pocket, pulling out a carefully folded page.

Jenny smoothed out the creases, Mitch's handwriting stark against the faded paper.

> *Dear Gracie,*
>
> *If you're reading this, then something has happened to me, and you need to understand what's at stake. Clarence and Judy named me trustee of the County Brickyard Legacy Property Clause.*
>
> *When I found out Hamish had them declared dead, without proof. I realized he was willing to erase his own family. And I had reason to believe he wouldn't stop there.*
>
> *So, until I can verify his intent for the sale of County Bricks, I've hid the documents in a place I know he'll never appreciate.*
>
> *The quilts hold more than history, Gracie. They hold truth. Keep it safe. When the time comes, don't be afraid to pull the threads and let the truth out.*
>
> *Examine the echoes, Grace. When the time comes, you'll know what to do.*
>
> *—Mitch*

Jenny exhaled, her heart squeezing. She'd finished his work. Mish had unraveled, the truth had come out, and County Bricks was safe.

A creak at the garden gate caught Jenny's attention, as Mena slipped by and knocked on Grace's front door.

Jed answered, his usual guarded expression softened as he stepped aside to let Mena in. No sign of the thick bandage he'd worn on his shoulder. No trace of the bruises and exhaustion that had marked his face just weeks ago.

Grace watched them disappear inside. "Mena's checked in on him every day," she said softly. "He's got five months left on house arrest. She says they're just friends, but I think they'd be good for each other."

Jenny hesitated. She wanted to encourage Grace to believe in anything that made her smile like that, but Mena had lost Lanny. And Grace hadn't seen what Jed and Mena had been through. This wasn't about romance. This was about two people who had walked through fire and come out burned but alive.

Sometimes, the only ones who understood were the ones who had survived the same flames.

A loud *clunk* caught her attention. Across the yard, Ron rummaged through an old trunk, his sleeves rolled up, grease smudged on his forearm.

"Hey, Jen!" He straightened, holding up a vintage tin train. "This is perfect for my office."

Jenny lifted a vintage metal iron she'd found for her own collection. "And this is perfect for mine."

Ron studied the two items. "We should display them together. We can start a vintage favorites shelf in the kitchen."

Jenny laughed, shaking her head. "You know, that's an idea." She stepped closer, pressing the iron into his free hand. "I'm not sure it will work but if you want to see it through go for it."

Ron's eyes warmed with his smile. "I think I will."

With a brief kiss of appreciation for this man who loved her and met her in her creativity and passion, Jenny turned.

Taking in the familiar scene of laughter and friends, Jenny's heart hummed with gratitude. This was what she fought for, the chance to rebuild, the air scented with fabric and dust, the friendships growing around her. The people worth binding together for a lifetime.

THE END

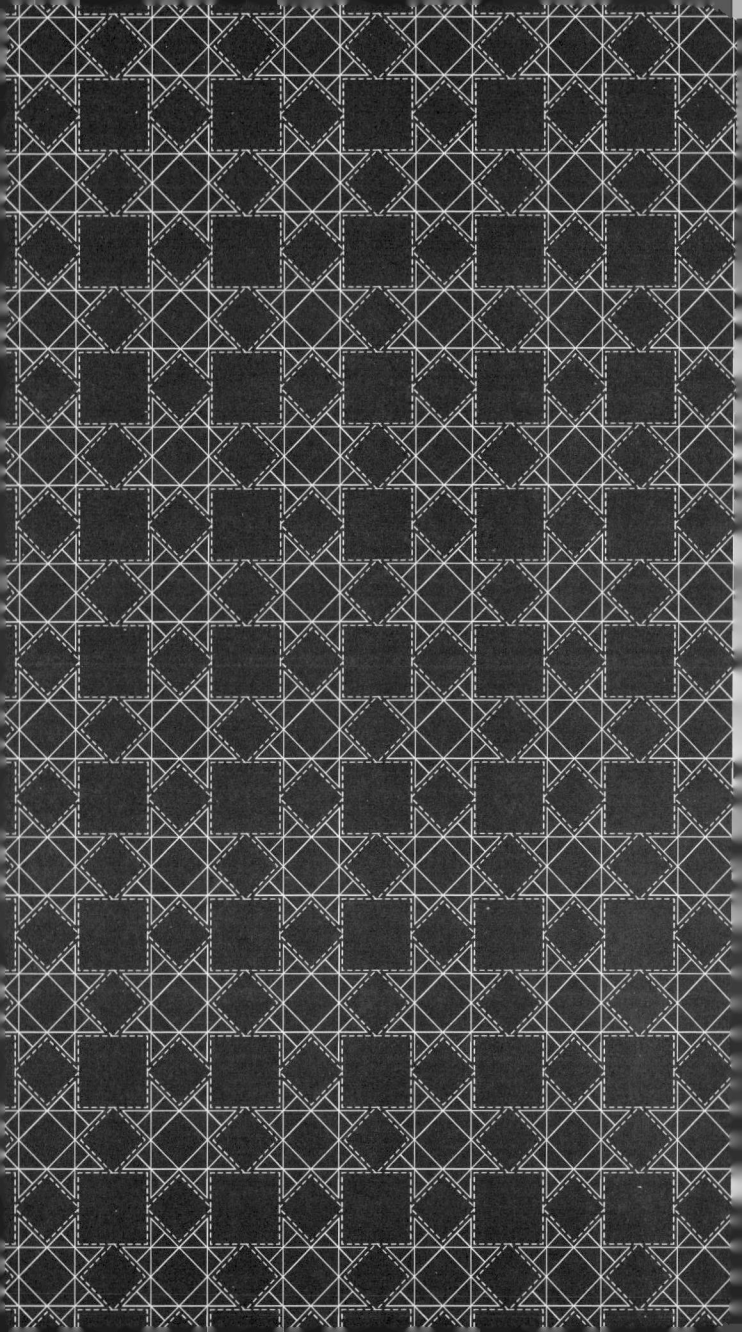

Flyaway Home Full Quilt

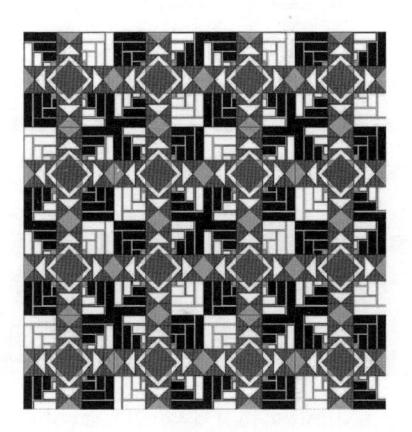

FROM QUILT BLOCK TO QUILT!

Now that you've made a Flyaway Home block the rest will be a walk in the park!

Make the block as directed, simply multiply the materials by how many blocks you want in your quilt. 👉

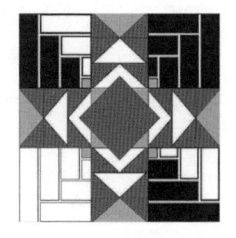

Laying out the blocks of Flyaway Home

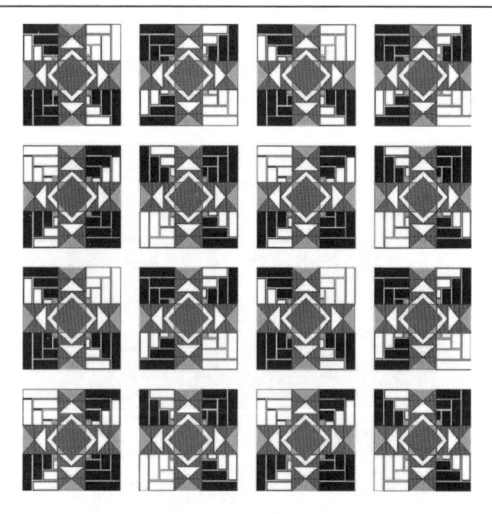

The diagram shows a 4 x 4 layout. (A set of four blocks sewn 2 x 2 should measure approx. 28 ½" square)

Example measurements are as follows —

- ✓ 4 x 4 (56 ½" sq)
- ✓ 6 x 6 (84 ½" sq)
- ✓ 6 x 8 (84 ½" x 112 ½")

✓

Final Thoughts on Flyaway Home

Here's the list of supplies per block so you don't have to go looking.

Supplies for the log cabin portion —
- ✓ 2 – DK 10" sqs
- ✓ 2 – LT 10" sqs

Supplies for your HST flying geese —
- ✓ 2 – HC 10" sqs
- ✓ 1 – POP 10" sq

(NOTES: I put the blocks together creating a pinwheel with the log cabin sections and a four patch from the solid-colored corners. You may consider putting the blocks together in sets of four to show off the pinwheel effect to its best advantage.)

More from the
Missouri Star Mystery Series

Chain Piecing a Mystery

A Body in Redwork

The Haunting of Quilter's Square

New to Quilting?

Never quilted before? Here are some good things to note. They may or may not be common sense. Read it before sewing, please!

Quilt tip # 1) Always keep your rotary blades closed when not in use! If your quilty mentor didn't tell you this, they don't actually quilt or maybe they trust you too much. Don't be offended, close your blades! Go now! Close them!

Quilt tip # 2) Double check your measurements before cutting. It stinks to cut your whole fabric swatch into 2 ½" strips only to realize you used the 2" line or your 2½" strips were supposed to be 2" and now you're out of fabric.

Quilt tip # 3) Have extra fabric! Mistakes happen! And if this is a new adventure, I promise you they will. (If they don't call me! Or send video proof! I will send you the biggest high five you've ever had.)

Quilt tip # 4) If in doubt watch a tutorial! Jenny has lots of videos online and there are so many others for all the ideas and possibilities out there! You've got this!

Quilt tip # 5) The Quarter Inch Seam. Quilts are generally sewn using a seam stitched ¼" from the edge of the fabric. I was a clothing seamstress *cough, sort of, cough* before I did much quilting and when I saw what a true ¼" seam was, it was much thinner than I thought. There are tools to help keep a good ¼" seam or you can put a strip of painter's tape on the bed of the sewing machine. Whatever you do, don't stress! However wide you sew it, be consistent. If you start with a ½" seam keep going that way. Your block will still turn out—just a little smaller than expected.

Helpful Basic Sewing Supply List

If you've never quilted before, here's some things you might need to get started.

Sewing Machine

Sewing Machine Needles

Fabric and thread — These are the very basics of sewing something. If your thread and fabric aren't a great color match, I advise choosing thread in a similar but darker color. Darker thread usually hides better than lighter. But trust your eyes and your gut. You got this!

Cutting Mat — Small is fine. Jenny has portable mats from 6" square to worktable cutting mats that are 3' x 5' feet across. Having a mat as large as your ruler is helpful, but whatever you can get is workable, I promise!

Rotary cutter — Please Note: No cutting mat, no rotary cutter! You don't want to use this incredibly sharp blade on a counter, floor, or any other surface that's not a cutting mat. Scissors are an option, but they are difficult for quilting. A rotary cutter is more precise.

PLEASE, DON'T HURT YOURSELF! Or accidentally cut your bedspread to shreds. It's been done. Consider yourself warned.

Clear Quilt Ruler — This is what you use to measure how much of a block, strip, or fabric piece to cut. Preferably find one marked with a grid system. 1", ½", ¼", & ⅛" inch lines are great. I like having as many dimensions as I can get on there. My only other recommendation is to try and get one a little longer than the cut you need to make. – cutting 10" squares? A 12" ruler is plenty. Cutting fabric yardage? You'll want something longer.)

Rotating Cutting — I mention a rotating cutting mat in my directions. It's not necessary but nice to have. It's simply a smaller cutting mat, mine is circular, but I'm sure they have other shapes. It allows you to cut your fabric or quilt block and not have to move it before cutting in a different direction. It helps keep the fabric and/or pieces lined up and saves you one more headache.

Quilter abbreviations & definitions cont.–

RST = Right sides together — When two pieces of fabric are placed with right sides facing each other, typically in preparation to sew them.

Sq(s) = Square(s) — A common shorthand reference for a square.

HST = Half-Square Triangle — Two triangles of fabric, sewn together on the long edge to form a square. The four at a time HST method is my favorite and what I describe in these patterns.

Pre-cut fabric & common sizes = Fabric pre-cut in commonly used sizes by fabric manufacturers. Often sold in packs of 30-40 fabrics from a single fabric line or coordinating colors. Pre-cut sizes and amount of fabric in a pack vary but the most common sizes are—

Squares come in 2 ½", 5", & 10"
Strips come in 1 ½", 2 ½", & 5"

Quilter abbreviations & definitions cont.–

Press open = Ironing the block flat — Iron the closed seam, then open the fabric and press again. Seams can be pressed both to either side or split open.)

Square the block = Trimming the excess fabric off a finished or partially finished quilt block, so it reaches a specified measurement.

WOF = Width of fabric — The width of the fabric is how wide the fabric is. This is a common quilting reference in patterns when cutting strips of fabric ... Let's be real, I don't use this abbrev. in this book and I'm only including it because I love the story about my mom, Jenny, first learning to quilt and she didn't know what WOF stood for. She just cut strips and barked at the fabric woof, woof, every time she cut a strip and hoped she did OK.

Acknowledgments

I am so grateful for the opportunity to share this experience of creating stories and adventures with such a wonderful team of people. I couldn't do this without my husband, Quintin, and my writers' group, Heidi Boyd and Tamara Hart Heiner. You three are my team, and I love you each dearly. ♡ I've learned and grown through so many experiences, and I'm thrilled to have found my place with all of you at my side.

I can't thank my daughter Phoebe Sperry enough. Phoebe tested both quilt block patterns we included in the book, as well as several others that I promise I will use eventually. Thank you so much for the gift of your skill, talent, and willingness to make things happen.

This next moment is for the beautiful cover art. Please join me in a big thank-you to Olivia Burbidge, one of my lovely daughters with her fabulous artistic skills. Your talents grow every day, and you astonish me with your gifts and creative intuition and drive as you develop them into your heart's passion.

My family will always have the less desirable knowledge of how much it takes to be an author. The mother they know in the middle of a deadline and the mother who is between books are completely different. I am so grateful that somehow your love continues to have no bounds. Thank you for the understanding and support you share that blesses me every day. We are, in every sense, a family quilt made of individuals and individual strengths, and through the effort of each, we've been stitched together in creativity, patience, and love.

To my readers, a truly heartfelt thank you! Your love of cozy mysteries, quilting, and small-town charm makes all of this possible. Whether I'm laughing or crying, your encouragement, reviews, and kind messages remind me why I sit down to write each day. Your willingness to be part of my patchwork story has given me wings to fly. And when I don't feel like flying, I make feathered quills, and I keep writing.

— Hillary

Hillary Doan Sperry is a cozy mystery author, quilter, and creative at heart. She's happiest with a fabric bundle in one hand and a plot twist in the other.

Her favorite colors change with the seasons, from turquoise and coral to pink and gray, and every year on her birthday, her family wears mustard yellow just to make her smile. She loves ice cream, chocolate cheesecake, strawberry pie, and the glorious smell of walking through a fabric store.

You can find her books through your favorite library, online retailer, or at hillarydoansperry.com.

Thanks for reading!

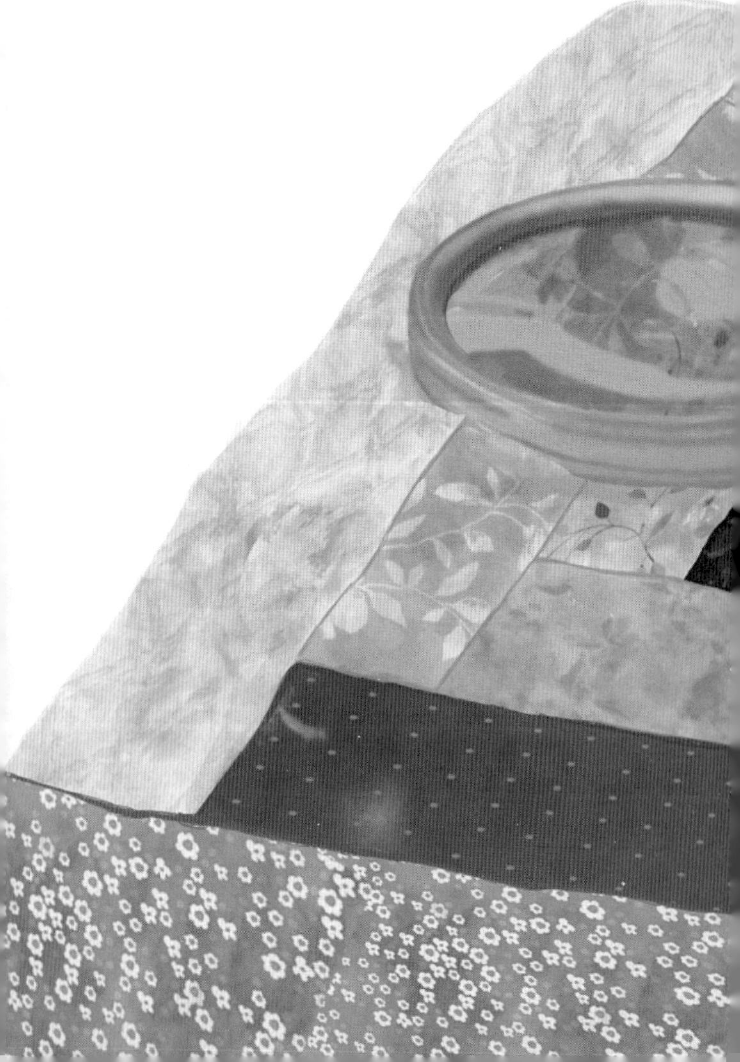